DIARY
OF A
DEAD MAN
ON LEAVE

Books by David Downing

The John Russell series
Zoo Station
Silesian Station
Stettin Station
Potsdam Station
Lehrter Station
Masaryk Station

The Jack McColl series
Jack of Spies
One Man's Flag
Lenin's Roller Coaster
The Dark Clouds Shining

Other titles
The Red Eagles

DIARY
OF A
DEAD MAN
ON LEAVE

DAVID DOWNING

Published in the United States by

Soho Press, Inc.
853 Broadway
New York, NY 10003

Library of Congress Cataloging-in-Publication Data

Downing, David, 1946- author.
Diary of a dead man on leave / David Downing.

ISBN 978-1-61695-843-5
eISBN 978-1-61695-844-2

I. Title
ClPR6054.O868 D53 2019 823'.914—dc23 2018046837

Interior design by Janine Agro, Soho Press, Inc.

Printed in the United States of America

10 9 8 7 6 5 4 3 2 1

To all the dead men and women on leave, past and present.

Correctly anticipating a sentence of death at his trial in 1919, Eugen Leviné, the leader of the Bavarian Soviet, famously announced that "we Communists are all dead men on leave." This proud utterance was subsequently adopted by those agents of the Communist International who worked outside the Soviet Union in the interwar years.

DIARY
OF A
DEAD MAN
ON LEAVE

Introduction

The man I knew as Josef Hofmann wrote this journal in my mother's house in 1938. I have appended an explanation of how it was found half a century later and brought the stories of those involved up to date as best as I can. Otherwise, I have left the journal to speak for itself, even when the temptation to explain my own feelings and behavior was almost irresistible.

Walter Gersdorff, November 1989

SATURDAY, APRIL 23

It is almost midnight. I am sitting at a small table by an open window, in the north German town of Hamm, writing these first lines. The rest of the house is quiet, but voices rise and fall on the street below, some talking quietly, others loud with drink and the end of a working week.

It's now been almost twenty-eight hours since I boarded the overnight train in Rotterdam. The papers I acquired in New York passed inspection at the German frontier; in Cologne, where I changed trains; and at the ticket barrier in Hamm. I took a cab from the station to the district surrounding the railway yards, intending to ask after lodgings in as many bars as I had to, and struck lucky at the first—one of the barmen knew a place nearby where someone had just moved out.

It was a large house on a T-junction corner, probably a manager's house in prewar days, when managers still lived among the workers. A canal ran parallel with the upper arm of the T, and beyond that the freight yards stretched away under a haze of smoke. A small Nazi flag hung limply over the front door.

A boy of around eleven or twelve answered my knock. I asked for Frau Gersdorff, the name I'd been given at the bar, and he stood and stared at me for a few seconds, as if he had trouble understanding. "My mother," he said eventually. "I'll fetch her." Halfway down the hall he stopped, turned, and told me with great seriousness that his name was Walter, as if it was really important that I knew who he was.

He reappeared a few moments later with a harassed-looking blonde woman in her late thirties or early forties. I introduced myself as Josef Hofmann and agreed to the rent and terms that she briskly outlined. Seeing in my papers that I'd only recently arrived in Germany, she asked where I'd been, and when I said Argentina, she gave me a look that mingled surprise and suspicion in roughly equal measure. I told her it seemed like a good time to return to the fatherland. "Of course," she murmured, but her eyes said: "What an idiot!"

She took me up to the vacant room, a large, airy attic with a fine view of the distant hills to the south. Away to the right I could see the railway yards where I was expecting to find work.

I said it would do. Frau Gersdorff told me that the guests' bathroom was on the first floor and that supper was served at six-thirty, breakfast at seven. Walter watched from the door-way, and when his mother left, I got the feeling it was only her gentle push that prevented him from staying.

I unpacked my suitcase, visited the bathroom, and made my way downstairs in search of the promised supper. There I met the first of three—as I later discovered—other lodgers. This one, a thin man of average height with short black hair, sunken eyes, sucked-in cheeks, and a thick black mustache hanging over a small mouth, introduced himself as Aksel Ruchay. He was wearing an immaculate Reichsbahn uni-form, which—as my father would have said—suggested that he rarely went near an actual train. The small enamel swastika in his lapel matched the *Völkischer Beobachter* in his lap.

A second lodger appeared almost immediately. He was probably five years older than Ruchay but seemed much less sure of himself. He was a short man, slightly overweight, with hair thinning at the front over a worried but kindly face. He checked his hands before shaking mine, the sure sign of a workingman. His name, he said, was Jakob Barufka.

Supper was being served by the time the final lodger appeared, a young man with slicked-back blond hair in his mid to late twenties. After apologizing to Frau Gersdorff for his late arrival, he told me his name was Rolf Gerritzen, and volunteered the information that he worked as a junior manager at Islacker Wire and Cable. He too wore a Nazi pin in his lapel, mostly, I suspect, because he prefers to swim with the tide. He ate his sausage, cabbage, and potatoes twice as fast as anyone else and seemed incapable of sitting still in his chair between courses.

As we devoured our apple-cake dessert, I told the three of them where I'd supposedly come from and why, and that I was hoping to get an administrative job on the railway. Ruchay nodded sagely when I said I had thought it a good time to return to Germany, and Gerritzen could hardly contain his enthusiasm for the Reich's future. Both Ruchay and Barufka confirmed the party's information that the Reichsbahn, like every other sector of the Reich's economy, is experiencing acute labor shortages—they were sure I would have no problem finding a job. "Success breeds its own difficulties," Ruchay murmured wisely, which prompted another panegyric from Gerritzen. It was ridiculous, but I found myself rather liking the young man. I told myself that in any other time and place, he'd just be another decent young man with more energy than he knew what to do with.

There were others in the house. I heard Frau Gersdorff

talking to someone in the kitchen, and while sitting at the table, I saw a tray being carried down the corridor that leads to the rear. A short while later a young man came in through the front door and disappeared into that part of the house. After Ruchay and Gerritzen had left—the one to his room, the other to the cinema with his sweetheart—Barufka filled me in. The cook's name was Verena; she lived a few streets away. Later I saw her leave, a pretty, dark-haired woman in her late thirties. The tray was for Anna's—Frau Gersdorff's, Barufka corrected himself—blind and bedridden father, who lived in one of the rooms at the back. The young man was her elder son, Erich, who was a "bit wild" but nice enough when you got to know him.

I reserved judgment on all of this: Barufka, I already suspected, was one of those people who tends to see the best in others, and sometimes only the best. He told me some of his own life story over the course of the next couple of hours: four years on the western front as a gunner, the railways ever since, a marriage that had failed soon after his return from the war. He had a grown-up married son in Hamburg whom he greatly loved but rarely saw. Since his divorce he had lived in lodgings, saving money, which he sent to his son. Barufka thought Anna—Frau Gersdorff, he corrected himself again— ran a very good lodging. He was, I realized, more than a little in love with her.

He asked me about my life, and I gave him the official version, the facts of service on the eastern front sliding into the fiction of a career in Argentina. He was interested in the latter, and I talked with some authority about the wonders of Buenos Aires and the Pampas, taking care not to mention my brief acquaintance with the prison system and deportation process.

At a minute to nine, Ruchay reappeared, and turned on the lounge wireless for what was obviously a ritual hearing of the news. When the reader announced, with barely suppressed excitement, that Czechoslovakia's Sudeten Germans had demanded full autonomy, Ruchay's face seemed to light up, and I felt obliged to force a smile of satisfaction to my own lips. It is still hardly a month since Austria was gobbled up by the Reich. The slide into war is gathering speed.

After the news everyone retired to their rooms. Frau Gersdorff hadn't appeared since supper, but Walter was loitering on the first-floor landing, idly kicking the foot of the stairwell bannister. "How many days did the boat take from Argentina?" he asked.

"Twenty-two," I told him, erring on the plus side.

"What was the name of the ship?" he wanted to know.

"The *Antilla*," I said, adding that it was a Dutch freighter, not an ocean liner.

"Oh," he said, clearly disappointed.

"It was cheaper," I explained, and he smiled for the first time.

For a moment neither of us spoke, and then just as I was lifting my foot onto the second flight of steps, he suddenly said, "We can be friends, can't we?"

I told him I didn't see why not.

He smiled again, said good night, and half tumbled down the stairs.

I suppose I should describe my room.

There is an old but comfortable bed, a cupboard and chest of drawers, and a small table beside the window at which I am now writing this. There is a fraying but serviceable armchair and a basin for water on the chest, and two ill-matched rugs cover most of the wooden floorboards. The wallpaper has almost faded to a uniform cream color, which goes quite well with the green paintwork on the door and window. When compared to most of the several hundred other rooms I have occupied in the course of the last twenty years, this one feels almost bourgeois.

In my room I sat by the window for a while, listening to the irregular clanking of freight cars in the floodlit yard, watching the occasional express steam by on the main lines beyond. I hadn't had any sleep for thirty-six hours, but I still felt wide awake. I'm not sure where the idea for this journal came from. On the train from Rotterdam, I had this strange feeling of too many memories clamoring for attention, begging for some sort of context and order. I bought the notebook in a stationer's opposite Cologne Cathedral, thinking I might write down a few, but not with any more definite purpose in mind.

Most of my comrades—not to mention my superiors—would find such a failure of discipline impossible to condone. They would consider it criminally reckless, and in most situations they would surely be right. They would say that it reflects an unhealthy level of interest in one's own individual thought processes, and there's probably more than a grain of truth in that as well. But then again, why should the bourgeoisie have a monopoly on self-reflection? I think I'm writing this because of an almost irresistible desire, after twenty years of living with history's truth, to immerse myself in the ordinary, day-to-day kind. And I think I've earned the right to this minor self-indulgence, always assuming it doesn't compromise my work.

There, of course, is the rub. I don't have the right to risk other comrades or to jeopardize the mission. I shall have to minimize the chances of the journal ever being found—not a straightforward task in a single room, but one that my father's tuition in joinery makes that much easier. I have already selected one space for concealment inside the window frame that will hold both the journal and my emergency supply of gold coins. A second, more obvious cache under the floorboards for a dummy journal seeded with meaningless names, times and dates should satisfy all but the most rigorous of searchers.

If I sound as if I'm trying to convince myself, perhaps it's because I am. Obfuscations always give clues, and no place is immune to discovery. There will be risks, to others as well as myself, and all I can promise is to make them as small as I can. Small enough, I hope, to balance out this compulsion I feel to make sense of my past and present by putting them down on paper.

SUNDAY, APRIL 24

A reader of this journal—should there ever be one—will need to know why I have come to this small German railway town.

I work for the International Liaison Section of the Communist International. The Comintern, as those of us who work for it understand only too well, is now essentially an arm of the Communist Party of the Soviet Union, the world's only worker's state. The leaders of the party believe that another European war is only just over the horizon, and they wish to know what, if anything, is left of what was once the world's second-largest Communist party—the KPD. More precisely, they want to find out whether there are still enough Communists in Germany brave or foolhardy enough to constitute a significant fifth column inside Hitler's Reich.

Hamm, and particularly its railway industry, was once a major stronghold of the KPD, and the significance of that industry in any future war would be enormous. I have a memorized list of nineteen party members who were working here when the Nazis took over, and my job is to find out if there are enough still living and loyal to put spokes in the wheels of Hitler's trains.

I have good qualifications for the job. Over the last fifteen years, I've been sent on similar missions to many different countries, and I've become quite an expert when it comes to judging the political potential of any given place and time. Here, in the country of my birth, the country I have fought for as both a soldier and a revolutionist, I don't anticipate any difficulty in sizing up the situation. I know these people, at least in this sense: I know when they are willing to fight and when they are not.

I'm also at home in the railway industry. My father worked in it all his life, and as a child I spent many hours in depots and on footplates. During the civil war in Russia, I put this secondhand knowledge to good use, organizing schedules and even driving locomotives on a couple of occasions. I have no firsthand knowledge of the Argentine railways, but received such an exhaustive briefing from an Argentinian comrade in New York that I feel I know all Buenos Aires's termini like the back of my hand and have no trouble visualizing a pair of silver rails running through grasslands toward the snowcapped Andes.

On the other hand, I don't want to overstate my importance. I am confident that Comrade Stalin is neither anxiously awaiting news of my mission nor overly concerned by the high possibility of my capture and execution. I am sorry to disappoint my Gestapo readers, but I am just a revolutionary journeyman and utterly expendable. Both I and my bosses in Moscow are very aware that this mission is as likely to prove fatal as not.

Despite this, I woke up this morning feeling strangely pleased with life. If I eventually report that there are still comrades and networks left to reengage, and if Moscow gives me the green light to do so, then will I have to begin my game of Russian roulette, exposing my identity to those KPD veterans who have, one way or another, survived five years of Hitler. But that decision is still many weeks, perhaps even months, away. For the moment I am relatively safe, doing a job that seems important, and that I know I can do well. A job that seems easier to live with than many others I have done in the last few years.

This morning's breakfast was depressingly instructive. Herr Ruchay obviously likes to read out loud from his newspaper whenever he comes across something suitably uplifting, and this morning he treated us to extracts from a speech by the Sudeten German leader Henlein, a speech as long on threats and short on truth as we have come to expect from the Nazis and their friends. I nodded my agreement as amiably as I could while Barufka concentrated on his food and Gerritzen's enthusiasm fought a valiant battle against an obvious hangover. The young manager was wearing an SA uniform, in readiness, as he told me, for the day's marathon march. Units of the local party, SA, and SS would be demonstrating their endurance by carrying heavy packs up into the hills and back again, ending with a parade through the town center.

Frau Gersdorff was also dressed for the outdoors and looked rather less harassed than she had the previous day. She told me that the party arranged so many events on Sundays that she had been forced to give up Sunday lunches. The cook would make sandwiches if asked, and the main meal was served in the evening. I asked her where she was off to and watched her suppress the desire to tell me to mind my own business. She and Walter often went cycling in the country on Sundays, she said rather abruptly, and then gave me a smile to compensate for the abruptness.

As suggested, I requisitioned some sandwiches and headed out to take a look at the town. I have been to Hamm twice before, but only for the shortest of periods, once waiting a few hours between troop trains during the war, once stopping over for a single night during my escape from Germany in 1923. The couple I stayed with on that second occasion were both killed by Freikorps a few weeks later, and as far as I know, I have never met any other comrades from the town. Since I have lived in Germany for roughly half of my forty-three years, there is always the chance that I'll run into someone who recognizes me, but the odds are on my side.

As I walked, I saw lots of families out enjoying the sunshine. Most looked happy and healthy enough. The saddest face I noticed belonged to a pastor standing outside his church, and seeing him slip back inside, I was curious enough to put my head around the door and catch a glimpse of his meager congregation. If, as the Comintern hopes, there are thousands of Germans seeking an organization that is willing and able to take on the Nazis, then the church doesn't seem to be it.

After walking back toward the lodging house, I ate my lunch by the canal. Fishermen punctuated its banks at regular intervals, most of them probably railwaymen enjoying their day off. Behind me, the yards and workshops where they worked were mostly silent, and by this time the sun was shining out of an almost cloudless sky. Sitting there, eating simple liverwurst sandwiches and watching the lines arcing out across the dark water, I discovered a painful awareness of the Germany inside me, and of how at home I feel here. Later, watching Gerritzen and his fellow marathon marchers manfully trying to strut their way down Ritterstrasse—many seemed to be suffering agonies from their shiny new boots—I was reminded of the Germany I had rejected, the Germany of flags and uniforms, of caste and obedience.

Sunday dinner followed the pattern of the previous day, a pattern that I presume will be repeated ad nauseam. The food was tasty enough, if a trifle bland after my years in Latin America. Ruchay lectured; Gerritzen bubbled—leaving Barufka and me to murmur approval or disapproval as required. I asked Frau Gersdorff if she and Walter had enjoyed their trip, and she said they had, volunteering the additional information that Walter was doing his homework. Ruchay interjected that he supposed the boy would be joining the Hitler Youth this coming summer. I saw anger flash in her eyes, but only for a moment. "There's plenty of time to decide about that," she said, as if it were a matter of little importance.

Ruchay was unabashed. "It would not look good to have two sons at odds with the new Germany," he told her pointedly. She looked as if she wanted to slap him, but he didn't seem to notice.

After dinner Barufka and I walked across to the local bar, mostly to escape Gerritzen's endless bleating about his blisters and the overwhelming smell that seemed to be seeping out of his boots. Over a couple of beers, I asked what had happened to Herr Gersdorff. He was dead, Barufka told me. He had died a long time ago, when Walter was only an infant. He had been much older than Anna and had left her the house.

Erich, however, was not his son. Anna had been married twice, and her first husband—Erich's father—had died in the war. Locals had told Barufka that she had married Walter's father during the Great Inflation, mostly for Erich's sake. Those had not been good years for raising a small child on your own.

When I asked him what Ruchay had meant by his comment about two children at odds with the new Germany, Barufka looked at me, weighed me up, and apparently decided that I could be trusted. Erich was involved with one of the youth gangs, he said. The Traveling Dudes. Despite having a regular job at the works—and he was a good worker, Barufka said—Erich had had several run-ins with the local police. "They go into the hills and start fights with Hitler Youth groups," Barufka said, a small smirk lurking at the corners of his mouth. "So it's important that Walter is a good

National Socialist. Otherwise they will start to think the family has faulty genes."

WEDNESDAY, APRIL 27

My intention of writing something every evening has quickly come to grief: a full day's work, as I should have remembered, makes a bed look so much more welcoming than a desk. Tonight, though, my brain seems too active for sleep. I should probably have refused the second cup of coffee, but there have been too many days when I hungered for one.

At 8 A.M. on Monday morning, I presented myself at the Reichsbahn offices, and I emerged a half hour later with a job as an assistant dispatcher. The labor shortage is as acute as everyone said it was, and I had the pick of a dozen jobs that needed filling. The man who interviewed me seemed so overwhelmed by the fact of an applicant that he barely glanced at my meticulously forged qualifications. He was more interested in why I had chosen Hamm for my reentry into German life, and for a second I was tempted to tell him I'd stuck a pin in a map. But I didn't. I stuck to my script: an Argentinian friend who had grown up here before the war had told me it was both a railway center and a nice place to live. My interviewer shook his head rather sadly at that and asked me what I thought of the new Germany. I told him that so far I was impressed, but that I'd been here only a few days.

He directed me to the offices of the German Labor Front, the Nazis' national union, where I was interviewed again, with rather more purpose, by a spotty-faced young man in a crisp uniform. So crisp, in fact, that I imagine it would have stood up on its own. He checked all my papers, asked me what he probably thought were probing questions, and reluctantly provided me with the official workbook I needed to start my new job. Having done that, he seemed to relax, and insisted on providing me with an exhaustive list of the Strength through Joy outings and holidays I could now apply for. He himself had recently been on the Baltic cruise, which he thoroughly recommended.

An hour later I started work in an office with a dozen or so desks overlooking the yards. Over the last few days, I have discovered that three shifts keep these in permanent use, checking freight in and then checking it out in the right direction. It's not difficult work, but the labor shortage means that there's a lot of it, and there isn't much time for thought. Tea breaks are taken outside if the weather is good, and for lunch we walk down the tracks to the locomotive works canteen. The food is cheap and plentiful, particularly by the standards I've grown used to over the last few years.

Two of my fellow dispatchers have helped settle me into the job, one because he was told to, the other because he obviously enjoyed doing so. The former has yet to say anything of a remotely political nature. He has the air of an old Social Democrat, but he might just be uninterested in politics. The latter, Otto Tikalsky, is on my memorized list of former KPD members in Hamm. He is now wearing a swastika badge and making the most of every opportunity he gets to praise the regime. He might be a genuine convert or a frightened opportunist; he could be an undercover infiltrator. Finding out which is unlikely to be easy. But not doing so may well prove fatal if and when I tell him who and what I really am.

Herr Ruchay—who is now one of my bosses, albeit a very distant one—represents another possible danger. For reasons best known to him, he has taken a liking to me, and seems intent on taking me under his wing. As we were walking home from work yesterday evening, he blithely informed me that he had given my name to the railwaymen's Social Club committee, along with the suggestion that I give a talk on National Socialism's appeal in South America. I expressed a modest reluctance to do so but was quickly made aware that refusal was not an option. It was left for him to fix a date, something he has now done—I face my audience two weeks from tomorrow.

I should record that I have taken an almost violent dislike to the man. Not for his politics, anathema as they are, but for the way he treats everyone else in the boardinghouse. He never misses a chance to pour scorn on Barufka and endlessly patronizes the mostly oblivious Gerritzen. On one occasion a few days ago, I came across him and Frau Gersdorff talking in the hall downstairs, and had the distinct impression that he was bullying her about something. I think he would be a bad enemy to make.

On another matter—over the last few days, I have had a few fresh doubts about the wisdom of keeping this journal, but have decided to ignore them. I have created the necessary hiding place in the window frame, and if I say so myself, it's invisible to all but the closest scrutiny. Not that the Gestapo would probably bother to look. For one thing, everyone knows that Comintern reps are strictly forbidden to put anything in writing; for another, the men in black have much more fun extracting information through broken teeth.

THURSDAY, APRIL 28

After this evening's supper Frau Gersdorff intercepted me at the bottom of the stairs. Walter had apparently decided that I was the perfect person to help him with a particular piece of homework; she didn't want him making a nuisance of himself, but she wondered if I would mind. I told her I'd be happy to help.

Walter arrived at my door about the same time I did,

though rather more out of breath. I sat him down at the small table with his book and took the armchair. His homework topic was German "living space," and he was supposed to explain the need for more of it.

He already knew all the government's arguments—overpopulation, the need for more farmland and raw materials to make the nation self-sufficient, the theft of Germany's colonies in 1918, the basic right of the strong to subdue the weak—but seemed less than completely convinced by them.

"If we have more living space, that just means other nations will have less," he said, looking at me questioningly.

"That's true," I said, "but maybe they don't need all they have."

He thought about that, screwing up his mouth as he did so. "You mean we Germans can do more with it?" he asked.

"That's what the Führer believes," I said. I realized I had no idea how much trouble boys his age could get into for questioning party dogma.

"Do you think the Führer's always right?" he asked, looking me straight in the eye. I was tempted to just say yes—and I should have. I had heard enough stories about children reporting their parents and other adults to the Gestapo—any other answer was asking for trouble. But I knew instinctively that the idea of reporting someone would never occur to him, that he simply wanted to know what I really thought. And that he would know if I lied to him. So I told him no, I didn't think that anyone was right all the time. He nodded at that and asked me whether anyone could be wrong all the time. I laughed, and so did he. "My brother . . ." he started to say, but stopped himself. I think he was about to tell me that Erich did believe Hitler was wrong about everything. I told him that his brother sounded like an independent sort of lad. "I'm only his half brother," he said, as if this were a weakness.

We had strayed a long way from "living space," but I had realized by this time that Walter was much more interested in making friends than in getting practical help. He examined the book by my bed—Theodor Fontane's *Effi Briest*—and asked me whether I'd heard of Tom Shark. I hadn't, but my ignorance was about to end. Tom Shark, it turns out, is the "King of Detectives," and I was treated to a lengthy exposition of his latest and—need I say it?—most dangerous case. I managed to avoid another plot by claiming, rather shamefully, that knowing it would spoil my enjoyment of the book itself, whereupon Walter promptly changed the subject to football. Apparently England are coming to play Germany in Berlin next month, with the World Cup to follow in Paris in June. I was at least able to say something intelligent about the latter, having studied reports of the riots that had recently taken place in Buenos Aires after the Argentine football authorities decided not to send a team. Any kudos I might have gathered from knowing that story promptly vanished when I failed to come up with a favorite club team in Argentina—I simply couldn't think of one. Walter's team is Schalke 04, which plays in nearby Gelsenkirchen. His favorite player is Fritz Szepan, who is the captain of both Schalke and Germany. "I have a signed photo in my room," he said. "You could come and see it."

We went down to his room, which was much tidier than I expected. I was examining the photograph when Frau Gersdorff suddenly appeared, looking less than happy to find me in the family's part of the house. I explained why I was there, agreed to Walter's request for future help with his homework, and beat a hasty retreat up the stairs. On the way up, it suddenly occurred to me—and I have no idea why it took so long—that both Frau Gersdorff and Herr Ruchay may have taken me for a possible Gestapo informer. Which, I decided, was somewhat ironic. But perhaps usefully so.

→ → →

SUNDAY, MAY 1

I suppose I must start with the train. The wonder train. Its visit to Hamm this afternoon was the sole topic of conversation at last night's supper. Ruchay was full of it, and so was Barufka. For once, they were in perfect harmony, swapping facts about speed, fuel consumption, internal decor, and God knows what else like a pair of enthusiastic schoolboys. The line drawing in the local evening newspaper was passed around the table like some kind of sacred relic, and when Frau Gersdorff confessed under questioning that she was not taking young Walter to the station, I half expected Ruchay to call the Gestapo.

This morning, circumstances—and perhaps Walter himself—conspired to change her mind. She was called away to look after a sick friend and left Erich—whom I'd previously seen only in glimpses—to ask me if I'd take Walter to the great event. Erich, a tall, rather gangly lad with dark hair flopping over his ears and collar, looked a less-than-willing messenger. He was wearing what I presumed was a gang uniform: a checked shirt with flower-emblazoned metal pin, dark shorts, and dazzling white socks.

He gave me the message and waited, with an almost imploring look, for my reply—no doubt he had plans for the day that didn't include babysitting his younger brother. I just looked at him, struck by the faintly ludicrous disconnect between young men in white socks who spent their weekends looking for Hitler Youth groups to beat up and the murderous war my party had fought against the brownshirts only five years earlier. For all I know, Erich and his friends are as serious about their politics as we are about ours, but he looks like an innocent, and innocence, in Nazi Germany, presupposes historical amnesia. The thought crossed my mind that Hitler had managed to slip Germany off its old moorings, to put clear water between the pre-Nazi past and the present. Which was not good news for the Comintern.

I told Erich I'd be happy to take Walter and got a big smile in return. Walter, when I picked him up downstairs twenty minutes later, was as excited as Ruchay and Barufka the previous evening, and by the time we reached the station, I must have known as much about the train as the workers who made it. The station was packed—one platform was reserved for local party bigwigs, the other three overflowing with lesser mortals—but we managed to get a good vantage point on the footbridge at the western end, and were soon rewarded by an excellent view of the train entering the station from the east. The streamlined, blood-colored locomotive, its golden swastika glinting in the sun, came to a halt not thirty meters away from us, and like everyone else, we were struck dumb by its futuristic beauty. It was more like a rocket than a train. When it left a mere fifteen minutes later, there was a sense of wonderment and joy on the faces of the dispersing crowd. In those fifteen minutes, half a town had been persuaded that Hitler's regressive nonsense of an ideology was really a glittering vision of the future. I could almost hear the wheels going around in Walter's brain. Maybe Hitler is always right. Surely trains like this deserved a bigger country, more running space.

TUESDAY, MAY 3

I read in this morning's paper that the kaiser's grandson has married a Romanov duchess. Both bride and groom were described as "throneless." A progressive word if ever I heard one.

~ ~ ~

THURSDAY, MAY 5

I am not sure whether the cries woke me or whether I was still awake. There were several of them, rising to a climax of apparent panic, and then, suddenly, silence. I lay there for a few moments, wondering whether or not to investigate, until curiosity got the better of me. I slowly descended the two flights of creaking stairs and stood motionless at the bottom, listening.

Anna Gersdorff's low voice seeped out of the silence, reassuring and full of love, and I stayed where I was, drinking in the sound, as if it were I who needed comforting. The murmur ceased, and before I could retreat up the stairs, she had emerged from Walter's room and seen me. "I heard a noise . . ." I began.

"He was having a nightmare," she said.

I went back to my room but not to bed. Instead I sat by the open window recalling another night, on the other side of the world. Then it was Chu wailing up the storm, and Lin lifting him out of his cot and bringing him back to our bed. Lin, a party member's widow who had been my amah for almost a year and my lover for only a fortnight.

The dawn was sufficiently advanced for me to study the graceful lines of her back and neck, and it was only when Chu quieted down that we heard the gunfire in the distance. I remember the sudden turn of her head a few seconds later when someone knocked on our outside door.

It was Chen Lu, sent to fetch me. I went back inside to throw on some clothes, and when I turned in the doorway to throw Lin a kiss, she laughed and did the same.

I never saw her again.

Eleven years have passed since then, eleven years of

roaming the world as a Comintern rep. Eleven years in which, I must admit, I have been largely content to let my actions speak for themselves and to willingly function as an anonymous and inseparable part of something much bigger than myself.

Sometimes, lately, I wonder if I'm reaching the end of that road. If I am, I'm not sure what it means or what it implies for my future. There is no other road I wish to travel or, indeed, know how to travel. Europe teeters on the edge of a precipice, and I have no intention of abandoning the job I was sent here to do.

SUNDAY, MAY 8

What have I learned in my first two weeks of work about the political state of the German proletariat? Quite a lot, but nothing particularly clear-cut. As was bound to be the case, the labor shortage has given the workers better cards to play, cards which, in any normal bourgeois economy, might add up to a winning hand. But this is not a normal bourgeois economy—it is Nazi Germany, and the political winners are already decided. So all the arguments have become workplace arguments—about conditions, hours, pay. Since full employment has been reached—a couple of years ago, I guess—the workers and the authorities have been banging up against each other. Wage rises have been ruled out, so the workers have tried to increase their pay by changing jobs. The authorities have now brought in new rules that prevent workers from doing this, and the workers retaliate by taking unofficial holidays and being generally less cooperative. They argue more—I've already witnessed several blazing rows—and take less care with their work, their tools, and their machinery. They are thoroughly pissed off.

But will all this obvious discontent escalate into something really serious? If, as seems inevitable, the regime intends to keep depressing wages and lengthening working hours in a situation of labor shortage, then it will need either more coercion or a very persuasive diversion. War conditions, of course, would provide it with both. In the meantime, assuming that the regime doesn't do anything too stupid, the workers will probably take noncooperation as close to confrontation as they can without actually challenging the powers that be.

Can we do anything to change this situation? Probably not, but I haven't given up hope. Barufka and I have spent the last two Saturday evenings at the railwaymen's Social Club, which would have been a stronghold of Social Democrat and Communist activity before the Nazi coup. Jakob knows practically everyone, and I have shared in several group conversations, all of them critical of the regime in one way or another. Yesterday, I shared a table with two men who were analyzing recent German developments in thoroughly Leninist terms, albeit without using Marxist terminology or mentioning the great man. These two ordinary workers understood that the Nazi economy is designed for war and that someone is eventually going to have to pay for the war machine Hitler is building. They can see that the regime will lose much of its popular support if it asks the German people to pay through taxation, that the money can come only from abroad through conquest, and that war is therefore inevitable.

There are probably millions like these two. The party had fifteen years to explain how societies work, and it will take longer than five for its teachings to be forgotten.

Still, understanding is one thing, daring to fight quite another. When I eventually have to approach people—and, of necessity, make my own position and loyalties clear—the responses are likely to cover a wide range. All will want convincing that I'm who I say I am and not a Nazi agent provocateur; beyond that the responses will range from an enthusiastic welcome to downright alarm that their world has suddenly turned upside down. And one or more of them may seek safety in betrayal. Men and women prepared to risk their lives for political beliefs are always in a minority—there are so many Ruchays and Gerritzens eager to be seduced, so many Barufkas who want a quiet life. Minorities can win if they are large and determined enough, but is this the case in Nazi Germany today? I doubt it. We lost in 1933, and life for most Germans was a lot worse in those days than it is now. There were no wonder trains then.

None of which guarantees a prudent response from my bosses in Moscow. The true situation in Germany is not the only thing they'll bear in mind when coming to a decision— all those involved will also be mindful of their own status and safety in the shark-filled sea of Kremlin politics. As we discovered in China, the percentage required for successful action abroad comes down dramatically when someone in Moscow thinks he needs something to happen.

This morning Walter showed me the spread of photographs the local paper had printed to commemorate the wonder train's visit, and I found myself remembering a very different train, almost twenty years before, in a small Ukrainian town. We arrived one afternoon in our agitprop-instruction train, and handed out desperately needed food. Our medics gave treatment and medicines to those in need, and that evening we set up our screen in the local church and showed our film about the revolution. I can still see the light as it flickers across the upturned faces, and the hope that shines in their eyes.

The train that Walter and I saw last Sunday was beautiful to look at, powerful and efficient, a miracle of modern technology. The one in Ukraine had a heart.

➤ ➤ ➤

MONDAY, MAY 9

I walked to work with Ruchay this morning. Usually he's several minutes ahead of Barufka and me, but today, either by accident or design on his part, he managed to arrive at the front door at the same time as we did.

Outside it was another cold, dry day, but Ruchay was more interested in the Italian weather—rain had spoiled the open-air opera Mussolini had laid on for the last day of the Führer's stay in Rome. Still, Ruchay thought the Italians had put on an excellent show, all in all. The Axis was clearly bringing out the best in them.

He nodded in agreement with himself and then pointed out, as if it had just occurred to him, that there were a lot of Italians in Argentina. And, of course, a large German community. It seemed like the ideal situation for National Socialist success, a nation with a homegrown Axis, so to speak. He hoped that I would be exploring this possibility in my talk on Thursday.

I made an encouraging noise, and resisted the temptation to point out that the Germans in Argentina, who were mostly upper-class, and the Italians, who were almost all workers or peasants, had as much in common as exploiters and exploited anywhere. This, I guessed, was Ruchay's way of making it clear that I was supposed to deliver an uplifting message.

Having done his duty, he returned to what passes for gossip in Nazi Germany. "The Führer's in Florence today," he told us, as if he were sharing an important secret. "Visiting the famous galleries. He returns to the fatherland tomorrow."

We parted company outside the office in which I work.

Inside, a shock was waiting for me. I was hardly in my chair when a figure loomed above me, hand outstretched. A tall man around forty with closely cropped black hair, large brown eyes, and a badly misshapen nose, he introduced himself as "Dariusz Müller, your section boss." I had been told that Herr Müller was in Berlin for a fortnight on a military transport–planning course. I hadn't been told that his first name was Dariusz, making him one of the men on my list. The last time I'd seen his face was in the dossier Moscow had sent to our New York office.

Worse still, in the moment of meeting, I realized I'd seen the face long before that. Not close up and not to talk to, but I remembered it from somewhere. Sitting here writing this, I'm still certain of that but no nearer remembering where or when. Given his age and my long absence from Germany, it must have been back in the early twenties, in a party office or at a demonstration. Among comrades.

He showed no sign of remembering any previous meeting. He welcomed me to the section, hoped I was happy with the way things were going, and told me to come to him with any difficulties or complaints. "I expect things are run differently in Argentina," he said with a grin, "but no doubt you'll be telling us all about that in your talk."

I watched him walk away down the aisle between the dispatchers' desks, conscious of my heart thumping inside my shirt. When Hitler came to power in 1933, Dariusz Müller had been the deputy secretary of the local party organization in Hamm, and he had, according to Moscow's dossier, played a leading role in the desperate struggles that followed. In April of that year, he had disappeared from view. Moscow had received no notification of his capture or death but had concluded that one or the other must have befallen him. And now, five years later, here he was, a shift boss in one of the most important yards in Germany.

His survival implied betrayal but not necessarily a change of allegiance. Had he really changed sides or just pretended to do so? And if he had bought his position with the names and blood of former comrades, had he intended the bargain to serve the future needs of the party or only himself? I had no way of knowing.

He showed no sign that he had recognized me, either then or later in the day. He had brought new tasks back from his meetings with the military, and whenever a gap appeared in our normal duties, two other dispatchers and I were set to work on a timetabling exercise, clearing paths for west-moving military trains with minimal disruption to the regular flow of industrial freight. No dates or contingencies were specified, but it seems to me that such dispositions must have something to do with strengthening the French frontier in case of a military confrontation with France's ally Czechoslovakia.

My co-workers don't seem that concerned. Like most of the men I've talked and listened to over the last two weeks, they seem to have abdicated all responsibility for their fate to the Führer. If he can save them from war, then of course he will. If he can't, then no one could. Ruchay isn't the only one—I heard two other apparently sane men talking of Hitler's return from Italy as if it really mattered to them.

I suppose Stalin has acquired a similar hold over the Soviet Union, but he never goes anywhere.

TUESDAY, MAY 10

This evening I had another visit from Walter. Our last joint homework pleased his teacher, and Anna had given him permission to enlist my assistance again. "But only if you don't mind," Walter added, poised over the upright chair by the small table.

I said I was happy to help.

This time, believe it or not, he was supposed to write two hundred words on *The Protocols of the Elders of Zion.* "It sounds convincing," Walter said, "but it doesn't make sense."

"It's a forgery," I said without thinking. "At least, some people think it is," I added, in an almost comically inadequate attempt to repair the damage. "What makes you think it doesn't make sense?"

"Well, Herr Skoumal says that the Jews have been blowing people up and trying to take over the world for at least fifty years, but there's no sign of them succeeding, is there?" He gave me an owlish look. "If they're so dangerous, you'd think they'd have taken over more than one country by this time. I know the party is stopping them from getting anywhere in Germany, but there are lots of other places."

The logic was hard to dispute, but I wasn't sure agreement was the wisest course. Instead I asked him which country they *had* taken over.

"Russia, or at least that's what Herr Skoumal says. He calls it the 'Jewish-Bolshevik world conspiracy,' but that doesn't make sense either. I mean, Jews love money above everything, don't they? But the Bolsheviks abolished money when they had the Russian Revolution. Why should they and the Jews be partners in a conspiracy? It doesn't make sense."

Sometimes the Third Reich feels like a cross between Kafka and *Alice in Wonderland.* "Maybe they're not partners in a real sense," I said, "but if they're both enemies of the Reich, then I suppose they might join forces out of convenience."

"But that wouldn't be a conspiracy," Walter argued. "And what about the *Protocols*—who thinks it's a forgery?"

Some people in America and Britain, I told him.

"But America is run by Jews, isn't it? Herr Skoumal will say that they're bound to think it's a forgery."

"I'm sure he will."

"So what can I say?"

I told him to say that many people believed it was true and many didn't. That if there was a conspiracy, it seems to have failed.

"But I shouldn't say it's just a load of nonsense?"

"No."

He gave me the sort of earnest look that only a preadolescent can manage. "Because it's not true or because I'll get in trouble if I do?"

"Because you might get in trouble," I answered just as seriously. My superiors in Moscow would be astonished to know that I'm putting honesty to a boy I barely know above the security of the mission, but then I'm pretty astonished myself. Sometimes I think that there's something about Walter that demands nothing less, sometimes that something has happened to me, that years of living lies has finally made me desperate for some truth.

"Sometimes I almost want to," Walter said, as if the idea had just occurred to him. "But I know I mustn't." He looked down at the carpet and changed the subject. Had I ever been married? Did I have any children?

Thinking of Lin, I told him no.

"Why not?" he asked. "Did you ever meet anyone you wanted to marry?"

I said yes, wondering if it was true. "But she died."

"Oh, I'm sorry," Walter said, staring at his feet. "My father died," he added, as if in compensation.

"I know. Did you know him?"

"Not really. I don't remember him. But I do miss him." He raised his head and looked out of the window. "I worry about my brother. I worry about my mother too." He turned to me. "She says what she thinks, no matter who's listening."

Then you have reason to worry, I thought.

"She doesn't like Herr Skoumal, but I don't think she particularly likes Jews or Bolsheviks either," Walter went on. "I tell her to be careful," he added, and suddenly smiled. "Just like she tells Erich."

He sighed and stood. "I must go and write this." Halfway to the door he turned and asked if I'd take him around the depot one weekend. "Herr Barufka took me last year," he said, "but I think I was too young to appreciate it. And he was afraid all the time that I'd hurt myself. I think he did it more for my mother than me. No, that sounds ungrateful . . ."

"This Sunday," I told him, "if you're here." With my talk coming up on Thursday, I wanted something to look forward to.

The room felt empty after he'd gone. I sat in the chair he'd vacated and opened the window, despite the chill of the evening. I followed the pinpricks of light into the distance, over the horizon, and around the spinning world, just the way I used to from my bedroom window as a boy. According to Ruchay at supper, Florence station had been lit by three thousand candles for Hitler's farewell, and the words were no sooner out of his mouth than I was back with Lin and Chu, by the lake in Canton's Yuexiu Park, surveying the myriad floating candles lit to celebrate the Lantern Festival.

They say you can never go back, but sometimes I feel as if I'm running a race with my past, and am about to be overtaken.

WEDNESDAY, MAY 11

It's almost midnight, and I've finally completed a rough draft of my lecture for tomorrow. The whole business is a complete pain in the behind, and I can't believe I let Ruchay talk me into it so easily. It shouldn't have been that hard to find an excuse. I have often heard Comintern comrades say they had to guard against carelessness in the first few days of a foreign mission and wondered why I seemed immune. Now I know that I'm not.

The situation would make a good exercise for the Comintern school. Question: How do you give a talk about political matters to a politically diverse audience without irritating or angering half your listeners? Answer: by playing the innocent. If I sound even remotely left wing, Ruchay and co. will be appalled and probably suspicious to boot. If I sound as right wing as that lot would like, then half my fellow workers—the ones I need to talk freely in my presence—will be afraid to do so. So I'm stuck with middle-of-the-road naivety—lots of local color and railway stuff. I can please everyone with a few swipes at the English, who, in Argentina at least, are both antiworker and anti-German. And if I welcome the Argentinian Fascists' promise to break down class antagonisms and unite the nation, Ruchay and his friends will share my joy that Argentina looks set to follow Germany's example, and any secret Communists in the audience will pity my naive idealism. I shall, I hope, be all things to all men.

Before I stop writing, I must note down something I saw in *Der Stürmer* this morning, something that stayed with me all day. It was a photograph of Baron Ludwig von Rothschild, and the words beneath it seemed to sum up the people who run this country. *"This photograph was taken seven days after his imprisonment,"* the caption read. *"Here he still looks confident of success. Since then his assurance has left him."*

It sounds like gangsters gloating over a victim in a cliché-ridden movie. If only that were all it was.

FRIDAY, MAY 13

Yesterday evening was, to say the least, interesting. Ruchay escorted me to the Social Club after supper and, once we got there, insisted on buying me a drink. "To help with the nerves," he said. Of course he wasn't to know how many hundreds of workers' meetings I've addressed over the years. Once we were settled with our beers he seemed unusually devoid of anything to say, perhaps because he had only one listener. I tried to break the ice by asking him how long he'd been at Anna's rooming house but received only a curt "several years" in reply. And when I followed this up by saying how well I thought she ran the place, he looked almost angry.

I was saved by the sudden appearance of the club secretary, telling me it was time. We walked through to the adjoining sports room, which had been crammed with upright chairs for the occasion. To my astonishment most of them were occupied. I had expected an audience of between ten and twenty, but there were at least fifty workers present. Almost all were men, and most were drinking and smoking—the far end of the room was already obscured by a tobacco fog, despite the wide-open windows.

While the secretary was introducing me, I studied my audience. Many of the faces were familiar from the canteen, and most of my fellow dispatchers were there, including Dariusz Müller. When I caught Barufka's eye, he gave me a grin and a thumbs-up. Looking around, I could see no sign of the earnest, out-to-make-a-point faces I had feared—this audience, I decided, had come to be entertained, not educated. I was still taking comfort from this conclusion, when I heard the secretary promise a question-and-answer session at the end of my talk. It seems quite incredible to me now, but the thought that I would be questioned by people who knew Argentina better than I did had never crossed my mind.

I talked for about forty minutes, rambling on about the country's geography, peoples, railways, and general economic development. I stressed the manly virtues of the open frontier and explained the new "tango" style of dancing with what I hoped was a finely judged blend of slight disapproval and repressed lust. It was, I thought, quite a performance.

The first question, asked while half the audience members were still refilling their glasses, concerned my opinion of Buenos Aires, and enhanced my false sense of security. The second destroyed it. A worker I didn't know—a gangling man in his late forties or early fifties—asked what I thought about the current tension in Argentina between the German community and the national government.

Having no idea what he was talking about, I asked him to be more specific. And luckily for me, he had an obvious fondness for the sound of his own voice.

It turned out that in mid-April—when I was in mid-ocean—twenty thousand Argentinian Nazis had assembled at a swastika-bedecked Luna Park arena in Buenos Aires to hear a series of like-minded speakers from the fatherland. Afterward, suitably fired up, they had fought pitched battles in the surrounding streets against local leftists. The resulting backlash against this brazen display of foreign flags and power had included government threats to close German community schools and hospitals. What, my questioner wanted to know, should our own government say to the one in Buenos Aires?

"I don't think our government should say anything," I said. "South American governments admire strength, but they hate to be bullied. In many ways these governments are our natural allies, allies we may need in the struggles to come, and it makes no sense to antagonize them."

That didn't shut him up. He asked if I was suggesting that we should just leave German communities outside the Reich to the mercy of their governments. "Surely," he said, "Germany must put Germans first."

I said I agreed but that Germans who cared deeply about their German ancestry could always return to the fatherland, as I had. I realized I was sweating, and not just from the heat. The atmosphere in the hall had suddenly grown tense, and I wasn't at all sure why.

"Maybe the Sudeten Germans should just come home!" a voice shouted out, raising the stakes.

"They're at home where they are," someone replied from the other side of the room.

I ploughed on. The two situations were different, I said. While the Germans in Argentina were not being perse- cuted in any real sense, it seemed clear from reports in the press that the Sudeten Germans were. And they lived right next door—the international boundary could be moved to incorporate them in the Reich. The German commu- nity in Argentina had chosen to live in a faraway country that contained many other nationalities, and had to accept the consequences of such a choice. This did not mean us abandoning them: on the contrary, the importance of the German and Italian communities in Argentina should lead to a strengthening of the relationship between Argentina and Germany, which could only help everyone.

That shut everyone up for a few seconds, during which I noticed Müller giving me a rather thoughtful-looking smile. I wondered whether I'd overdone it.

The next question was about the wider gauge used by the Argentinian railways and prompted a discussion among the audience about some crackpot scheme of Hitler's to build an even wider-gauge super-railway across the Reich. The arguments for and against were scrupulously technical, but put with a virulence that suggested more was at stake than at first seemed apparent.

For my final question, I was asked whether I recom- mended emigration to Argentina. I hemmed and hawed, playing up the Argentinian outdoor life and wild scenery like a "Strength through Joy" brochure, but admitting that

I probably hadn't been back in Germany long enough to appreciate how much had changed. And it would be impossible, I said, to recommend leaving the fatherland at a time like this, when so much seemed possible.

At which point the secretary thanked me for a fascinating talk and encouraged the audience to give me a round of applause. I left as soon as I could and walked back to my room alone, feeling utterly exhausted. I went to bed immediately and fell asleep still wondering whether I'd been a little too clever for some of my audience.

It's probably too early to tell, but nothing happened today to confirm my fears. Several people—including Müller—told me they'd enjoyed my talk, and as far as I could tell, they meant it. At any rate, I shall not volunteer to give another.

SATURDAY, MAY 14

I went for a haircut this morning, and the barber's salon smelled just the way I remembered from my childhood. There were several of the same products on the display shelves, some with the same packaging after more than thirty years. The only big difference was the picture of Hitler that stared down from one wall, as if daring us to ask for the same ridiculous hairstyle and mustache. No one was tempted.

A lively discussion was underway when I arrived, the main outlines of which only gradually became apparent. The subject was Baron von Cramm, who, I soon discovered, was a famous tennis player. Yesterday he was sentenced to a year in prison for having a five-year-long homosexual relationship with a Galician Jew, and this morning the whole story was spread across the papers. I could understand why Ruchay had not included this particular item in the digest he inflicts on us over breakfast each morning.

The problem, according to a pock-faced man sitting opposite me, was the shortness of the sentence. Buggery was a bad enough crime in itself, and obviously buggering a Jew was a damn sight worse. A year was almost an insult, the man said, and several other heads—including, to the barber's annoyance, the one in the chair—vigorously nodded their agreement.

I asked what had happened to the Galician Jew and was told, with some relish, that he had first blackmailed 30,000 marks out of von Cramm, and then used the money to emigrate to Palestine. While I was absorbing this, the young man sitting next to me entered the fray. The judge had got it right, he said. "It was really the wife's fault—the judge said so. Until von Cramm married her, and she fucked someone else on their wedding night, he was completely normal. That would send any man around the bend."

"Bah!" was the pock-faced man's reply. He agreed that a shock like that might induce a man to bugger a Jew, but not to keep buggering him for five years! And in any case, that wasn't the reason the judge had let von Cramm off so lightly. "He was from 'an excellent family'—that's what the judge said. And the bastards all stick up for each other, buggers or otherwise." There were murmurs of agreement—clearly the Nazis haven't been as good at eradicating class consciousness as they think they have.

The conversation soon turned to football and this afternoon's match against England in Berlin. The general opinion was that Germany would win, though the barber was doubtful. He turned out to be right.

We listened to the game in the common room—Ruchay, Barufka, Walter, and I. Ruchay knows even less about football than Barufka and I do, but he cherished the idea of a victory over the English. Walter, of course, was highly excited, not least because two of his beloved Schalke players were in the national team. Ruchay mistook the boy's enthusiasm for patriotic fervor, and for once did nothing to squelch it.

There was no missing the political undertones. The radio commentator prattled on about trains pouring into Berlin full of excited fans and was beside himself with joy when the English team raised their arms in the Hitler salute. He ran through the German team somewhat perfunctorily, and then listed the occupants of the Führer Box—Göring, Goebbels, Hess, and Ribbentrop among others—with breathless awe. Hitler wasn't there, however. He must know more about football than his disciples.

It was obvious from the way the commentator's voice slowly lost its jauntiness that the English were playing the better football. When they scored their first goal after fifteen minutes, you could hear the silence in the stadium, and imagine the gloomy faces in front of all the People's Radios. But then, out of the blue, an equalizer. Walter hopped around with glee—his two Schalke heroes had made and scored the goal—and Ruchay smiled with relief.

That was as good as it got. The English went on to score goal after goal, and the radio commentator's voice grew more and more depressed. I had a mental picture of the men in the Führer Box, lips twitching like Ruchay's in otherwise stony faces. Walter, by contrast, took defeat like a man, which impressed me enormously.

This evening Barufka and I went to the Social Club as usual. There was no sign that Thursday's talk had changed anyone's attitude toward me, or made them any less willing to talk in my presence. This afternoon's game was the main topic of conversation, the general opinion being that when it came to football, the government and its press were all talk and no delivery. The feeling that this criticism could be applied to other aspects of national life was left unspoken but is, I am certain, shared by most of Hamm's railway workers.

← ← ←

SUNDAY, MAY 15

I was going to say that I took Walter around the depot this afternoon, but really we took each other. He insisted on seeing absolutely everything, which turned us both into explorers. We walked the length of the freight yards, swapping the names of the far-flung outposts we found chalked or painted on rolling stock, from Cádiz to Danzig, Brindisi to Copenhagen. And in the process, my shrunken, claustrophobic Europe of Comintern defeats turned into Walter's mysterious continent, full of romance, full of possibilities.

I showed him my office—two-thirds empty on a Sunday—and took him up to one of the yard boxes, where we were lucky to find a friend of Barufka's. He made Walter's day by letting him set one of the signals. We then walked the aisles of the shed, clambering up onto several footplates. There were no shiny express locomotives, of course—Hamm is a freight depot—but Walter didn't seem to mind; he strikes me as a boy with remarkably few preconceptions and a corresponding openness to just about everything.

We watched as an engine was turned on the new vacuum turntable and then climbed up and over the coal stage and down the steps to the works, which seemed unusually busy for a Sunday. Between the workshop building and the canal, we found an engine graveyard—three lines of rust-eroded locomotives in various states of decomposition, all bearing the word "condemned" on some part of their anatomy. One locomotive at the end of a line—an Ellingen 4-4-2 that had been almost swallowed by the surrounding vegetation—somehow triggered a memory from my childhood. It was nothing special, just a vivid picture of my father in his best suit, arriving home one evening with a bunch of flowers for my mother. I must have been eight or nine years old, and I remembered feeling so happy for both of them.

Some of this must have shown on my face, because Walter, with his usual disarming directness, asked me what I was thinking about. I told him.

"Where was that?" he asked. "Where did you grow up?"

"In Offenbach," I said. "Near Frankfurt am Main."

Walter wanted to know if my parents were still alive.

I told him they had both died in the flu epidemic of 1918. I didn't say that I'd only found out three years later.

As we walked back toward the works, Walter plied me with a string of questions. What had my father done? What was my mother like? Did I have any brothers or sisters?

I couldn't even remember the relevant details from my false identity, which made it easier to tell him the truth. I told Walter that my father had worked on the railway, that he had started off as a cleaner and ended up a shed foreman. That my mother had been a full-time nurse before she met him and a part-time one after that. That I'd had an elder brother named Jens who was killed in the war.

"So you have no family at all," Walter said.

"No."

This obviously made him happy, but he did his best to disguise the fact. I felt flattered but also guilty, knowing full well that my time in Hamm would be limited.

Since we got back from the depot, I've been unable to shake off the subject of parents. Over supper Gerritzen was full of his own and how they had promised to lend him the money for a luxurious honeymoon cruise the following spring. Ruchay, not to be outdone, launched into an account of how his mother had single-handedly purged her village library of degenerate literature and been personally congratulated by the local gauleiter. I went out for a walk along the canal, hoping for a cool evening breeze to blow away both heat and memories. There wasn't one.

Over the last couple of hours, sitting on a bench in the spring twilight, I have been roaming the years like a masochist in H. G. Wells's time machine. I have revisited the house I grew up in, seen my mother at the kitchen door, my father lighting the evening fire. I have relived those two trips home from the front, the one to help bury my brother, the other to tell my parents the party had taken their place. I have heard the anger in my father's voice and tried not to see the terrible hurt in his eyes. I have listened as news of their deaths has appeared, like magic, in the middle of a conversation about printer's ink on a wet autumn day in Kiev. And I have calmly shrugged them off, as if they were remnants of some other life, some other age.

They have been dead for twenty years now. Their names were Matthias and Eva, and the longer I live the more I think I am deep in their debt.

MONDAY, MAY 16

Something distressing has happened. Or at least, that's what it feels like.

After supper this evening, Anna came up to my room. She didn't raise her voice, but she didn't need to—her anger was obvious enough. She told me that Walter had come home from school with a letter of reprimand from Herr Skoumal, and that he had been forced to stand in front of the class while the teacher poured scorn on his assertion that *The Protocols of the Elders of the Zion* were a forgery. "He can only have gotten that from you," she said.

I tried to explain, but she cut me off.

This wasn't Argentina, she said. "You know it's a forgery, and I know it's a forgery," she almost whispered. "But this idiot of a teacher probably doesn't. And even if he does, he won't say so, or he'll be out of a job. That's the way things are now . . ."

She stopped herself. Her anger had blown itself out, and fear was taking its place. She seemed suddenly aware that, like her son, she'd said too much. "I'm sorry," she said stiffly. "I know you were just trying to help."

I told her it wouldn't happen again. She looked at me for what seemed a long time, as if she wanted to say something else, but then simply spread her hands in a gesture of resigned acceptance, and left.

That was more than an hour ago. Since then I have sat by the window listening to two discordant voices, both of which seem to be mine.

One voice says I'm an agent of the Comintern, a small but vital cog in the worldwide struggle against Fascism. That I was sent here to do a political job, not to fill the place of one young German boy's dead father.

The other voice says that the boy needs me, that I don't want his name added to the lengthening list of those I have failed to help because I was too busy helping everyman.

The first voice is stronger, perhaps wiser. It has been my voice, for better and worse, for twenty years. But it is not as certain as it was. It occurs to me that Jesus was tempted in the desert and that these days Germany is a desert of the soul.

TUESDAY, MAY 17

Over breakfast, Ruchay read out an obituary in the *Völkischer Beobachter*. It was a nauseating paean to an SS NCO killed during an escape from a Thuringian Forest concentration camp four days ago. Two Communists have been on the run ever since, and I spent much of the day imagining myself in their shoes.

⬦ ⬦ ⬦

WEDNESDAY, MAY 18

I have finally met Walter's grandfather. The sound of someone thundering up the stairs soon after supper gave me a
momentary fright, but the knock on my door was reassuringly
hesitant. I found an out-of-breath, worried-looking Erich on
the other side. His grandfather had fallen out of bed and was
unconscious. Could I help lift the old man back onto the bed
and stick around while Erich went to fetch the doctor?

As we hurried down the stairs, Erich explained that Anna
and Walter were both out. He didn't say why I was his chosen
lodger, but I could guess. He hated Ruchay, and—according to Walter—was not overhappy about Barufka's passive
devotion to his mother. Gerritzen was doubtless out with the
girlfriend. Which left only me.

The old man was no longer unconscious. In fact, he was
cursing his inability to turn himself over or lift himself up
off the floor. His metal walking frame had ended up halfway
across the room, and an overturned bedpan lay in a pool of
spilt urine only inches from his white-haired head.

"We're here, Pops," Erich said, and there was a sigh of
relief from the prone figure. We lifted him carefully onto
the bed, but there were no cries of pain. He didn't seem to
have broken anything, but a cut on his forehead was bleeding profusely.

Erich seemed uncertain what to do next, so I told him to
go and get the doctor. When he'd gone, I got a washcloth
from the bathroom next door and held it over the wound
until the bleeding stopped. The old man had relapsed into
either sleep or unconsciousness, but his pulse was regular
enough. I fetched a bucket from the kitchen and mopped up
the yellow puddle.

I was examining the cut again when his eyes suddenly opened. They were as white as his hair. "Who's that?" he asked.

I told him my name and that I was a lodger.

"You're the idiot who came back from Argentina!" he croaked. "Walter likes you, though," he added before I had time to respond. "And he's a good boy," he rambled on.

I agreed that he was.

"They both are," he went on. "She's raised them well, despite everything. She should never have married that boy. Not because he was a Communist, though. Because he was a shit."

"Walter's father was a Communist?" I asked. I couldn't help myself.

"Ernst?!" He laughed so much that the blood started oozing from his forehead again. "No, no, no. That was just a bargain. Sex for security. Walter was the silver lining."

I pressed down on the cut and asked him how he was feeling. He shrugged, as if it hardly mattered and asked where I'd learned to take a pulse. In the war, I told him.

"That's when she met him," he said. "The first one. Erich's father. The shit."

I was about to ask the shit's name when I heard footsteps in the corridor. It was Erich and the doctor, a young man with a pleasant face who showed no sign of resenting the after-hours summons. I put a hand on the old man's wrist, said goodbye, and left them to it.

This family is full of surprises.

FRIDAY, MAY 20

Ruchay's sermon at breakfast was all about Göring's latest project, the Rhine-Main-Danube Canal, which is scheduled for completion in 1945. This new waterway, which will connect the North and Black Seas, was apparently dreamt up by Charlemagne, and is consequently being touted by the Nazis as the "culmination of a thousand-year-old dream." The Third Reich has every intention of extending itself that far into the future, but I'll be astonished if it's here for the inaugural passage.

At work this morning, everyone was talking about the rumors of troop movements in Saxony and Bavaria, and this afternoon we were busy clearing contingency paths for troop trains to the western frontier. Is this it? The papers are certainly preparing the ground—they are full of rabid Czech mobs hunting innocent Germans.

On a much more cheerful note, I've been invited to Walter's birthday party. It's on Saturday afternoon, and Verena has already baked the cake.

SATURDAY, MAY 21

I spoke to Verena Hanssen today. She's the woman who comes in six days a week to help Anna cook and clean, and the mother, it turns out, of the Negro boy I've seen waiting outside the house on more than a few occasions. He looks a year or so older than Walter, which makes it likely that he's one of the Ruhr-occupation babies. Verena must have either had an affair with one of the African soldiers involved, or been raped by one of them.

Marco seems a nice lad, and there are no obvious signs that he's being persecuted or bullied on account of his color. Which is surprising. Either he has very independent-minded teachers at school, or the Nazis are so focused on the Jews that they lack the time to thoroughly persecute anyone else. The other boys at Walter's birthday party certainly treated Marco like an equal, which verges on the miraculous in a state which classifies worth according to race.

Verena is very like Anna. They look different—Verena is slightly younger, more obviously attractive, darker complexioned, and darker haired—but they have the same perpetually harassed air, as if they need to keep on running in order to stand still. And they probably do. For all the mother worship that goes on here, single mothers have a pretty hard time of it.

Verena ended up standing beside me for a few minutes after she and Anna brought in the birthday cake. She asked me a few polite questions about Argentina and how I was finding things back home. I asked her what felt like an innocent question—how far away she lived—and saw fear in her eyes, if only for an instant. She told me but hurried back to the kitchen the moment a rather self-conscious Walter had blown out his candles.

There were five other boys there, all of whom seemed like fairly ordinary eleven- and twelve-year-olds. I was glad I'd been invited and told Anna so when I got the chance. "Walter wanted you to come," she said, leaving the impression that she hadn't. Realizing this, she suddenly smiled and almost admitted as much. "I'm sorry about the other day," she said.

I told her that Walter was a clever boy, that he understood some things as well as many adults did, and that most of the time he was fully aware that some things were better kept to himself. "But he's only a child," I said. "And sometimes he just can't help himself."

"And the teachers play on that," she said bitterly. "They try to trap the children into betraying themselves."

They did, I agreed, conscious that I was being far more open than was wise and not really giving a damn. And if he wanted my help in the future, I told her, and if she was willing to let me give it, then I'd make sure that he knew the difference between what was true and what was sayable.

She gave me a surprised look, as if she had suddenly realized that she was talking to someone she didn't know.

My false identity is beginning to feel like an itch I can't resist scratching.

SUNDAY, MAY 22

The Nazis have apparently decided to up the stakes in their political war with Czechoslovakia. Their papers are full of outrages against the poor Sudeten Germans, all of whom, it seems, are hungry for the chance to swell the legions of the Reich. More significantly, there's been a definite step-up in the preparations for military action. I and half a dozen others were called in to work this morning because the regular Sunday shift was insufficient to cope with the increase in military traffic.

The local paper, which I read over lunch in the canteen, had nothing to say about Czechoslovakia, but contained a long piece on the "gang" Erich belongs to, the "Traveling Dudes." Personally, I find it hard to criticize any group that lists beating up Nazis among its hobbies, but if I were Erich—or Anna—the tone of this article would worry me. It read like the opening shots of a crackdown.

It occurs to me that a reader of this journal might conclude from recent entries that I've abandoned the job I was sent here to do. I haven't. By briefly examining a few attendance cards each day, thoroughly perusing the various message boards, and innocently asking after long-lost colleagues, I have managed to place all but two of the nineteen names I memorized in Moscow. Nine are dead or have moved away, but eight are still working here in Hamm, and I've established some sort of contact with four of them.

Dariusz Müller and Otto Tikalsky both work in the dispatcher's office, and I've now had several weeks to ingratiate myself with the latter. I think I detect a faint undercurrent of irony in most of his pro-Nazi statements, but that may be wishful thinking on my part. Müller has been less available, which suits me fine—when I see my contact I'll be asking if Moscow can dig up any more information about his activities in the year that followed the Nazi takeover.

I've discovered that two other names on my list—Hans Derleth and Alfred Neubecker—belong to the pair with the Marxist analytical skills that I noticed on my second visit to the Social Club. I've been keeping an eye out for both over the last few days, but so far without any luck. Over the coming days and weeks, I hope to track down the remaining four, and to find out what I can about all eight. I may casually run into them on their way to work, or happen to find myself sharing their tables in the canteen or Social Club bar. I will take note of the men they choose to mix with at work and introduce myself to the latter, whenever the opportunity arises. In this way, I hope to sit in on conversations involving my actual targets and get the chance to work out where they stand without inviting the risks inherent in a more direct approach.

I will of course avoid saying anything even vaguely political in the first few encounters, and put my toes in the water, so to speak, only once some sort of trust has been established. And I will be just as interested in their unconscious reactions as in anything they choose to say. Things as simple as a reluctance to make eye contact or, even worse, a determination to do so. I'll be expecting wariness, hoping for a sense of inner stillness.

TUESDAY, MAY 24

My avoidance of Müller has had the opposite effect to that intended. He approached me at lunch today and said he'd been waiting for a chance to have a chat with me. Reckoning that there was nothing to be gained from a refusal, I allowed myself to be steered to one of the side tables for two, wondering how I was going to respond to an announcement that he'd recognized me.

But he said no such thing. He asked me how I was getting on, how I was finding the new Germany, how I found the work conditions, and how I thought they could be improved. And as the questions got more political, I sensed him weighing each answer—he was testing me in much the same way I've been testing others.

But for whom? I tried to pitch my answers somewhere between faint encouragement and polite rejection—to hint that I might be more forthcoming with him if he was more forthcoming with me. I was still getting acclimatized, I said, and I liked leaving politics to the politicians, but I was interested in union work. What did he think of the government's Labor Front?

He neatly deflected that question with a similar one of his own, and so on. Since both of us were trying to size up the other's true allegiance without revealing our own, it was a somewhat surreal conversation. I don't know what impression he went away with—the impression that I am who I claim to be, I hope. If so, and he remains loyal to the party, that may induce him to try and recruit me. If he's working for the Gestapo, it should persuade him to leave me alone. If he doesn't know quite what to make of me, then, whomever he's working for, I can expect more such conversations.

Which is hardly an enticing prospect. One of the two comrades from the concentration camp in the Thuringian Forest was captured yesterday. He was found hiding in a brickworks oven near Stendal and was immediately executed. He'd been in the KZ for two years, so they knew he'd told them all he was going to.

— — —

WEDNESDAY, MAY 25

It seems that Anna has decided to trust me. When I returned from work, she invited me into the family parlor, where Walter was sitting, pen poised over a blank sheet of paper. Herr Skoumal, Anna said, had returned from sick leave and immediately started picking on the boy. Walter butted in with the details: he had been given question after question until he got one wrong and had then been given extra homework. He has until tomorrow to write a short essay under the title: "Is There a Place for Jews in the Third Reich?"

"If Walter says yes," Anna said, "Skoumal will denounce him as a degenerate. If he says no, then Skoumal will have his victory, and he'll no doubt make the most of it. But it'll all be forgotten in a few days."

"Not by me," Walter said indignantly. "Lots of Jews fought for Germany in the last war. There was a place for them then."

"Who told you that?" Anna asked. "No, don't tell me—it was your grandfather." She sighed and looked to me for help.

"You can't win this one, Walter," I told him. "If you challenge this teacher, it'll only make him more determined—"

"But how can he argue with the fact that all those Jews gave their lives for the fatherland?"

"I don't know. Maybe he'll say they had no choice. It doesn't matter. Sometimes being right—and you are right—doesn't help. Sometimes you just have to survive to fight another day. And if you're interested in truth, that's what living in Germany is about right now—survival. Just write what he wants to hear. Make him think he's convinced you. The truth is always important, but sometimes you have to keep it hidden."

During this speech of mine, Walter's face went from

argumentative to thoughtful to downright surprised. I didn't want to look at Anna, but I knew I'd crossed a bridge with her.

"Josef's right," she said to Walter, and he sighed his acquiescence.

A little while ago, he brought up his finished work to show me. He's done a wonderful job—Goebbels could find him a job in his propaganda ministry.

He also had an invitation from downstairs. "My granddad would like it if you came to see him again sometime, to have a beer perhaps. He says you were in the war?"

I said I had been, and Walter settled back in my armchair as if preparing himself for the whole story. I told him I'd spent four years on the eastern front, had never won a medal, and had never even been wounded.

"But you did have friends who were killed?" he asked, as if he needed convincing that I'd fought in the real war.

"Yes," I told him. Every last one of them, I reminded myself.

"Was it hard to get used to peace again after all that?" he asked, switching from child to youth as only those who are stuck between the two can.

"I suppose so," I said. The truthful answer was that I never got the chance to find out—my war just slipped into another form, became a war that transcended borders, in which the battlefield could be anywhere. Even here in this room, answering the innocent questions of a twelve-year-old boy. "But I emigrated to Argentina," I said. "And Europe seemed a long way away."

"Granddad was at Verdun," Walter said. "And Passchendaele. That's where he was blinded by the gas."

I was surprised. He seemed older than that.

Walter must have read the thought in my face. "He was in the landsturm," he explained, "but he still had to lie about his age. You had to be under forty-five, and he was forty-nine in 1914."

I suddenly realized I didn't know the old man's name.

"Andreas," Walter replied when I asked him. "Andreas Biesinger. That's my mother's maiden name," he added somewhat unnecessarily.

"I'll visit him tomorrow," I promised.

THURSDAY, MAY 26

I wasn't sure what to expect from Walter's grandfather in this second encounter. What I got was a much more coherent man than the one I'd met just after his fall. He may be bed-bound and blind, but there doesn't seem to be much wrong with his brain.

We talked—mostly, he talked—about the war. He has no interest in why it had happened or why Germany had lost— his stock of anecdotes all seem to revolve around an essential disbelief that men could do such things to one another. And not just the cruel and violent things. In such conditions he finds man's humanity to man even harder to credit.

Over the last twenty years, I have met many men who refuse to talk about their experiences in the war, and a few, like Andreas Biesinger, who have found it hard to talk about anything else. Twenty years on, he still can't believe what he saw, heard, felt, smelled, in those years, and that disbelief has colored his every waking moment since. Listening to him, it's hard to disagree with those who say that something fundamental died in the trenches, something most people still haven't learned to do without. I don't know what you'd call it—a faith in progress, perhaps, or trust in humanity, even belief in God. Many of us filled that void with the revolution, but for those who didn't, the present and future must sometimes seem unimaginably bleak.

One thing is clear—he dotes on Anna. If it's possible for

blind eyes to light up, his did when she brought us both some hot chocolate. I'd been waiting for an opening to ask about her first husband and did so as the door closed behind her, despite a strong feeling that I shouldn't. "What happened to Erich's father?" I asked, as casually as I could.

"The Spanish flu," the answer came back like an unwanted coin from a slot. I knew he was lying.

"So Erich never knew his father," I went on, moving the conversation to safer ground.

"No. And he didn't like Ernst—Walter's father. But he has a good heart, that boy."

I came back to my room with my curiosity unsated. Had Anna's first husband—the Communist—just left her? Or had he died in the struggle? I told myself it was none of my business, but of course that's exactly what it is.

FRIDAY, MAY 27

I've made some progress over the last few days, picking up three further firsthand impressions of men on Moscow's list.

On Wednesday I managed to insert myself into a canteen conversation between Alfred Neubecker and a man I didn't know and was again impressed by Neubecker's essentially Marxist insights into the nation's fragile economy. And this time I also noticed the passion behind the analysis, which bodes even better as far as my mission's concerned. I suspect, like me, he saw his views of life and politics transformed by the war and its aftermath, and has hardly looked back since. Neubecker's at least a decade older than I am, but despite the thinning grey hair, he still looks reasonably fit, and advancing age has not dulled his mind. Strength of will is of course another story, and on that I'm reserving judgment.

This evening at the Social Club, I ran into two more of the

men on my list, Horst Franke and Richard Opatz. They were part of a long and scurrilously amusing discussion of Field Marshal Göring's personal habits, both known and imaginary, which somehow turned into something more somber as closing time approached. Horst Franke is around my age, plump, round faced, with longish brown hair and a generous mustache. At first sight he seems slightly clownish, but his serious purpose soon becomes apparent—a lot goes on behind his eyes. The man is parsimonious with words, but when he does say something, it's usually to the point. As yet I know nothing about his homelife, but he feels like a possibility.

So does his friend Richard Opatz. The two are clearly good friends and, as is often the case, seem like polar opposites. Opatz is wiry, prematurely bald, and serious looking, but someone who talks to fill silences. He works as a shunter in the freight yards and is probably ten years younger than Franke. Aware that he's less intelligent, Opatz almost always defers to the other. It looks as if they come as a pair, which is usually good news—personal and political loyalties tend to be mutually reinforcing.

SATURDAY, MAY 28

Today was the last Saturday of the month, the prearranged date for my first clandestine meeting in Germany. After breakfast I told my fellow lodgers that I was off to look up a distant relative in Dortmund, walked down to the station, and caught one of the frequent local trains. The ten-mile journey must have taken about half an hour, but I was too preoccupied by the imminent meeting to more than notice the parched countryside. Over the years I must have made a hundred such assignations, but the process never gets easier. The feeling of helplessness, of being so completely at the mercy of someone else's competence, luck, or good will, seems to speed and amplify the heart, to dry the throat, to leave that shrinking feeling in the stomach that a Chinese doctor once explained to me as a lack of communication between the heart and the kidneys. As I sat on that train this morning, I was acutely aware of the unknown comrade traveling toward Dortmund on another train, a comrade who might already have been compromised in one of half a dozen ways. If so, I told myself, I would soon be talking to the Gestapo. And all the horrors of memory and imagination filled my head, as they always have, as they doubtless always will.

I had more than the Nazis to worry about. Over the last few years, many comrades have arrived at clandestine meetings only to discover that their work abroad is over, that they are needed back in Moscow for "reassignment" or "retraining" or "review" or any of the other words Yezhov and his crew use to disguise the usually fatal fall from official favor. Lately, I have, somewhat to my surprise, begun to wonder whether I would obey such a summons. This would seem strange to my comrades, most of whom have, like me, spent the last twenty years believing that life outside the party would be essentially meaningless. It's a belief that's hard to abandon, and a year ago I would have had no hesitation in taking the train back to Moscow. Which, of course, is probably why no one has asked me to do so.

I digress. After arriving in Dortmund with almost two hours to spare, I walked down to the river for a look at the meeting place— an open-air, tree-shaded café close to one of the bridges—and then back into the city center in search of a good coffee shop. I found one with wonderful pastries near the Marienkirche and sat outside in the sunshine, sipping at the strong Viennese coffee and heroically struggling to keep the cream cake from oozing all over my shirt.

Someone had left Friday's edition of the *Frankfurter Zei-tung* on the adjoining table, and I glanced through it in search of the paper's once-famous liberalism. It was gone. Like the *Völkischer Beobachter* and our local daily, if a trace more elegantly, the *Zeitung* was spewing out Nazi propaganda. The lead story was the new "Strength through Joy Motorcar," the subject of Hitler's speech on Thursday morning, which had, like all his broadcast speeches, effectively brought the country to a halt. There's no doubt that the figures are impressive—the car's going to be on sale next year for around 1,000 marks, and families will be able to get their hands on one for weekly payments of around five. Calling it the People's Car is another touch of genius—Hitler understands that National Socialism needs to appear socialistic, even as he seeks to destroy everything in Germany that actually fits the description.

I digress again. At a quarter to twelve, I walked back down to the river and ordered myself another, much inferior, coffee at the outdoor café, and took a seat at one of several wrought iron tables that looked out across the almost dry bed of the Emscher. In the old days, we used to use novels as recognition signals in Germany, and before I left New York, the local ILS office spent several days trying to identify writers who were certain to remain unbanned. Goethe was the only one they'd come up with, so the previous weekend I'd purchased the copy of *Wilhelm Meister's Apprenticeship*, which I now laid down on the table in front of me.

A few minutes later, she walked across the river bridge. I knew her as Elise, which probably wasn't her real name. Like many comrades, she's someone I've come across at irregular intervals over the years, but never really gotten to know. I think I first met her at Karl Liebknecht House in 1922 or 1923, and our paths have crossed in Moscow on several occasions—the last, I think, in 1932. She's probably about thirty-five years old, with shoulder-length brown hair, brown eyes, and a figure just the right side of plump. Today, she was wearing a simply cut cream dress and cream shoes with blue bows, all of which made the most of her suntan. She certainly looked nothing like a Comintern regional agent.

She steered herself through the tables toward me. "Josef," she said, smiling and leaning over to kiss my cheek. "Have you finished your coffee? Let's walk."

As we started down the path beside the river, she put her arm through mine, and I felt a jolt of something—surprise, I suppose. It's been so long since I had that sort of casual physical contact with a woman, the sort of nonsexual contact that assumes an existing affection, whether sexual or platonic. It sounds absurd, but that touch was probably the most disturbing thing I experienced all day.

If she noticed, she gave no sign. Following standard protocol, she began by telling me the place and time of the next *treff*—if for any reason, we had to split up in a hurry, I would know when and where to go.

I then reported on the situation in Hamm, slipping back into the language of the party with an ease that felt almost insulting. I told her that there was considerable discontent on the shop floor, but that this was being channeled into purely economic demands by a combination of Labor Front carrots and the fear of Gestapo sticks, that, in short, there were no objective conditions for conducting political work. I said that there were probably enough committed ex-party members and sympathizers in the yards to set up an underground group for sabotage work, but that finding out exactly who they were would be like playing several games of Russian roulette with the same gun.

I told her about Dariusz Müller, that I thought he might have recognized me, but didn't know from where or when. One or more of our exiles living in Moscow might remember something useful, so could she put in a request for some digging?

She said she would. "Moscow's looking for optimism," she said, without apparent irony.

"They won't find much here," I said.

"I know. Everyone agrees about that."

"So what next?" I asked.

"You know how it works. They'll go through the reports, then make their decision. If war breaks out, just sit tight. If it doesn't, you'll probably get new instructions next month."

After we parted in the city center, I walked back to the station and caught the local train for Hamm. Sitting by a window as the countryside unfolded, I felt a strange mixture of elation and unfocused grief. The worst had not happened—I had another month of grace, of living what passed for a normal life in Hitler's Germany. It might be—it is—unreal. I am, of course, playing a part. But like the actor who loses himself in a particular role, I am feeling more at home in my role than my real life. I enjoy my work at the yard and the feelings of achieving something useful that accompany it. I cherish all those conversations, trivial and otherwise, which I share with my fellow workers in the canteens and bars. I have enjoyed, and am still enjoying, getting to know Walter. And I love these hours in my room, sitting in the armchair or close by the window, indulging in those greatest of luxuries—reflection and doubt.

SUNDAY, MAY 29

Erich has been arrested.

The first I knew that something serious had happened was when Anna thundered up the stairs late this afternoon and asked if I could keep an eye on Walter while she went out. He was busy doing his homework downstairs, but just in case . . .

I said of course I would. She offered no explanation for her sudden departure and, as I soon discovered, had said nothing to Walter either. But he knew his mother well enough to be worried. His math homework was finished, but mostly by me.

Verena had also been pressed into emergency duty, and while she and I struggled to finish the half-produced supper on time, Walter and Marco commandeered the kitchen table for a board game. A single glance was enough to tell me that Walter had at least one ear cocked toward the front door and his mother's eventual return.

She finally came back around nine, looking decidedly careworn. Walter ran to greet her and was quickly shooed into the family's part of the house. She told him to get ready for bed and thanked me for looking after him. I took my cue, and went back up to my room.

About half an hour later she knocked on the door. I invited her in, and for the first time in our acquaintance, she agreed to take a chair. "Erich was arrested today," she began. "Walter knows, so you should too."

She told me how it had happened. Erich and several of his friends from the Traveling Dudes had hitchhiked down to the Rothaargebirge on Friday evening for a weekend of hiking and camping. Late on Friday they had gotten involved in a shouting match with some members of the SA in a beer garden, but no punches were thrown, and the Dudes had thought nothing more of it. The storm troopers, however, had been less forgiving, and had alerted the local Kripo. These worthies had trailed the Dudes back to their mountain camp on the Saturday evening and hunkered down in the surrounding bushes to enjoy the gang's repertoire of anti-Nazi jokes and songs. Eventually, unable to tolerate any more slurs on their glorious leader, the mixed band of Kripo and storm troopers had emerged from hiding and attempted to arrest the youths. A fight had broken out, during which several Dudes escaped into the darkness and one SA man ended up in the campfire. Erich had received a blow on the back of the head and woken up in a police van an hour or so later. He and six others were now in a cell at the Dortmund Gestapo headquarters.

When Anna recited one of the offensive couplets—"Get out your cudgels and come into town / and smash in the skulls of the bosses in brown"—I couldn't resist a smile, and she noticed as much. "I could murder him," she said, "but it's hard not to feel proud of him too."

I smiled again, and we just looked at each other for a moment, sharing the recognition that we'd reached a new level of complicity.

I asked what would happen next.

She said the duty officer had told her Erich would be brought to court sometime in the next two weeks. "He's one of the oldest in the group," she added, "so he'll get one of the stiffest sentences. Three months, at least, I should think. And of course he'll lose his job."

I told her she shouldn't worry overmuch about that—the way things were he'd have no trouble getting another one. "And unemployment . . ." I was going to say, would probably be the least of his worries.

She picked up my unspoken thought perfectly. "We'll be at war in a year, won't we?" she half asked. "But will the English and French really fight for Czechoslovakia?"

At this point, I made a conscious effort to draw back. It would have been so easy—so comforting—to continue this discussion, to share my belief that the German economy needed a war, that Hitler's real ambitions were in the east, that the Soviet Union would have no choice but to fight. If her husband had been a Communist, then there was a good chance that she had been one too, and we would recognize each other in the ways we described how the world works. And that would have represented another, irreversible level of complicity, one I could not risk.

"I don't know," I said in answer to her question, and she seemed to sense my retreat from openness. She got up to leave and thanked me for listening to a mother's worries. I told her I'd be happy to look after Walter whenever she needed to visit Erich.

MONDAY, MAY 30

This morning's breakfast was a dramatic affair. Ruchay was in the middle of spreading cherry preserves over his roll when he came upon Erich's name in the list of those arrested in the Rothaargebirge. Knife suspended in midair, Ruchay read the appropriate bits out loud. "Did anyone know about this?" he asked the rest of us.

I made the mistake of admitting I did. "Frau Gersdorff asked me to look after Walter while she went to see the police," I explained, but Ruchay was far from mollified.

"We should all have been informed," he insisted.

"I don't see—" Barufka began, but at that moment Anna came back into the room with the second pot of coffee.

"You should have told us about this," Ruchay said angrily, waving the paper at her. "Not left us to read about it."

Her hand shook slightly in the act of refilling Gerritzen's cup, but her voice was steady—and cold—as a rock. "I don't believe it is any business of yours, Herr Ruchay," she said.

"Such behavior is everybody's business," he almost sluttered. "Particularly those of us who live under the same roof as your son. Something like this is bound to reflect badly on all of us."

"I'm sorry you feel like that," she said quietly. "If you are not happy here, and you wish to leave without the required notice, I will of course understand." And with that, she calmly walked out.

I felt like applauding, but Ruchay was less impressed. He stared at his coffee for what seemed an eternity and then got up and left the room without touching it. The rest of us listened to him walk down the hall and heard the knock on the family connecting door. We couldn't make out what he said to her, but it sounded for all the world like the hissing of snakes. He didn't come back for his coffee.

When I got back from work this evening, I found that Anna had gone to Dortmund, leaving Verena to cook and watch over Walter and Marco. She had left a message asking me to look after Walter and Andreas if she was not home by the time Verena and Marco left.

Supper was a much quieter affair than breakfast. I was expecting more tantrums from Ruchay, but he seemed strangely deflated, and had considerably less to say than he usually does.

Verena and Marco left after eight, and Walter was soon ensconced in my window seat. He was obviously upset about Erich's arrest but trying hard to be grown-up about it. He kept asking, in various ways, what I thought would happen to his brother, and I kept saying I really didn't know but that I doubted whether it would be anything terrible. "Because he's not a Jew or a Communist?" Walter wanted to know.

He talked about Erich, something he'd never done with me before. They're obviously not extremely close—five years is a big gap, after all—but there seems no trace of envy or hostility. Walter's angry with Erich for worrying and upsetting their mother, but he clearly admires his brother for the willful independence that leads him into such trouble. According to Walter, Erich's a "doer" rather than a talker, but that doesn't mean he's stupid. "He says if you know how things work, you don't need to know why."

We went down to check on Walter's grandfather and had just made him a cup of chocolate when Anna returned. She told us Erich was fine and that he'd probably be appearing in court at the beginning of next week.

I came back up here and wrote the above, conscious throughout of the feelings lurking at the back of my mind, feelings I have struggled to keep at bay throughout the day. There was another item in the paper this morning—a lurid, almost ecstatic account of the terror Japanese planes have been raining down on Canton for the last few days. The paper reported that five hundred people have been killed, nine hundred wounded, but as old China hands know only too well, such figures are almost always underestimates. The correspondent also wrote that thousands of Chinese had fled across the Pearl River in sampans, hoping for shelter in the international settlement on Shameen Island, only to be beaten back by soldiers and sailors of the imperialist powers. The correspondent seemed uncertain whether to condemn Germany's English and French rivals for behaving in such a degenerate colonial manner, or to congratulate them for showing the nonwhite races who's in charge.

It is eleven years since I was in Canton, but I can see that river, those sampans, the international settlement, as clearly as if it were yesterday. I can feel the heat, smell the streets, feel the sudden dryness in my throat when the reality of betrayal struck home. Most of the Chinese comrades I got to know in 1927 were dead within days, and I've never been back.

Lin's son Chu would have been thirteen this October, seven months older than Walter.

TUESDAY, MAY 31

I was enjoying my ten-minute break this morning, sitting outside the office in the sunshine, when Dariusz Müller sat down beside me. He said that a few months earlier he and a few other yard employees had set up an unofficial "Working Group" to discuss work-related matters. They met every few weeks in someone's home, and he wondered if I'd like to come along to this evening's meeting. I told him I didn't think I'd been back in Germany long enough to have many useful opinions of my own, but that I'd be interested to come along and listen. He told me the place and time—a street only fifteen minutes' walk away from my boardinghouse at eight o'clock. I said I'd be there and then spent the rest of the working day wondering whether I should be.

I took a roundabout walk to the house in question, partly out of conspiratorial habit, partly to enjoy the bright summer evening. Despite the late hour, the local park was full of small children making joyful noises and watchful parents sharing a chat and a smoke. There were lots of young couples out for a walk, and the benches were full of old people basking in the golden sunlight. And there was hardly a uniform to be seen. At such moments it's easy to forget the poison pumping through this country's veins.

The meeting was held in the downstairs front room of a small terraced house. The front door was opened by the tenant, a short man with an unruly shock of dark hair and worried brown eyes. He introduced himself as Joachim Wosz and went around the circle of seats naming the other nine men who were there. Müller gave me a smile; the other eight offered wary nods of acknowledgment. With the exception of Wosz, they were younger than I expected, in their late twenties or early thirties. I recognized all their faces from the works canteen, but Müller was the only one on my memorized list. As the meeting got underway, I found myself almost soothed by the familiarity of it all—the worker's room lined with books, the shabby furniture and serious faces, the feeling that everyone had one ear tuned to the discussion, one to the street outside.

We worked our way through a formal agenda, which consisted of issues likely to arise at next week's Labor Front meeting. There was talk of demanding an overtime ban, and of focusing attention on the rising number of accidents that have taken place since the recent introduction of a new safety regime. A long discussion followed about a particular dispute involving one of the yard managers—a friend of Ruchay's, I think—and one of the women canteen workers. She is facing a disciplinary hearing for dumping a bowl of soup in his lap, and while there seems to be general agreement that she did it on purpose, the man himself is considered a Nazi toad.

I listened, offered a few bland remarks, and did my best to read between the lines. It was clear to me that this Working Group consists of party activists who have spent several years out of contact with the émigré leadership. In the absence of any outside direction, they have made the best of a bad job, agreeing on political goals among themselves, and then using regime-sponsored forums such as the Labor Front to spread them among the wider workforce. They may also be involved in riskier activities such as printing and distributing literature, but probably nothing more than that. Their lack of ambition may reflect a sound grasp of the local reality, or it may be due to lack of direction. Or both.

When the agenda was officially exhausted, Frau Wosz appeared, as if by magic, with a tray of tea and biscuits. By this time everyone was standing, stretching their limbs, and as I circled the room, I noticed the framed family photograph on one wall. Joachim Wosz was in it, and next to him was another young man, presumably his older brother, with a face which I recognized from the Moscow files. Matthias Wosz had been a leading member of the Hamm KPD in 1933, but had been left off my list because he was known to be fighting in Spain with the International Brigades.

I felt someone at my shoulder. It was Joachim. "Your family?" I asked.

"Yes," he said, and changed the subject. "Did you find our discussion interesting?" he asked.

I said I had and offered the additional bait that I had been involved in union activities in Argentina.

"You didn't mention that in your talk," Müller said jovially, looming over my other shoulder.

I told them that I'd been unsure of my ground, that unions in today's Germany were probably very different from unions in Argentina, and as I was speaking, my eyes fell on the Wosz family wireless, a large and powerful-looking set that sat on a small cupboard in the corner. I had noticed it when I arrived, but only then saw that it was tuned to 29.8 on the shortwave. In January 1937 the Spanish Republican government had placed a powerful transmitter and this particular wavelength at the disposal of German anti-Nazi exiles for broadcasting back to the fatherland. Listening to it was the sort of criminal offence that earned you a stay in a KZ.

Sitting here in my room, I feel certain that Wosz leaving his radio tuned to this signal was mere carelessness. But at the time I had the sudden—and probably ridiculous—feeling that I was being tested. If I was who I said I was, this radio frequency would mean nothing to me, but if I showed any signs of recognition, I would betray myself, in their eyes, as a Gestapo informer. At best, I would receive no more invitations to meetings. At worst, I might meet with one of those serious accidents at work we had all discussed earlier.

"That's a wonderful radio," I said. "Do you know any good stations for dance music?" I asked, adding that that was one of the things I missed most about Argentina.

They didn't. I don't think dancing figures highly in their list of priorities, but then I can't claim that it has ever figured very highly in mine.

Müller insisted on walking part of the way home with me. It was dark by this time, the streets almost deserted but still warm. After we parted with a comradely smile, I had to remind myself that his resurrection remains unexplained, and suspicious. Then again, people like Joachim Wosz would have known him five years ago and must believe they have reason to trust him.

When I reached the house, I found Anna sitting on the steps outside, staring into space. She was smoking, something I hadn't seen her do before and something that testified to her state of mind—the regime officially frowns on women smoking in public. I asked her if there was any news of Erich, and she told me, as if surfacing from a great depth, that his court appearance has been set for next Monday. I left her in her angry solitude, a woman whose every instinct is to scream defiance but who knows that such defiance is a luxury she cannot afford.

WEDNESDAY, JUNE 1

The Nazi news machine continues to churn out uplifting entertainment for the masses. Ruchay was delighted to tell us this morning that the Warburg bank has been "aryanized"— three Warburgs and a Spiegelberg have been retired, and replaced by Germans with more acceptable racial ancestry. I innocently asked what had actually happened to the Warburgs and Spiegelberg, but Ruchay's search for an answer proved—rather annoyingly to him—fruitless. "They'll probably live abroad on the profits they have squeezed out of ordinary Germans" was his guess, but I wonder. You can usually rely on falling bankers to provide themselves with a soft landing, but Jewish bankers in Nazi Germany may be the exception that proves the rule.

Another of today's stories—as on any other day recently—concerned a fresh outrage in the Sudetenland. Yesterday two of Henlein's thugs were shot and seriously wounded in a Sudetenland café. The paper admitted that Henlein's men had attacked the Czechs, but claimed that they had been irresistibly provoked—the Czechs had requested that the café's band play a popular Czech number!

Ruchay read this bit out, but as I discovered later, there was more. A bed in Varnsdore that Henlein once slept in has become a place of pilgrimage for young girls. The sheets have not been changed since their encounter with the heroic Sudeten leader, and the girls are allowed to lie between them for a few seconds, sniffing as they do so for his lingering scent.

This kind of hysteria seems peculiar to the Reich and its minions—on the wireless you can hear the women screaming as Hitler drives by in his Mercedes, and most of them would probably kill for a sniff of the Führer's sheets. Where does this come from? What strange void is being filled here?

Walter came up to see me after supper. He seemed subdued, much like the rest of the house and, indeed, the rest of Germany. The country is bracing itself for a war that only the government wants, but that everyone else believes is inevitable. Walter is also bracing himself for bad news about Erich and his mother's reaction to that news. Last week he was full of the football World Cup, which, if I remember correctly, begins this Saturday, but there was no sign of that enthusiasm this evening. I hope Anna has been reminding Erich that judges appreciate remorse.

THURSDAY, JUNE 2

Jakob and I went for a drink at the Social Club this evening, and one of his driver friends had a fellow driver in tow, the seventh of the eight men left on my list. Artur Zerbe is around my age, with fair hair and a thin mustache. On first sight, he looks muscular enough for a Nazi sports poster, but there's too much amusement in his eyes. He gives the impression of enjoying life, which is hardly a political recommendation in the here and now, but nothing he actually said set my inner alarm bells ringing. He was not wearing a wedding ring and, if the way he flirted with a passing member of the kitchen staff is anything to go by, seems to fancy himself with the ladies. Having no responsibilities often makes men more prepared to take risks, but first one must know why they've chosen that sort of life.

I have the opposite problem with Alfred Neubecker, who was also down at the club. I've discovered quite a lot about him recently, and none of it good. His wife is chronically ill, but she insists on sending him out for his Friday drink while a neighbor stands guard. They have no children to look after her if anything happens to him. I have few doubts about his political integrity or loyalty to the party, but as I talked to him tonight, I reached the conclusion that he's not an acceptable risk. His wife is dying, and his faith in life and the future is dying with her—you can see it in his eyes, in the way he looks at people. If he's forced to choose between her and us, he won't think twice, and I've reluctantly crossed him off my list.

As usual I walked home with Jakob. I spend more of my time with him than anyone else, but he doesn't make many appearances in these pages. Some people are like that—comfortable to be with, fundamentally decent, unambitious, and uninspiring. I like Barufka. I think I could rely on him in a crisis, even if it meant a risk to himself. And that's more than I could say for some comrades.

I don't know if he's always been the way he is now, or whether, as with Neubecker, something happened to flatten him out emotionally. An obvious guess would be the war—nothing deadens like a surfeit of death. I suspect he came back from the trenches looking much the same, but diminished in a way his wife either couldn't or wouldn't understand. And when she left and took the child with her, he was diminished still further.

He loves Anna in a quiet, hopeless sort of way. He knows she simply likes him, and he would never do anything to upset or embarrass her. He's good to Walter, who repays him with largely unconscious disdain—Barufka is about as far from Tom Shark as one can get. He's one of those kind men living in an unkind world who even doubt their right to be here.

FRIDAY, JUNE 3

Over the last few days, I've belatedly come to realize that Jakob isn't the only lodger quietly obsessed with Anna. Ruchay is neither kind nor courteous to her—in fact he's often unkind and downright rude—but there's a personal edge to his behavior that goes beyond the regrettable manner in which single men often treat their landladies. And this evening at dinner I caught him looking at her in a way that was impossible to misinterpret.

An hour or so later, enjoying a beer with Anna's father in his room, I mentioned what I thought I'd seen.

Andreas grimaced. "He's always been mean to her, and we all know why. He wants her, and he can't work out why or what to do about it. So he takes it out on her by being mean and ill-mannered. I've told her to throw him out, but she says we can't afford to."

SATURDAY, JUNE 4

When I woke up this morning, the sun was streaming in through a gap I had left in the curtains, and I just lay there in bed for the better part of an hour, luxuriating in the light and the fact that it was Saturday. Days off are one of the great joys of an ordinary working life, perhaps especially for those, like myself, who are unaccustomed to the continuous grind of days on. I flung open the curtains just in time to see the first Berlin train of the morning steam by on the far side of the yards, its locomotive belching a picture-book pattern of white smoke into the blue sky as it eased up the incline toward the works.

The atmosphere around the breakfast table was considerably less sunny. Ruchay read his paper with lips pursed and for once found nothing he wanted to share with the rest of us. Gerritzen was just as uncommunicative. He ate with his customary gusto, but mechanically, his brows furrowed with worry. A row with his girlfriend perhaps, or maybe a promotion denied. Only Jakob seemed his normal reliable self, neither cheerful nor depressed, just there. As usual, his eyes followed Anna when she entered the room and mirrored the anxiety in hers.

Later that morning, while shopping with Jakob for a fishing rod, I caught sight of her across the street, deep in conversation with Dariusz Müller. There was nothing conspiratorial about the meeting—the two of them were standing in front of a shop on a busy street—but it was clear that both were taking their talk very seriously, which suggested more than a passing acquaintance. When I mentioned later that I'd seen her with my boss, she explained that she was asking about possible workplace support for Erich. This explanation would have seemed more reasonable if I hadn't seen the instinctive flash of alarm that preceded it.

Germany's World Cup match against Switzerland was a big disappointment. This time it was only Jakob, Walter, and I listening to the common-room wireless; Ruchay and Gerritzen either had other business to attend to, or had decided that one humiliation on the soccer field was enough for the spring. The game ended in a draw, a result that seemed to suit the mood of the house. It will be played again on Wednesday, during school and work hours. Walter seemed unconcerned—he is, unsurprisingly, more worried about Erich's fate than that of his footballing heroes.

The match was hardly mentioned at the Social Club, where everyone wanted to talk about the continuing rumors of war. The latest has it that Hitler has penciled in June 12—a week from tomorrow—as "The Day" for military action against the Czechs. Lots of men had pieces of evidence to support the rumor, ranging from the latest disposition of armor-carrying trains to their mother's intuition, but I can't see it myself. Hitler may be evil incarnate, but he has shown no sign of being a political idiot, and fighting for something he can get through peaceful means would be the act of one. The obvious lack of Anglo-French interest in an alliance with Moscow is a clear signal that they are unwilling to fight for Czech rule over the Sudeten Germans, and once Hitler has their mountains, he can roll over the rest of Czechoslovakia at any time he wants. I could be wrong, of course. He may be so eager for a military triumph that he throws political wisdom to the winds.

I didn't say any of this. The old Comintern adage—"Listen for an hour; speak for a minute"—has become almost second nature. I can remember first hearing the adage from one of my instructors in Moscow, a man named Piakov who could never stop talking.

SUNDAY, JUNE 5

When Anna went to see Erich this afternoon, Walter and I took ourselves off to the cinema. The main picture was a military drama set in the 1813 War of Liberation. It was well-made, up to Hollywood standards, I would guess, and seemed to satisfy the audience. The hero, a Prussian officer much given to stirring speeches and staring into the distance with a visionary glint in his eyes, was clearly intended to evoke thoughts of the Führer. Everyone poured scorn on his insistence that French spies were at work in the area, but he was of course proved right in the end. I found myself wondering whether the many children in the audience would draw the obviously intended conclusion and place their trust blindly in Hitler or draw what seemed an equally valid but clearly unintended conclusion, that they should follow their own hearts and brains.

The American newsreel that preceded the main film was also strangely bereft of reality. It was subtitled "The Land of Unlimited Possibilities," but made no mention of those, such as racial harmony or health care for the poor, that a modern Jefferson or Lincoln might wish to realize. Instead we watched men walk tightropes strung between skyscrapers and survive being packed into barrels and washed over Niagara Falls. The impression left behind—of a nation that couldn't be serious—was rendered starker still by the main feature and its hero's inability to be anything but.

Walter gave it all his rapt attention, but as we walked home, I could feel his anxiety build. Anna, back before us and working on the evening meal with Verena, said Erich was fine, but she looked worn out with worry. Over supper, Ruchay and Gerritzen looked no happier than they had at breakfast. The whole house seemed sunk in gloom.

Back in my room, I half expected a visit from Walter, but for once he failed to appear. I spent an hour reading Ernst Jünger's *Storm of Steel*, a book that Ruchay thinks "inspirational." It's how an overexcited Nietzsche would have described the Great War, all bloodred sunsets and delirious heroism. Jünger can write, but I wish he couldn't. I hate to think how many boys will march off to the next war expecting a religious experience only to find themselves caught up in the usual circus of useless pain. One old comrade, long since dead, told me the worst days of his life had been the four that followed the beginning of the Somme battles in 1916. During those days he had listened, whenever the guns were silent, to the howling, moaning, and piteous pleading of the hundreds of wounded British soldiers left behind in no-man's-land. With the ending of each artillery bombardment, this ghastly chorus grew thinner, fainter, until finally, on the morning of the fourth day, a blessed silence hung over the churned-up fields. My comrade was fond of repeating a line from an American poem he'd read somewhere: "After such knowledge, what forgiveness?"

MONDAY, JUNE 6

Erich received his sentence this morning—six months in a hard labor camp. The news was all over the canteen by lunchtime, and there were a lot of sympathetic noises: the older men don't have much time for youth gangs like the Dudes— even those who share their hatred of the Nazis—but Erich never brought his gang life to work, and he's known as a good worker. Some thought the sentence rather harsh, considering that no real crime had been committed, but others thought he'd been lucky, and I agreed with the latter. He's not going to a concentration camp, or even a regular prison, and provided he keeps his head, the experience won't do him any lasting harm.

Anna announced the outcome over supper. Erich realized he'd behaved badly, she said, and had no complaints about his punishment. Barufka said, with his customary awkwardness in her presence, that we all felt sorry that this had happened and hoped that Erich would be none the worse for the experience. Ruchay opened his mouth to say something and then closed it again.

When Walter came to see me later, he wanted to know what sort of hardships his brother was in for. I said I didn't really know—I have, in fact, never been locked away in the land of my birth—but that I thought he'd be sharing a barracks rather than sitting alone in a cell and that his days would consist of a lot of hard physical labor. "They don't want to break him," I said; "they want him to see the error of his ways."

Walter thought about that. "I don't think Erich will ever see the error of his ways," he said glumly.

I agreed he might not, but said I thought him clever enough to make them believe that he had.

"I hope so," Walter said with his usual earnestness.

After he'd gone down, I had the sudden, sobering thought that I would probably not see Erich again. One way or another, my work in Hamm should be over before six months have passed.

TUESDAY, JUNE 7

The atmosphere in the house seemed very different this evening, as if a load has been lifted. And in a way, I suppose it has. Erich still has his six months to serve, but twenty-four hours ago Anna and Walter were waiting for doom to fall, and now they can start looking forward to Erich's release.

I envy them. I have nothing to complain of in the present, but the future looks bleak, and the past keeps grabbing me from behind. Canton was in the papers again today: the Japanese have been bombing the city for eleven days now, and over eight thousand people have died. The *Völkischer Beobachter* reports, with scarcely concealed admiration, that hospitals have been deliberately bombed. Last week the same paper was hailing the German bombing raids on Republican-held Valencia.

One thing seems certain—the next European war will be very different from the last. It will be a war of planes and tanks, with ordinary soldiers asked to secure the territory that those machines have conquered. The government here seems to understand this—there's a steady stream of items in the press about tank and aircraft technology—but I don't think those in Moscow or Paris do. The party gives the impression it's still fighting the civil war, and the Maginot Line isn't much more than a fancy concrete trench.

I read the Canton accounts in several papers, and one of them mentioned the destruction of—my hand seems reluctant to even write out the words—the Shao-lin Hotel. That was the destination Chen and I set out for that night, half walking, half running, the occasional spasm of gunfire growing steadily louder as we crossed the Chinese part of the city. It was only about nine o'clock, but all the doors and shutters were closed, all the lights extinguished. I had no sense of people sleeping, though. On the contrary, it felt as if thousands of furtive eyes were mapping our journey through the darkened streets.

My fellow German Heinz Neumann and the Georgian Vissarion Lominadze were the Comintern chiefs in Canton, and when Chen and I reached the Shao-lin Hotel, we found the former nervously pacing the lobby. More than a little drunk and sweating profusely, Neumann looked less like a German Communist than a young colonial gone to seed. I remember thinking that the whole scene reeked of Hollywood: the palms in their pots, the lazily spinning fans, all the white men wiping their brows while the locals looked impassively on.

Moscow had ordered an insurrection, Neumann told me. Ignoring my protests, he said I'd been chosen to persuade Hai San, a warlord currently encamped with his twenty thousand men about fifteen miles outside the city, to throw his forces behind the newly proclaimed Canton Soviet. I could hardly believe my ears. I had met Hai San on several occasions and knew I had next to no chance of persuading him into such a suicidal course of action. The Kuomintang had two armies in the area larger than Hai San's, and half the workers in Neumann's mostly imaginary commune were Chiang Kai-shek supporters.

Neumann read it all in my face. "Ours not to reason why," he said, and I still had enough residual faith in Comintern orders to assume that the leaders knew something I did not. As it happened, the Comintern had issued no such directive—Neumann and his friend Lominadze had decided on making this grab for glory all by themselves—but I didn't find that out until several weeks later.

After a ridiculous argument over who should take the only available motor—Chen and I or those delivering leaflets announcing our commune—the two of us drove out of the city in search of Hai San and his army. Finding them both early next morning, we spent the next thirty-six hours trying and failing to persuade the general that he and his troops should board our sinking ship.

On the night of the fourteenth, a night of ferocious rainfall, we drove back into Canton. The rain had cleared the streets of the living, but the carpet of corpses forced us to abandon the car. At the Shao-lin Hotel, the surviving Chinese leaders of the commune seemed almost deranged by the calamity that had befallen them; Neumann and Lominadze, we discovered, had not been seen for twenty-four hours.

I tried to make my way home, but soon ran into a Kuomintang patrol. I ran and was shot in the side. They came after me, but I managed to lose them in the teeming rain, reach the canal, steal a boat, and make it across to the international settlement. The French soldiers who found me bleeding profusely on their doorstep were inclined to give a white man the benefit of the doubt and commandeered a rickshaw to take me to their hospital. Over the next few days, as I lay there in bed slowly regaining my strength, the terrible news filtered in. Thousands had been killed. Communists, friends of Communists, friends of their friends. Any enemy of China, as decreed by the Kuomintang and Chiang Kai-shek. Even Chinese women who wore their hair in European styles. Women like Lin.

It wasn't safe for a European to leave the international settlement, but I managed to persuade one of the Chinese orderlies to cross the river and find out if Lin was all right. When he returned that evening, the look on his face said the answer was no. Finding the house empty, he had asked the neighbors and been told that the soldiers had come looking for me, and made up for their disappointment by killing her and the child. When I asked how, he just gave me a look, and I let him spare me the details. Later I would think I should have been stronger, but at the time I managed to convince myself that knowing would serve no useful purpose.

WEDNESDAY, JUNE 8

Walter came up to see me, as he does almost every evening. He doesn't often ask for help with his homework these days, but he likes to talk about it and anything else that's on his mind. I've gotten used to him sitting there in the upright chair by the window, to the range of facial expressions that are his and his alone, to the way he sits, half-slouched with his feet just about touching the ground. He sat there this evening, his knees dirty from an earlier game of football, his hair still sticking in all directions despite a weekend trip to the barber.

He brought a piece of homework to show me—a map of the proposed Rhine-Main-Danube Canal, which has been much in the news of late. The drawing was beautifully done, both accurate and easy on the eye. He smiled when I told him so. "I like geography," he said. "It's certain. No one can argue about where the Rhine is."

"Like science," I suggested.

He gave a Walter-like grimace. "We were learning about the atom in physics a few weeks ago, but Herr Borchers was scared to answer any questions about it. According to Fahrian—he's a boy in my class—that whole area of physics is now called Jewish physics, just because the man who discovered it was a Jew." He shook his head in bemusement. "What if the man who discovered the source of the Nile was Jewish—would that make it Jewish geography? It's all so silly."

I brought up something I'd been meaning to ask him for some time—how was Marco treated at school?

"All right, really. It's weird. Some of the teachers are pretty rotten to him, but others are especially nice, as if they're trying to make it up to him. Last year Herr Ehrmann told him he couldn't wear a swastika badge, but Frau Hanssen went down to the school, and he carried on wearing it. The PE teacher's always picking on him. Marco's good at games and things like climbing ropes, but he's always put with the boys who aren't."

"What about the other boys? How do they treat him?"

"All right. Even the boys you think wouldn't. Stefan Wilden, he's got blond hair and blue eyes and he's tall, and he's always being asked to stand at the front of the class as an example of the perfect Aryan, and he's one of Marco's best friends. It's weird," he said again.

I sat there wondering, not for the first time, where Walter gets it all from. I've never known a twelve-year-old so willing to question what he was being taught, but I suppose I haven't known many twelve-year-olds, and much of what passes for sanity in Nazi Germany would strain anyone's credibility. Maybe there are thousands of Walters out there, but I doubt it. He has a precocious commitment to logic that is all his own. There's a famous English author—I can't remember his name—who said that wisdom was all about making connections, and Walter makes them better than most of the adults I've known. But it's more than that—it's logic in the service of fairness. I guess this moral sense has to come from Anna, and perhaps Erich. And given how much Walter loves Tom Shark and how importantly Tom rates fairness—I read one of the books last week—he's probably as influential as mother and brother combined. Or maybe it's just who Walter is. Millions of German boys read Tom Shark, but I doubt many notice that their hero's moral outlook is completely at odds with the country they're living in. Walter does.

As usual he asked me a lot of questions about my opinions and my past. Sometimes I think he suspects that I'm not who I say I am but is either too polite to say so or scared of finding out that his suspicions are justified. But he picks away nevertheless and sometimes seems to be checking my answers for inconsistencies. This may just be paranoia on my part, but it's a strange feeling being interrogated by a twelve-year-old.

THURSDAY, JUNE 9

Asking Walter about Marco was probably a mistake. I expected the usual visit this evening, but it was Anna who knocked on my door and sat down in the seat by the window. "Walter said he'd talked to you about Marco," she said. She was quick to add that she wasn't accusing me of anything—she just wanted to know what had been said.

I told her he had seemed pleasantly surprised by how well most of the boys and teachers treat Marco. "Why? What's happened?"

She sighed and pushed a stray wisp of hair back behind an ear. "One of the teachers let him down," she said dryly, and told me the story. During PE an obstacle course had been set up to separate "the courageous" from "the cowardly," and one of the obstacles had involved using a constantly moving rope to swing across a gap between two vaulting horses. According to Walter, when Marco reached this stage of the course, the PE master had deliberately held the rope out of his reach. Marco had hesitated, and the master, Herr Memering, had immediately branded him a coward. At which point Walter had been unable to restrain himself. "He told me it was just so obvious that he had to say something."

"What did he say?" I asked.

"He said that Marco hadn't been given a fair chance. Which, of course, was like showing a red rag to a bull. Walter was marched across to the headmaster's office, where Memering explained what a troublemaker he is. Walter wasn't allowed to say anything, just sent home with a letter for me. I've been warned that his conduct is 'highly unsatisfactory' and that I would be foolish to take his continued attendance at the school for granted. There's even a reference to Erich—some rubbish about Walter needing to work twice as hard to overcome the stigma of his brother's disgrace." She hugged herself a little tighter, as if the air had suddenly turned cold. "But what can I do?" she went on. "I wrote a letter about how important it is that children learn to stand up for what they believe is right, read it through, and tore it up. It would only make things worse. I'm always telling Walter he has to accept their authority, even when he can't respect it, but I used to say the same to Erich, and look how well that worked. I just can't see an end to all this; I really can't. And then I've got Herr Ruchay to deal with . . ." Her interlinked fingers completed the sentence, turning white as she tightened the knot.

"What's Ruchay up to?" I asked.

"Oh, nothing new," she said evasively, and then changed the subject so abruptly and aggressively that it almost took my breath away. "Why did you come back?" she asked. "You hate them as much as I do."

There was no point denying it. "Because it's home," I said simply. It wasn't true, but it could have been. Most people find it hard to abandon the country of their birth.

"For better or worse," she murmured.

I nodded, and she took that as a signal to leave. As her footsteps faded on the stairs, I wondered about Ruchay. Why would a man like that want a woman like her? They're roughly the same age but in all other respects seem about as incompatible as two people can be. Is it just that she's the only woman he has any real contact with? A lonely obsession?

More to the point, why does she feel threatened by him? He must have some influence with the local authorities, but what could he actually threaten her with? Or is he just pestering her at a time when she has more than enough to cope with already?

Why do I care? Because I like her and care what happens to her and Walter. I was lying when I said I'd come back to Germany because it was home, but this house of theirs feels increasingly like one. I've lived in many places over the years, and some of them—the Hotel Lux in Moscow; sundry lodgings in Canton, Sofia, and Rio—have come to feel like somewhere I belonged. We all used to say that the party was our real home, but it isn't. Those who work in the Comintern's external sections spend most of their time as cuckoos in others' nests.

I'm a cuckoo in this house, of course. One who feels more and more at home in his foreign nest. Maybe all cuckoos are prone to this delusion, but I should know better.

FRIDAY, JUNE 10

The other Communist who escaped from the Thuringian Forest KZ has been captured in the Sudetenland, and the Nazi government is applying for his extradition. Since a refusal would be interpreted as a deliberate provocation, I suppose the Czech government will send the man back to his death.

I have decided that the chances of any significant political action at the yards, in either peace or war, are practically nonexistent. The best we can hope for is an underground sabotage unit, and the chances of that surviving for more than a couple of operations are not good. Those operations might be worth the cost in lives. An efficient disabling of the locomotive turntable, works traverser, and yard brake retarders could shut the place down for several days, delaying the transport of troops and armor to the front. Such actions—like any number of parallel operations elsewhere—could make the difference between success and failure on some far-off battlefield. Of course, I cannot know for certain that they would, and neither can the people I report to. They can only play the odds, and if that involves sacrifice on a grand scale, then so be it. "It's just mathematics," as a NKVD colonel told me several years ago, and at one level he was absolutely correct. If Moscow prevails over Berlin, the survivors won't be questioning Stalin's methods.

As for those sacrificed—well, they at least got to feel better about themselves. Losing one's life in the war against Fascism is a lot more appealing than a bullet in the neck from one of Yezhov's thugs.

Or maybe that's just the beer talking—Jakob and I each had

an extra glass tonight to celebrate the opening of Göring's new Master School of Painting. According to the *Völkischer Beobachter*, "Art shall bloom again and again be strong and German." We laughed so hard we almost cried. I hope none of my fellow drinkers were offended, or my own war against Fascism will end rather sooner than expected.

SATURDAY, JUNE 11

Painfully aware that I'd had too much to drink last night, I left the Social Club earlier than usual tonight, hoping for an enjoyable hour or two of reading. I'm halfway through a biography of Frederick the Great that I found in the club library. The Führer would be proud of me.

But I got to the book later than I expected. I was happily nearing home when Gerritzen's voice leapt out of the darkness. He was sitting on one of the canal-side benches, and considerably drunker than I had been the previous evening. He insisted I join him. "Please, please, please," he went on, in the manner of a spoiled child. "I really need someone to talk to."

Curiosity triumphed over contempt. I'd been wondering for a week what had gotten into him and was apparently about to find out. I sat down, accepted one of his cigarettes, and let him talk.

Liselotte was the problem. Had he got her pregnant? No, it was much worse than that. His father had employed a private detective agency to investigate her ancestry and discovered that she was one-eighth Jewish. "Her great-grandmother Eva," Gerritzen lamented. "From Silesia," he added mournfully, as if that clinched matters.

I knew that you needed at least two Jewish grandparents to be defined as a Jew, and that only one qualified you for the higher status of a Mischling. Surely one great-grandparent wasn't anything to worry about?

It was. "My father will have nothing to do with her," Gerritzen said. "He says an infection is an infection—it doesn't matter how many germs there are."

"That's not what the law says," I told him.

"Maybe not now," Gerritzen lamented, "but who knows in a year's time, or two years? I love her; I really do, but what sort of life would we have? I have to break it off. For her sake as much as mine."

I felt like hitting him, but I didn't. I felt like telling him to act like a mensch, but that seemed inappropriate.

SUNDAY, JUNE 12

Anna caught me on my way out this morning and asked if I could spare a few minutes. When I said yes, she led me through to her small living room at the back of the house. Walter was nowhere to be seen.

I'd had a glimpse of the room on the night her father had his fall but had never been in it. A small settee and armchair sat on either side of a fireplace, a table and two upright chairs under the window in the opposite wall. A somber landscape painting of birds flying over a marsh at dusk or dawn hung above the settee. A small and well-stocked bookcase stood against the wall behind the door.

She gestured me to the settee and sat in the armchair, leaning forward with her hands on her knees. "I need your help," she said.

"Of course," I said.

She said she'd been thinking about Walter and how to keep him "safe" since the headmaster's letter and that she'd come to the conclusion that they could no longer go on the way they were, keeping their distance from the new Germany and hoping that no one would notice or be offended by their lack of enthusiasm. They had to make more of an effort to fit in, had to put up a better pretense. "For one thing," she said, "Walter will have to join the Jungvolk."

"The Hitler Youth?" I asked.

"The junior section—boys between ten and fourteen. All boys are expected to join, but it's not compulsory, not yet. And Walter has always refused. Mostly because Marco can't join. I think he'll actually enjoy a lot of the activities, but he'll see it as a betrayal."

"Ah," I said, finally understanding her need for help.

"If you could talk to him as well. He trusts you."

I probably winced at that.

"It's for his own safety," she said.

"I know," I said. "I understand. I think you're right. And of course I'll talk to him. When will he start?"

"I'll put his name down this week, but he can start in September when he goes back to school. I'm hoping to send him to my aunt's family at the end of July for a month, so there's no point in starting now."

I was taken unaware by the pang of emptiness this announcement provoked. "Walter hasn't said anything about this," I said.

He didn't yet know. She'd only just written to her aunt's daughter Sofie—a farmer's wife in the East—and wasn't planning to tell Walter until everything was finalized. "It'll do him good to get away, to get out of this house, see a different sort of life," she added. Sofie and her husband, Harald, ran the family farm, and Sofie and her sons, aged eight and six, were Walter's only cousins. "It'll be exciting for him—the train rides, summer in the countryside. He'll love it." She smiled ruefully, a smile that turned into a sigh. "But what can I say to Verena?" she asked. "Walter's right—it is a betrayal. I just can't see another way."

"You tell her the truth," I said. "That Erich's sins have put

Walter at risk. She'll understand. And it might even help her and Marco. Walter galloping to Marco's rescue certainly won't. Not the way things are."

She stood. "I do think Verena will understand," she said. "I would in her place. But I still feel as if I'm letting her down." She gave me a fierce, challenging look. I surprised myself by opening my arms, and I think she surprised herself by letting them enfold her. We embraced for what seemed a long time but was probably only a few seconds. As we pulled apart, she kissed me lightly on the cheek.

I set off on my Sunday morning walk in a state of some confusion. The news that Walter would be gone for a month had upset me more than I would have thought possible. And the fact that I found it so upsetting was upsetting in itself—what sort of Comintern operative in the field allowed himself the luxury of forming an emotional attachment to a twelve-year-old boy? For one thing, it was dangerous for both of us. For another, I was letting Walter become emotionally dependent on someone he was bound to lose. I was promising something I couldn't deliver.

And—I must be honest—the embrace with Anna had also upset me. There was nothing sexual in it—Anna's an attractive woman, but I've never felt any spark between us, or felt more than a flicker of desire for her. I tried telling myself that the physical pressure of another body is always slightly shocking, particularly for those of us who live deep within our own skins, but I knew it was more than that. Anna's embrace was a demonstration of trust, and it was that which unnerved me. In another world I might be worthy of the faith Walter and his mother seem eager to place in me, but in this one I seem fated to let them down.

What choice do I have? I shall talk to Walter and do my best to keep him safe. From everything but his faith in me.

At least last week's rumors of imminent action against the

Czechs have proved groundless. Hitler has either suffered a momentary loss of nerve or is simply toying with his opponents, rather like a cat with an injured bird. I think he'll make his move in the early autumn, when the rivers are low and before snow blocks the mountain passes.

MONDAY, JUNE 13

Monday is usually a hard day at work, but not today. Today everyone but the drivers and signalers were told to down tools and listen to Herr Goebbels for almost three hours. I was in the canteen when he began and sat there with around two hundred others listening to a diatribe on the "Beauty of Work" campaign. This government has verbal diarrhea—if there's a war, they'll end up talking the enemy to death.

We were treated to an endless list of achievements—sports fields and gardens laid around factory walls, swimming pools next to ironworks, cleaner facilities—he couldn't bring himself to say "toilets"—for just about everyone. He had a neat line for everything—"Good lighting means good work" was my favorite. He obviously hadn't seen the scrawled response in our own newly lit workshop: "NOW WE CAN REALLY SEE THE CRAP WE'RE WORKING WITH!" At one point I found myself staring at the "GERMANY NEEDS COLONIES" poster on the canteen wall and imagining this lot rigging all of Africa and Asia with their loudspeakers. A vision of hell.

The talk with Walter was easier than I expected. "I'm joining the Jungvolk," he said by way of greeting, and I tried to look surprised. He didn't seem that upset by the prospect. "It's to help Erich," he explained. "Mama says we all have to do things we'd rather not do. She says she's going to be nicer to Herr Ruchay."

"How about Marco?" I asked.

"Oh, I talked to him about it. He wants me to get him one of the daggers if I can."

I was lost for words.

"We went to the toy shop after school," Walter went on. "They've got a new set of infantry soldiers—there's even two dead ones, and they look really real." He must have seen the look on my face. "I'm sorry," he said. "Does that make you think about, you know . . . ? But it is more real, isn't it? Soldiers *are* killed in war."

I had to agree that they were.

He was quiet for a moment, thinking—I assumed about the soldiers. But he wasn't. "What will happen to Marco?" he asked.

I told him I didn't know, but that I thought Marco would have a hard time of it. Nothing worse, I added hastily, just a hard time. In every contact with officialdom, he'd be made to feel inferior, but as long as he had a mother and friends who knew he wasn't, and who made him know that they knew, then he'd be all right. At least he wasn't Jewish, I almost added, but had the sense not to.

"Maybe one day he'll go to Africa," Walter said. "That's where his father lives," he explained.

"And maybe one day people will accept each other for who they are and not which race they're born to," I said.

He gave me the classic Walter look, the one that says, "You may be the adult, but who do you think you're kidding?"

TUESDAY, JUNE 14

Gerritzen hasn't spoken to me since his drunken outburst on Saturday night, but if his occasional glances in my direction are anything to go by, he's wishing the encounter had never taken place. He has seemed deflated at the dinner table but also harder, as if he's seeking someone other than himself to be angry with. One anti-Jewish comment at breakfast seemed completely out of character. This, I think, is how political poison infects a whole culture—it enters the bloodstream through the cuts and bruises of personal disappointment and feeds on hearts wounded by feelings of inadequacy or rejection.

Ruchay has also changed, if only in the way he deals with me. There's no overt hostility—he's never less than polite, but there's a coldness that wasn't there before. I may have stepped across some line—particularly where Anna is concerned—that only he can see. Or it may just be that I'm not deferential enough. I'm torn between trying to improve matters and letting him stew.

He won't be pleased to hear that I've been invited to go for a picnic next Sunday with Anna, Verena, and the two boys. Not that I care a jot for Ruchay's feelings. A few weeks ago I would have worried about upsetting Jakob, but I think he knows by now that I have no romantic interest in Anna and that I've been invited more as Walter's friend than hers. Anyway, it seemed such a nice idea when she asked that I accepted with barely a second thought, and the possible risk to my mission only occurred to me hours later. Marco's mere existence is provocation enough in this country, and I will be seen as the responsible male if anyone chooses to challenge his right to be present wherever we happen to be. My old instructors in Moscow would be horrified. So, two months ago, would I have been.

Eleven days from now I'll find out what Moscow has in mind for me. Even dead men on leave deserve the occasional picnic.

WEDNESDAY, JUNE 15

If my writing seems a little shakier than usual, it's because my whole body is still revolting against the inaction my brain forced on it a few minutes ago. Müller and I were on our way home from the Working Group—only a couple of streets away from here—when we rounded a corner and saw a bunch of SA thugs kicking a young man to death. There was no warning—there was no talking or shouting from the storm troopers, only the rasping breath of men doing hard physical work. Their victim had probably already lost the ability to produce sounds, and the houses that lined the streets were silent and still, despite the fact that the light had only recently begun to fade.

Müller and I looked at each other, realized we had reached the same conclusion—that intervention would result, at best, in our arrest—and shrank back into what shadows there were. It was, as my instructors would have said, the correct course of action, but that didn't make it feel any better. And from what I could judge, it cost Müller as much as it cost me.

Seconds, perhaps minutes, went by. The flurry of activity came to an end. One of the men said something; others laughed. They marched off, happily for us, in the other direction.

"At least we can take him to the hospital," Müller said, as the boot steps faded. But there was no point. The victim, a man in his early twenties, was beyond help. There were bloody dents on one side of his head, and his throat had been comprehensively crushed. "I know who he is," Müller said, almost in a whisper. "His name's Rolf Hangebruch. He lives—lived—a few streets away. He was a homosexual. And not afraid to let people know it."

We stood there for a moment just looking at him. "No point hanging around," I said. Müller gave me a sharp look, but nodded. At the end of the next street, we parted without another word.

All my instincts tell me that Müller can be trusted, but those instincts have sometimes led me astray. I need a believable account of his last five years. How long was he in custody? How did he get his current job? Is he even the Dariusz Müller I think he is or someone else with the same name—a cousin, perhaps? Elise may have some answers for me at the end of the month. If she doesn't, then I'll have to do some digging of my own.

This evening's meeting, like the last one, was held at Joachim Wosz's house. At last Friday's Labor Front meeting, the workers' official representatives had given up their demand for an end to compulsory overtime in exchange for a promise of new gymnasium equipment, and most of our meeting was taken up with wondering whether we could make any political capital out of the resulting derision and discontent. The real answer was no, but it was decided that we should sound out the workforce over its willingness to undertake some sort of action. Looking around the faces, I could sense that everyone shared the same feeling, that we were just going through the motions, and we knew it.

There was one exception, however. Paul Giesemann, a chubby young worker with a Bavarian accent and an almost permanent smile, was apparently more frustrated than anyone else and never missed an opportunity to suggest bolder paths of action. The others, who have clearly known him for quite a while, seem more amused than concerned by Giesemann's reckless suggestions, but he smells like an informer to me. Someone else for Moscow to check on.

It's completely dark now, and I suppose the young man's corpse is still lying in the street where we left it. Most of the time it's hard to take Nazi Germany seriously—the ideology is so ludicrous and so utterly transparent to anyone who knows anything about the way societies work. And no one who has lived outside his own country for more than a few weeks could swallow the nonsense they talk about national and racial hierarchies. If Walter, a twelve-year-old so-called Aryan, can see through it all, then why can't everyone else?

But they can't. And watching those SA men kick that young man to death was like watching a rehearsal for the bigger spectacle, when bigger German gangs start kicking the rest of Europe to death. Absurd they may be, but not taking these bastards seriously will be the death of us.

THURSDAY, JUNE 16

There's a parade through the town center on Saturday, and Walter tells me that Ruchay has asked Anna to watch it with him. Much to Walter's disgust she not only accepted the invitation, but also insists that he comes along. I now understand why Ruchay could hardly stop smiling over supper.

There's been a reply from Anna's cousin Sofie—her family is happy to have Walter for four weeks in August. Walter clearly has mixed feelings about it all. A month at the mercy of virtual strangers is a bit daunting, and I think he's also worried about deserting his mother for such a long time. But he's excited as well, particularly by the prospect of the journey itself. Anna will take him as far as Berlin, Sofie the rest of the way.

Walter says he will write to me once a week. He also says that if his mother marries Herr Ruchay, he's not coming back.

I had a short chat with Otto Tikalsky this afternoon, when we both found ourselves scouring the stores cupboard for carbon paper. He asked me if I'd seen the early edition of the local evening paper and, when I said no, told me that a young man's body had been found in Hamm that morning. According to the paper, Rolf Hangebruch was a hit-and-run victim, knocked down by some local youth gang members enjoying a nocturnal ride. "I knew him," Tikalsky told me, sadness lurking in his eyes. "He lived on my street. Everyone knew he was queer, but everyone liked him anyway. He was always cheerful, and he went out of his way to help people. And I'll bet you a million marks he wasn't hit by a car."

SATURDAY, JUNE 18

I spent some of the afternoon sitting out in the yard at the back of the house with Andreas. It was a hot, sunny day, and I rolled him out in the makeshift contraption Erich constructed from an old rocking chair and some rusted wheels last year. Andreas loves the heat and says that he can feel the brightness even if he can't see it.

It was the first time I'd been out back. There's not much in the way of garden, only a few window boxes with flowers and one climbing plant. Walter, and sometimes Marco, use the space for football practice, and there's a chicken run up against the end wall.

In the course of a long and rambling conversation, I learned a little more about Andreas's life. He grew up in the Ruhr and worked there until the war as a local government administrator. After the war he lived with his wife until she died, and then with Anna. "I could have gone to my sister, Meta," he said, "but death will be more exciting than East Prussia."

I read to him for a while—something both Anna and Walter do every day. The current book is Dickens's *Great Expectations*, which both of us have read before. After about ten minutes, he fell asleep, and I sat there in the sunshine wondering how Anna and Walter were getting on with Ruchay. When the breeze was in the right direction, I could hear the distant music of the band.

They came back an hour later. Walter looked relieved, while Anna's face was an absolute mask. Ruchay seemed rather pleased with himself.

SUNDAY, JUNE 19

Marco has a bad summer cold, so he and Verena missed out on the picnic. Anna, Walter, and I took a special hikers' train south to the Sauerland and got off after about an hour at a small village station. Another train arrived from the opposite direction at the same time, and it seemed for a moment as if half of Germany's youth was milling around the station area. There were enough bronzed limbs and blonde pigtails on display to keep Goebbels's propaganda artists at work for weeks. I caught Walter staring at a well-shepherded troop of Hitler Youth, half-fascinated, half-contemptuous. They marched off singing the "Horst Wessel Song," and I wondered whether any remnants of Erich's old gang would be waiting for them in the forest.

We took the same path at a slower pace, and their voices soon faded. A mile or so up the valley we could have been alone in the world, surrounded by sun-dappled trees and a tapestry of birdsong. After two miles, the path emerged from the trees by the side of a mountain lake. There were lots of picnic tables, many of them already filled with families, and canoes for hire. We picked a place to lay our rug and unloaded our bags. Anna suggested that Walter and I take a turn on the water while she organized the food.

The lake was about a kilometer in length and never more than two hundred meters wide. I wondered why so few people were swimming until I felt the water—it was freezing. We paddled to the far end and back again, managing to keep a reasonably straight course. The last person I had shared a canoe with was my brother, Jens, on a lake like this one, several years before the war. I sometimes wonder what he would have made of my life these last twenty years.

It wasn't even noon, but we fell on the feast as if it were midafternoon. There were cold sausages and ham, potato salad and sauerkraut, tomatoes and rye bread, and a heavenly blackberry tart for dessert. Much to his delighted surprise, Walter was presented with a bottle of Coca-Cola, leaving Anna and me to share a bottle of Riesling and a thermos of coffee. I haven't enjoyed a meal so much for years.

Afterward, Walter announced that he was going to walk around the lake. Anna stretched out on the grass, eyes closed, mouth set in a half smile. She looked more relaxed than I'd ever seen her and, with her thin blue dress molded to the shape of her body, more desirable too. I imagined her as a young woman, undoubtedly beautiful, and alive with those enthusiasms and passions that the succeeding years have dulled or forced into hiding.

I wanted to ask about her earlier life—it is, after all, something people usually do as they get to know someone—but I didn't. I didn't want to spoil the day, to overload it with the weight of the past. And it didn't feel right. I couldn't tell her the truth about my life, so how could I ask for the truth about hers? I thought about giving her half the story—admitting my Communist career in postwar Germany, keeping quiet about my subsequent work for the Comintern—but a half-fictional life seemed no better than one that was wholly false. I solved the problem by falling asleep.

Walter woke us both up and pointedly asked why we'd come all this way if we were just going to sleep. Suitably shamed, we allowed ourselves to be talked into a rowboat. I rowed us down the lake, but Walter insisted on rowing us back and sat there facing the two of us with what looked like a matchmaker's glint in his eyes.

While walking back down through the woods to the station, I felt, for a few minutes, an almost overwhelming sense of loss. With the late afternoon sun still pouring down through the trees and Anna's blonde hair dancing on her shoulders in front of me, I needed all my discipline to keep from crying. Nothing tears the heart like a glimpse of happiness.

MONDAY, JUNE 20

The first name on my list belongs to an inveterate drinker. Hans Derleth is always sober at work, but the reddened nose and bloodshot eyes raised my suspicions, and after taking time to follow him home on three occasions, I no longer have any doubts. He stops for drinks at the first bar he comes to and again at the second and third. He drinks spirits rather than beer, and he drinks them at a punishing rate. By the time he gets home, he can hardly walk straight, and on two of three occasions, I watched him fall up the stairs. He may be sober again each morning, but a functioning drunk is still a drunk. Another one crossed off my list.

WEDNESDAY, JUNE 22

There's hardly ever any South American news in the German papers, but this morning's *Völkischer Beobachter* carried a lengthy article about those fresh travails of German immigrants in Argentina and Brazil that one man had raised at my Social Club talk. After reveling in their original homeland's resurgence, these German expatriates are now finding that their new countrymen expect them to abandon old allegiances, and behave more like Argentinians and Brazilians than Germans. Setting up German-speaking schools and filling their children with love of a distant Führer has not gone down well with the locals, and "transparently reasonable" objections by the German foreign ministry to the resultant protests have caused a "storm of unwarranted criticism."

Ruchay's indignation rose as he read out the article, and he concluded by turning to me—the supposed South American expert—with an accusatory "What do you think of that?"

I shook my head, as if I were just as appalled by such ungrateful behavior. I explained that the governments over there were incredibly intolerant of anything they thought posed a threat to their authority. They were of course mistaken in this case, and would probably realize as much before too many weeks had passed.

"I should hope so," Ruchay retorted, and returned to his paper in search of better news, leaving me to my coffee and memories of that continent. My years there had been among the happiest and most rewarding of my life. True, I had spent a third of them in prison—six months in Buenos Aires for "sedition," eighteen in Rio for my small part in organizing the failed Prestes rebellion—but the conditions had been relatively benign by contemporary European standards. I was seldom hungry and rarely beaten—and then not badly—and you do eventually get used to being bitten by every species of insect and spider under the sun.

During the four years I was free, I did useful political work in several countries, setting up presses, helping to organize slowdowns and strikes, establishing parties and courier networks. And the sheer beauty of the Andes and Altiplano are hard to exaggerate: picture a line of distant volcanoes leaking wispy trails of smoke into a cornflower-blue sky. Maybe the thin air at three thousand meters does something to the brain, but rolling along a Bolivian mountain road with a bunch of comrade miners in the back of an open truck some-times felt like happiness defined.

Speaking of mountains, the papers are full of one called Nanga Parbat. I had never heard of it, but Walter filled me in before he set off for school. He told me it's at the western end of the Himalayas and at 8,126 meters is the ninth-highest peak in the world. Many have tried but no one has ever reached the top, earning Nanga Parbat its "Killer Mountain" nickname.

The current German expedition is the fourth in six years. The 1932 one wisely turned back; the next in 1934 was caught in a storm and perished almost to a man. In 1937 an avalanche did the damage, burying all but one of the seven-teen-strong party. Walter's class at school is painting a mural of the current attempt, and Walter himself seems excited by it all, so I bit back the comment that came to mind about turning an Asian mountain into a German cemetery. Even as a child, I could never see the sense of doing difficult things just because they were there to be done. I still can't, though these days I am willing to concede that those who enjoy such challenges are not necessarily idiots.

It is past one in the morning, but I can't go to bed—like everyone else in the house, I am expected downstairs in front of the wireless when the big fight begins at 3 A.M. Max Schmeling, Germany's finest boxer, is taking on the Ameri-can Negro Joe Louis for the second time, having beaten him two years ago when Jim Braddock held the heavyweight crown. Since then Louis has beaten Braddock, so the crown is at stake in this second fight. As with the "Killer Mountain," most of my information comes from Walter, who has read every inch of the papers' fulsome coverage and whom Anna has promised to wake in time for the actual fight.

Schmeling has been in America for seven weeks, blowing the Nazi trumpet, telling all and sundry that Germany has never been so united and that the reports of ill-treatment

of Jews have been wildly exaggerated. Until recently Goebbels and his editors here have been careful not to stake the
Reich's reputation on Schmeling—fearful, no doubt, that he
might lose—but as the excitement has mounted over the last
few days, they haven't been able to help themselves. I don't
suppose it'll make that much difference. After all the Nazis
have said about race since they came to power, their credibility was bound to be on the line. A Schmeling victory will
prove them right; a Louis triumph will be a resounding slap
in the face to all they hold dear.

Ruchay has been swinging between bluster and nerves all
day, and I imagine half the country is in a similar state. It's
going to be an interesting hour or so.

THURSDAY 23 JUNE

An interesting two minutes, as things turned out. There we
all were—Ruchay, Gerritzen, Barufka, Anna, Walter, and I—
still settling in for a long and grueling battle when the whole
thing was suddenly over.

The fight seemed briefer for the overlong buildup. By the
time Walter fetched me downstairs soon after two, the broadcast had already been underway for over an hour. According
to Walter, the excerpts from a book by the famous boxing
commentator Arno Hellmis had been really interesting, the
pieces of music considerably less so. Soon after I sat down,
the German commentators in New York began to describe the
stadium setup, weather, and crowd, none of which they
liked. There was chaos where there should be order, fear-
some heat, which might sap their hero's strength, and as
for the people . . . well, Americans were certainly different.
Exactly how was never spelled out, but we were left with an
impression of unruly children or animals, unschooled in

self-discipline, a rung or two lower than Germans on the evolutionary ladder.

When Barufka and I went out for a short walk, we found more windows lit than not—the nation was certainly listening.

Shortly before three, Hellmis himself appeared on air, sounding, I thought, slightly hysterical. Soon after that the two fighters made their appearances, Schmeling getting the louder cheers. It sounded as if much of the white American crowd was putting race above nation, and Hellmis duly said as much in a suitably gloating manner, before noting how serene Schmeling looked amid all the chaos.

The German again got the bigger cheer when the fighters were introduced, and Ruchay's smile was almost ecstatic. According to Walter, Joe Louis had been disappointing in his last few fights, and it felt like he was up against it here.

How wrong can one be? The fight lasted 124 seconds and, from what we heard, could well have been stopped even earlier. I know little about boxing, but I didn't need to know any more than I did. Hellmis started off describing punches, but barely ten seconds had passed before his commentary unraveled, turning first into strangled cries of disbelief— Schmeling was down!—and then to despairing pleas—"Stop him! Hold on! . . . Get up, Max!"

Looking around at my companions, I noticed that all but Anna had their mouths open. She was trying to hold back a smile.

And then it was over. "The towel!" Hellmis shrieked in despair. "Max Schmeling is beaten!" he shouted twice, as if he needed to convince himself.

The words seemed to echo around our room. Ruchay's face was grey, Gerritzen's mouth an angry pout. Barufka looked shocked, Walter confused. "Is it over?" he asked.

"I'm afraid so," I told him, but I think he was more surprised than disappointed.

Hellmis had recovered some of his own composure by this time, but still seemed half in shock. He praised Schmeling's honesty and courage and put the result down to "the meanness of fate." He still hadn't mentioned Louis when the broadcast suddenly came to an end, and the sound of the New York crowd gave way to the wretched "Horst Wessel Song." A rendition of "Deutschland, Deutschland über Alles" was followed by a single spirited "Heil."

And then we were sitting in silence.

"Well, he did his best," Barufka said.

Ruchay gave him a contemptuous look and stood. There would be reasons we knew nothing of, he said. He couldn't believe it had been a fair fight—Louis had cheated on the previous occasion, and we would doubtless find he had done so again.

Ruchay, as I discovered today, was far from alone in his suspicions. The late-morning editions were full of dark hints, and during the course of the workday, I overheard several men voicing their feeling that there'd been something crooked about Schelling's defeat, but by evening someone in Berlin had decided that acting the good loser was the better option, and the later editions followed that line. Walter at least was pleased—as Joe Louis's representative in Hamm, his friend Marco had a day of being bullied by teachers that was only partly offset by the newfound admiration of several fellow pupils. Now that Goebbels has given the result his blessing, Marco should be less of a target.

FRIDAY, JUNE 24

Right after work this evening, I went with Anna to see the Gestapo. She braved their lair a couple of days ago to inquire about Erich's whereabouts—after the trial they had promised

to let her know within days—and was offered an appointment with one of their "overworked" officers. Thinking she
might be taken more seriously with a man in tow, she booked
a time when she knew I was free and then asked if I would
mind going with her. I should have made an excuse—why
give them a face to remember?—but I just said yes. I knew I
was putting an individual's immediate needs above the prob-
able needs of the party but felt no real regret.

We hardly shared a word on our walk into the town. I had
no real reason to feel nervous, but no one takes the Gestapo
lightly, and a lion's mouth is a lion's mouth. Anna was clearly
anxious: mostly, she admitted as we neared our destination,
about losing her temper. If I thought she was getting too
aggressive, she said, I should give her a gentle nudge in the
side.

The police building in Hamm was tucked just behind the
town hall, and the Gestapo had a small suite of four offices
right at the front. There were, I guessed, no more than eight
or ten men involved, and the man in charge—if the plaque
on the only closed door could be trusted—was Kriminalinspektor Herbert Jagusch. We, it transpired, after a lengthy
wait in the reception area, would have to make do with one
of his underlings, a portly young man with thin blond hair
and glasses. He didn't offer his name, and when Anna asked
him for it, he pulled out a warrant card and crisply informed
us that was all we needed to see. After that, I expected him
to question my right to be present, but being a "friend of
the family" turned out to be good enough. And, I have to
admit, he was much more willing to help than Anna or I had
expected.

Despite our having an appointment, he had no information to hand, but an exhaustive search ensued, which gave
us time to marvel at the sheer volume of paperwork even a
small Gestapo office could generate in a little over five years.

And ten minutes later we had the information we had come for: Erich was in Work Camp 37, close to the Belgian border, about forty kilometers south of Aachen. He might be moved at a later date, but six-month sentences were usually spent in one place.

Anna asked if she could write to him and was told that Erich could neither receive nor send letters. "He is being punished," the Kriminalsekretär reminded her, as if she had forgotten.

"But so am I," she told him, "and I've done nothing wrong."

He gave her a look that suggested her lack of mothering skills might have played a part in Erich's fall from grace, but merely repeated that these were the rules. She took a deep breath, and I readied myself to apply the requested nudge, but in the end none was required. Anna simply asked to be informed if Erich was moved, thanked the Kriminalsekretär for all his help, and even held out a hand. He looked surprised but shook it anyway. Three Heil Hitlers later we were on our way out.

It had, I thought, gone better than we had hoped it would. Anna thought so too. She knew it was foolish but felt much better just knowing where Erich was. And Walter would too. They would look up the place in his atlas together.

SUNDAY, JUNE 26

This month's *treff* was yesterday. The train was a fast one, stopping only in Unna and Hagen before it reached Barmen, which these days forms part of the new urban aggregation that stretches down the Wupper valley. My destination was the old Elberfeld station, now christened Wuppertal-Elberfeld.

The train was close to full, mostly, it seemed, with

middle-class families out for the day, but the weather was poor for summer, with a dull leaden sky and clinging damp air that never quite turned into rain.

Elise was sitting in the buffet, nursing the last of a coffee. She was wearing a dark raincoat over the same cream dress but without the last occasion's matching shoes. The low-heeled ankle-high boots she wore instead had a decidedly Parisian elegance, reinforcing her disguise and, I suspect, providing an element of guilt-free pleasure.

After greeting each other like affectionate siblings, we left the buffet and station, and as we started down toward the river, she reached inside her handbag for a packet of cigarettes. When I asked if that was wise, she gave me a look and said, "Probably not," but lit one anyway. "If we see a uniform, I'll pass it to you."

The Wupper, with its famous overhead monorail, was only a couple of minutes away, and as we approached it, a train slid past on the framework of girders that straddled the river. Had Walter ever been here? I wondered. I'd been well into my twenties when I first rode on one of the underslung trains, and I'd still found it exciting.

There weren't many people on the paths on either side of the river, and for once in Hitler's Germany, there wasn't a uniform in sight. I told Elise that Engels had grown up nearby, which brought forth the dry rejoinder that a pilgrimage probably wouldn't be wise. I told her the Nazis had probably torn the house down.

She leaned against the bankside railing and gazed gloomily down at the fast-running water. After one last drag on the cigarette, she tossed the butt into the wet bushes below and pulled herself upright. "So, Dariusz Müller," she said, taking my arm and steering me westwards along the path. "He joined the Spartakusbund in 1917, and was an active member until 1933. According to comrades in Moscow, he was involved in a lot of street fighting both before and after the Nazis came to power. In fact, right up until the moment he was arrested. His wife was too, and she was killed that spring."

So the current wife was his second, I thought. "Did they have children?" I asked.

"Not that anyone recalls. Müller was released in December 1934 and back at his job a week or so later, which looks suspicious. But according to Moscow, no one who knew him believes he would turn traitor."

Which wasn't a great help. I asked if she knew where Müller had been during 1921 through 1923, my two years in Germany.

"He's always lived in this general area," she said. "First Essen, then Gelsenkirchen, then Hamm."

"I must have run into him during those years. I'm sure he remembers me."

Elise shrugged. "So tell me how you've been doing."

The first things that came to my head were Erich's imprisonment and Walter's travails at school, but they weren't what she needed to hear about. I told her about Müller's group for discussing workplace issues and what I thought it really represented. It might be a gift, I told her, a ready-made unit that needed only Moscow's direction. But if, as I suspected, at least one of its members was a Gestapo informer, it might serve us better as a stalking horse, distracting attention away from a newly created group.

"If Müller's a traitor, then his group must be flypaper," Elise said. "What about the list you started with?"

There was no one behind or ahead of us, so I handed over the preliminary reports I'd written on the seven I'd met who were still working at the yards, and asked her to let Moscow know how grateful I'd be for any further information that the German comrades in exile might have. I'd used numbers rather than names, so we spent ten minutes sitting on a bench crafting a mnemonic out of the names for Elise to remember. This proved strangely enjoyable, and as we were completing the task, a line of red balloon-bearing children hurried past, causing Elise to smile for the first time.

It was only briefly. "I guess that's it," she said, looking up at the grey sky. "The next *treff* will be in Essen, same time, at the Café Hummel on Frohnhauser Strasse."

I told her I knew it but added that I hadn't been inside it for fifteen years.

"But you won't be meeting me," she added, almost as an afterthought. "I've been called back to Moscow."

It was probably my imagination, but she seemed to grip my arm a little tighter as she said it. I almost asked if she'd obey the summons and realized that meant I wasn't sure I would.

We parted with another cursory kiss, like a brother and sister used to such separations. I watched her walk away across the station concourse and saw the male heads turn to follow her progress. I wondered if sex appeal would save her in Moscow and decided it probably wouldn't. Her bosses might be tempted, but there was too much independence in her eyes.

I was back in Hamm by three, and as I walked back home through the town, I found myself noticing how familiar so much of it was. The lettering on the signs, the meats in the butcher's window, the faces and tones of speech. Things like the color of light that you notice only when you've lived outside northern Europe. This is where I'm from, but that's all it is—it brings no warmth to my heart.

I looked for changes, and there were plenty of them. So many flags, so many women in pigtails, so many buildings boasting loudspeakers, which for once had nothing to say. And, I have to admit it, the people seem fatter, fitter, happier, than they did in the early twenties. Or at least less miserable.

I suspect the eventual cost will surpass their worst imaginings, but for the moment it's easy to understand why few feel the need or desire to stick their heads above the parapet.

And sometimes it all just seems too ludicrous for words. One of Walter's weekend homework assignments requires him to provide evidence of Nordic racial superiority, and earlier today he turned up at my door with the pages of mimeographed quotes his teacher had helpfully provided to assist him in the task. Walter read one through, and if I had it in front of me, I would quote it in full. The gist, as I remember it, was this: Nordic peoples' mouths have a better shape, allowing them to talk and sing more clearly, whereas inferior races have inferior mouths, with which they can make only clumsy and indistinct sounds, like barking, snoring, and squeaking. The proof of this theory is found in birds, which have beautiful voices because they have Nordic-shaped throats and mouths.

"It can't be true, can it?" Walter asked doubtfully after he'd finished reading the passage.

No it couldn't, I thought, but that's what they rely on— that smidgen of doubt. Anyone who'd listened to a Negro gospel choir or an Italian opera diva would know such ideas for the rubbish they were, but few had been so lucky, especially in a place like Hamm. When most people here saw an argument like this in print, delivered as fact in such relentless detail, their instinct would be to believe it.

No, I told Walter, it couldn't be true, because I'd heard beautiful singing everywhere I'd been, from every racial group under the sun.

Walter nodded. He'd come to the same conclusion from another direction. Both he and Erich had Nordic throats, and when either burst into song, someone would tell him to stop.

"You do know how to write this essay?" I asked.

He did. He would list all the good things about Germany—the bullet train, the zeppelins, Nobel Prize winners, Beethoven, Bismarck, and Goethe—and simply ignore all the bad stuff.

I suggested it might be wise to include the Führer in his list.

"Right at the top," he said with a grin.

TUESDAY, JUNE 28

Jakob and I went to the Social Club this evening, and the pair of us had an enjoyable time, drinking slightly too much and even winning a few pfennigs at the skat table. None of the men on my list were present, so for once I was able to forget why I'm here.

The last few days have been unusually hot, but the spell seems to be ending—sitting here by my open window, I can see forks of lightning on the western horizon and occasionally hear a faint roll of thunder. After all last week's excitement, the house has felt much calmer in recent days. Gerritzen has been the only one showing any animation—a new girl, I suspect, whose distant ancestors his father will surely be double-checking. Anna has seemed less anxious since finding out where Erich is, and her newfound optimism has rubbed off on Walter. Ruchay, like any true believer, has found a way of turning Schmeling's defeat into victory—according to him, given that everyone knows Louis cheated, the refusal to lodge an official complaint shows how superior Germany actually is.

And I of course feel that much calmer after the *treff* in Barmen. I have another month to gather information and impressions, and no immediate need to put my life at risk.

The next *treff* is on July 30, two days before Walter leaves for East Prussia. I know I will miss him greatly, but his being gone will make it easier to concentrate on the work I was sent here to do. A terrible admission for a veteran rep like myself, but undeniably true.

WEDNESDAY, JUNE 29

I spent most of this evening sitting outside with Andreas. He seems better lately. There's more color in his face, and his mind is as sharp as anyone's. The hot weather obviously suits the old man, and most days someone pushes him and his modified rocking chair out into the yard.

It doesn't get dark until after ten, and this evening was particularly pleasant, still warm with the slightest of breezes under a clear blue sky. I read to Andreas for an hour or so—a recent novel about the war that he obviously found entertaining, in spite of— or perhaps because of—its almost comic lack of authenticity.

When I put the book down, he asked if I'd ever read *The Good Soldier Schweik*.

I told him I had.

"They banned it of course."

I wasn't surprised—it mocks all those things the current leadership holds dear. Things like patriotic duty, unquestioning obedience, glorying in slaughter.

"I loved it," Andreas admitted cheerfully. "But probably better not to say so these days."

"Not to say what?" a voice said behind me.

"Ah, our noble block warden," Andreas said. "Have you two met?"

We had. Herr Clauer had come to introduce himself the day after my arrival, and I'd been pleasantly surprised by his affability. Anna had later told me that they were lucky, that the warden was an old friend of her father's.

Andreas said we'd been talking about *The Good Soldier Schweik* and was willing to bet that Clauer had read it.

"Not since it was banned," Clauer said jovially enough. He asked how I'd settled in at work and joked that I might not have come back from South America if I'd known how many shifts I'd be working. "And then you have to spend your evenings looking after this old Red!"

I must have betrayed my surprise, because he put a friendly hand on my shoulder and reminded me that the Duce had once been a Communist. It was what you did these days that mattered.

Well, Andreas said, he just sat around, thanking his lucky stars that he was too old to go to war, and that at least one of his grandsons was too young.

Clauer observed that the other one hadn't exactly covered himself in glory.

"He's learning," Andreas said.

Clauer hoped so. He had come around to suggest a new flag for the front of the house. With Erich under a cloud, it wouldn't do to look mean, and Clauer had guessed that with all her worries Anna might not have noticed how ragged the current one looked.

Andreas thanked him for pointing it out, then suggested that any time Clauer fancied wheeling him down to the nearest bar, he might even buy him a drink.

"Not tonight," Clauer told him. "I've got a lot of people to see. But soon!"

Once he was gone, Andreas filled me in on their history. They'd known each other in Essen before the war and had served in the same unit on the western front until Andreas lost his sight. More coincidentally, they'd both ended up moving to Hamm, and only a few houses apart.

I said that Clauer seemed a decent man, and Andreas agreed. They'd always disagreed about politics, but in a friendly sort of way. Franz Clauer was one of those men who always thought the best of people, "whether it's you or me or the Führer." They were lucky to have him, Andreas said, because most of the block wardens just liked sticking their noses in and using whatever they found to make themselves look good. But Franz thought he was helping people, and sometimes he really was. If he hadn't put a word in for Erich with the local Gestapo, it might have been more than six months.

I asked Andreas if he thought Erich had the sense to keep his head down.

The old man laughed. "Maybe, maybe not." But Erich was tough; it was Walter that Andreas was worried about. The boy was "too decent for a world like this one."

He'd hardly finished saying it when Walter himself appeared, characteristically out of breath, sweater in hand. "Mama says you should put this on."

Andreas did as he was told, and for a moment I thought I saw tears in his eyes.

THURSDAY, JUNE 30

I have worked at the yard for nine weeks now, and have, I hope, established myself as a fairly easygoing chap with an interest in workplace issues but no political ax to grind. I'm pleasant and undemanding company, who's not going to upset anyone's day by being prickly, intrusive, or particularly clever. A Barufka without the cloak of sadness.

I have now had—or overheard—several conversations involving the seven men on my list whom I've managed to meet. I've also brought their names up in various settings and listened to any opinions that others were willing to offer. I've followed a few of them home and chatted with their neighbors. I have done what spies do, and I know as much about these men as any stranger could. It's not enough of course, but then it never can be. People do stupid things for sensible reasons, and vice versa. All I can do is play the odds and try to minimize the risks.

And today I finally met my eighth man. Gunter Schulte is a tall, thin, dour-looking individual who works in the locomotive repair shop. He nearly always eats alone, reading a paper as he forks in the food, but today he was sharing a table with an engineer named Weber whom I slightly know, and I wasted no time in joining them. Weber seemed put out, but Schulte was more welcoming than I expected and almost immediately asked my opinion about the subject they were discussing, which turned out to be the "Jewish problem" in general, and the regime's treatment of German Jewish war veterans in particular. "I am saying that a man who fights bravely for his country—bravely enough to win an Iron Cross First Class— should be honored in that country," Schulte said, his obvious anger just about under control. "Honored for life. Forever. If you have a problem with too many Jewish bankers and lawyers and doctors, fine. Introduce quotas; redress the balance. But don't try and rewrite history. Those men were every bit as brave as your so-called Aryans."

Weber was unabashed. "An enemy is an enemy," he said. "We can't afford to make exceptions."

I thought Schulte might hit him, but Schulte simply shook his head and laughed. "Have it your way," he said. "I suppose we must assume the Führer knows best," he added with more than a hint of sarcasm.

"Yes, we must," Weber said, getting up. "And you should be more careful what you say, Gunter," he added, with a glance in my direction.

Schulte watched him walk away, then turned a calm face to me. "My late wife was Jewish," he said. "And both her brothers won Iron Crosses."

⟶ ⟶ ⟶

FRIDAY, JULY 1

The Anschluss is fewer than four months old, but already it seems clear that Hitler has no intention of resting on his laurels. Having swallowed his native Austria whole, he now seems intent on nibbling away at the German-populated edges of Czechoslovakia. The wireless this morning carried news of the latest outrage and German protests—teachers in Czech schools are apparently encouraging their pupils to sing rude songs about the Führer. In revenge, the announcer characterized the entire Czech population as an "urchin-like rabble."

He also described the situation as "untenable," which is probably close to the mark. Hitler and his wrecking crew won't be happy until every last German is under their control. The Czech Sudetenland looks certain to be next on their list, and after that who knows? There are sizable German populations in most of the neighboring countries.

Not that extending Germany's borders to bring them all inside the Reich would satisfy Hitler. And he has never pretended it would. Anyone who wades through *Mein Kampf*—as I did ten years ago when his ravings still seemed more crazy than real—will read that Germany's eastern border should follow the Ural Mountains. All the land now occupied by Poles, Russians, Ukrainians, and others is earmarked as "living space" for the more-deserving Germans. Add to that his hatred of Communists and Jews—whom he bizarrely conflates into a single enemy—and its clear that the Soviet Union is his prime objective.

This "living space" can't be taken peacefully, so building up German military strength must be Hitler's top priority. Which brings us back to Czechoslovakia, and not just the parts where Germans live. The Czech heartland has large and efficient arms and motor industries, both of which the Wehrmacht badly needs. If and when the Sudetenland goes, the rest won't be far behind.

If I can see all this, then surely Stalin and the Western leaders can see it too. If they can find a way of stopping Hitler in his tracks and thereby prevent him from keeping the Reich economy afloat with the bounty of serial conquests, then the whole Nazi project should start to fall apart. But first they have to stop him, and I see little sign that they're even willing to try. The Soviet Union has no common border with Czechoslovakia, so even if he wanted to, Stalin would find it hard to provide any meaningful help, and I don't think he'll stick his neck out that far. As for the British and French, they seem to be hoping that the Nazis either belatedly learn to behave or—in the likely event that this proves beyond them—take out their resentments on others. The Soviets, say.

SUNDAY, JULY 3

An excellent day. As promised, the heat wave abated overnight, and this morning I went for a walk by the canal. Out in the open countryside, the scene was positively idyllic, a hazy blue sky hanging above the golden cornfields, with only a distant song of church bells rising above the whispers and murmurs of nature.

This afternoon I took Walter and Marco to see a Hollywood double bill at the cinema. The supporting feature, a Western called *Outlaws of Sonora*, had a ludicrous plot about swapping identities but was mercifully short. The German newsreel conspicuously failed to cover Max Schmeling's humiliation in New York, giving over its sports section to the upcoming Grand Prix season, which started today in France.

Walter's favorite driver is Rudolf Caracciola, but Walter can list about half a dozen other German track stars, together with the makes and colors of their racing machines.

The main feature was *The Adventures of Robin Hood*, which I must admit was highly entertaining. Walter and Marco loved it, and spent their first hour back at the house staging imaginary sword fights up and down the stairs with tightly rolled newspapers.

Ruchay has been away visiting his mother in Hannover, and this evening Gerritzen was out with his new girlfriend, so dinner was a much more pleasant affair than usual. Verena and Marco ate with Anna, Jakob, Walter, and me, and it felt like a family occasion. A taste of how things should be, but so rarely are.

It brought back memories of my own family at dinner, before the war in our Offenbach home. My mother in her pale blue apron, my father still in his foreman's uniform. Jens making all of us laugh with an impersonation of one of his teachers.

MONDAY, JULY 4

When Jakob and I arrived at work this morning, the yard was swarming with uniformed Orpo, and two Gestapo cars were parked in front of the director's office. I knew that if they'd wanted me, they'd have come to the house, but my heart beat a little faster nevertheless.

So why were they there? Slogans in the toilet, an acquaintance I passed in the corridor told me with a contemptuous smirk. Whether the contempt was for the sloganeers or those who'd come to catch them wasn't clear.

In the dispatch office, no one seemed to be working, but there was only the one topic of conversation. There was nothing new about political slogans on toilet doors—we had all seen the hammers and sickles and pleas to shoot Hitler sharing space with varied carnal ambitions—so we could surmise only that someone had finally thought them worth reporting. A few minutes later, Müller walked in, hushed the room with a rap on his desk, and told us that a new and particularly offensive slogan had been discovered on doors in several different buildings. These had been reported to the local police, who had promptly involved the Gestapo.

When someone asked what the slogan was, Müller admitted that he didn't know. I wondered what it could have been—what could the Nazis find more offensive than scribbled pleas to shoot their leader? The Gestapo, Müller added, had set themselves up in the canteen and would be questioning every worker in turn.

One man remarked that lunch would be a cheerful affair. Others were more concerned about the toilets—were any still accessible?

Müller went to find out, and returned a couple of minutes later with the welcome news that only one of our toilet's cubicles was out of use, and only for the time it would take to paint over the offending slogan. And no, he hadn't been able to see what it was, but no doubt we'd find out soon enough. In the meantime, we should all get back to work. The Gestapo would tell us when we were needed.

An Orpo officer arrived with the first three names. The choice suggested alphabetical order, which told me I would be one of the following three. Once called, two of us were told to wait outside the canteen's door while the other one was questioned. The Gestapo officers had taken the table farthest from the serving hatch and kitchen, where several women were already preparing lunch. It seemed that no one had asked them to keep the noise down, and the low murmur of my colleague's questioning was interspersed with clanging saucepans and slamming drawers.

My turn soon came. There were two men seated at the desk—the Kriminalsekretär I'd seen with Anna and a Kriminalinspektor whom I assumed was the Hamm chief, Herbert Jagusch. He was probably still in his thirties, with greasy swept-back hair that was starting to recede and a sharp-boned face beneath a wide brow. Two other agents hovered behind them, ready to fetch and carry if the need arose.

I handed over my papers and offered the Kriminalsekretär a friendly smile while his superior looked through them. The smile wasn't exactly returned, but perhaps a lip twitched ever so slightly.

The Kriminalinspektor repeated what he'd read—that my name was Josef Hofmann, that I'd recently returned to Germany from Argentina, where I'd worked on the railways.

I nodded.

He noted that I'd left Germany in 1923, the year that many Communists had fled the Reich following the collapse of their criminal uprising.

I said I'd never been a Communist, that I'd left Germany because my Ruhr homeland was occupied by foreigners and because the Great Inflation had destroyed half the local jobs. Having no family, I'd decided to try my luck abroad, in a country where Germans were known to be welcome. And why had I come back? Because thanks to the party, there were jobs to be had once more, and Germany's future looked bright.

He gave me a look. "We will be investigating your past," he said, as if offering me one last chance to get my story straight.

I told him I had nothing to hide.

His almost imperceptible shrug conceded that might be the case. He assumed I was aware that inflammatory slogans had been discovered in several different toilets, in several parts of the yard.

I said I assumed they must be inflammatory but had not seen any myself and had no idea what they said.

"Mostly the usual Communist nonsense," he said, by which I presumed he meant hammers and sickles and pleas to shoot Hitler. "But this is the one we are interested in," he went on, handing over a sheet of paper. This slogan, he added, had been found in a number of locations.

"Hitler and Stalin—brothers under the skin!" was the message in question. One I was cautioned not to repeat.

"Of course," I said, as if shocked by the thought.

He asked me what I thought the slogan meant.

I was wondering that myself, and also wondering—a separate question—what to say if I was asked.

Looking suitably perplexed, I said it could mean several things. That our Führer and the Soviet leader, though clearly worlds apart in most respects, did share certain attributes—strength in leadership, perhaps. But I had to admit it was strange—you would expect a Communist to love his leader and hate ours, while we of course would feel the opposite.

A Trotskyist would consider both men equally murderous, but my fictional self wouldn't know that. The Kriminalinspektor patiently waited, apparently hoping I'd say something more, so I settled for simply looking bewildered and was duly rewarded with a curt dismissal.

The questioning continued for most of the day. I could see the Gestapo cars through the window opposite my desk, and when they eventually drove away, one of the young apprentices was with them. He looked around sixteen, and as if he might burst into tears at any moment. He didn't seem like an author of ambiguous political slogans.

No one in our office knew anything more than his first name, which is Gregor, but Jakob, with whom I shared the walk home, had further information. Since his hiring a few weeks ago, the boy has performed menial tasks at the shed—mostly shoveling coal, ash, and sand. His father, who has an administrative post elsewhere in the yard, is one of Hitler's most fervent supporters and—that rarest of things— a friend of Herr Ruchay's.

Not surprisingly, the topic came up over supper. Ruchay claimed he was sure of the boy's innocence, but could hardly contain his outrage at the crime. For him, the thought of Hitler and Stalin sharing anything was truly appalling, and as I listened to him rant, I began to appreciate why the Gestapo was taking the business so seriously.

Later, up here in my room, I admitted to myself that part of me shared the man's outrage, albeit from a different perspective. The sloganeer, whoever he is, has hit a nerve, and I spent some time in my chair trying to work out why. Any fool can see similarities in the means Stalin and Hitler use, but the ends—socialism and a slave state built on eugenic nonsense—are just as obviously worlds apart. So why does the comparison upset me? We have told ourselves for twenty years that harshness is the price we pay for breaking the status quo and its tenacious supporters, that the end justifies the means. Am I beginning to doubt it? To fear that the means employed might contaminate the end?

As I sat here, I recalled a story someone told me years ago, of how Lenin once asked his writer friend Maxim Gorky to turn off some beautiful music because, with the revolution still in the balance, Lenin couldn't afford the sort of human feelings the music evoked. And I remember thinking, when I heard this, that it made perfect sense. As of course it does in terms of realpolitik. But realpolitik has its limits, and now I wonder if Lenin was wrong and whether a revolution that puts aside such feelings can ever get them back. A sobering thought for a Comintern rep.

But one good thing has come out of my reflections. The sloganeer, I realize, has given me a tool. If I am disturbed by his words, then so will other comrades be, and their reactions could provide me with an indication of where their loyalties currently lie. With the slogan the talk of the works, no one will consider it strange if I ask his opinion, and I may learn much from people's answers.

TUESDAY, JULY 5

A single Gestapo car arrived at the works soon after our shift started and left again ten minutes later after somehow squeezing four apprentices into the back seat. Two of the latter were returned after a couple of hours, looking more than a little relieved. Over lunch Barufka passed on the news that the first apprentice arrested had owned up to an unflattering picture of Göring in the repair shop toilet, but had denied drawing anything else or writing a single slogan. According to one colleague, the boy's portrait of the Reichsmarschall is both witty and well executed and, for reasons best known to the Gestapo, has not yet been painted over. Does anyone in Germany like Göring?

Barufka and I agreed that the Hitler-Stalin slogan was written by someone a good deal older than the young apprentices the Gestapo had taken away. I was pretty sure the author was or had been a Communist, and over his doubtless superior lunch, Kriminalinspektor Jagusch apparently came to the same conclusion. He was back in midafternoon to requestion five of the men he'd already seen, all of them on Moscow's list. But this time no one was taken away.

WEDNESDAY, JULY 6

At lunch today I was able to try out my brain wave. Spotting Horst Franke with Fritz Angermund, the youngest of my fellow dispatchers, I took my tray over to join them, hoping to bring up the slogan. I needn't have worried—they were already discussing it.

"They both say they're in it for the ordinary guy," Angermund was saying, taking care not to speak too loudly. "They both believe in state planning, and they both insist on political unity. They both even have mustaches." He grinned. "But seriously, what are the differences?"

Horst was already shaking his head. That was crap, he said. How could Fascism and Communism be the same when one was on the right and the other on the left?

That was just what they called themselves, Angermund argued. They could still behave in similar ways.

Horst's head hadn't stopped shaking. Like me he wanted to talk about ends but knew that that would be a step too far, even among friends. And I wasn't one. "We shall see" was all he said. "Where Germany is in ten years and where Russia is. We shall see the difference then."

He's a Communist all right, at least in his mind. Why else would the slogan upset him so? But being a Communist isn't enough. He has to be willing to risk his life for that belief.

There was a Working Group meeting this evening, and I wasn't the only one keen to hear others' opinions of the slogan. The others are not yet sure of me, so it came as no surprise when I was the first one offered the chance to give myself away. Being among fellow socialists would have made things easier, if I hadn't been half-convinced that one or more of the others was an informer.

I claimed ignorance. There were obviously similarities between Hitler and Stalin, but I wasn't sure how deep these were. Stalin was authoritarian, but possibly out of necessity, whereas Hitler believed that dictatorship was the natural order of things. At this stage, I concluded pathetically, it was impossible to know which system would do the most for the workingman.

I could tell from the faces that nobody much liked my answer, but then no one seemed enraged by it either. Others were keener to point out the differences—the new Soviet constitution, the rights of Soviet women, and the wonders of free health care were all brought up. No one shouted or got overly emotional, but it was clear to me how much the slogan had offended these men's sense of what was right. And then I realized why. They were all talking about the Soviet Union of five years ago, the one that still existed when the Nazi takeover cut off their links with Moscow, before Kirov's death and the terror that followed, before you really could make a case for Hitler and Stalin being brothers under the skin.

Paul Giesemann seemed the most offended of all, railing against the notion of any equivalence between Nazis and Communists. Hadn't they shed enough of each other's blood in recent years? Weren't the KZs still full of comrades?

I would be certain the young man is an informer if not for the fact that the group is still meeting. Are the Gestapo playing a long game, letting us chat as long as that's all we do, hoping that more and more flies will stick to Elise's flypaper?

THURSDAY, JULY 7

Most weekday evenings we four lodgers still gather in the living room downstairs to listen to the nine o'clock news broadcast. Barufka looks bored most of the time and, I suspect, just turns up for the company, but Ruchay and Gerritzen see it almost as a duty, as if their keeping abreast of the Third Reich's relentless advances is somehow part of the process. They treat the whole thing like a football match, the various announcements like goals scored by their side. You would think that some of the stuff the regime puts out would test anyone's credulity, but these two lap it all up, and I'm sure they're far from unusual.

A few days ago we were given the news that the German and Polish education authorities have reached agreement on the impartial teaching of history in their respective schools. Past conflicts between the two nations are to be covered objectively, without passion, and each side has offered to remove from its textbooks anything the other finds offensive. More astonishing still, they have promised to extend this agreement to subjects other than history. Which? I wonder. Are there different German and Polish laws of physics? Disagreement on where the world's coalfields are? Even Jakob raised an eyebrow at this, and the whole idea is clearly ludicrous, but Ruchay and Gerritzen just sat there nodding and smiling, as if it all made perfect sense.

This evening we learned that a new Reich Institute for Colonial Administration will soon be offering courses in how to run colonies. Germany currently has none—a cost of losing the war—but Hitler clearly has hopes. When the "day of justice" arrives, and Germany either gets the old ones back or conquers new ones, there will be a corps of administrators ready and waiting to run them on the Führer's behalf. The courses, we were told, will combine lessons from Germany's prewar experience with new ideas from the National Socialist canon, thereby combining the best of past and future. By which I suspect they mean that yesterday's traditional thuggery will be infused with modern sadism. Racial theory will obviously play a big part, and when the Nazis say that they intend to "balance the interests of homeland and colony," I assume they mean Germans at home and Germans abroad. I can't see how the natives—whoever they happen to be—could be anything other than virtual slaves in a National Socialist colony.

According to the announcement, the new administrators

will all be married men, presumably to avoid the perils of miscegenation. Though why anyone would think that being married would keep these chosen ones on the straight and narrow eludes me. Perhaps castration seems too severe, or a deterrent to recruitment.

Ruchay appeared riveted by this item, and after the news was over, we learned why. His father was involved in the building of the Central Line railway in German East Africa before the war, so the Reich's colonial future is something Ruchay feels he has a personal stake in. But that wasn't all. Answering a question from Gerritzen, he revealed that his father had never come home. Taken prisoner by the British soon after the outbreak of war, he had ended up in an internment camp, where he eventually fell ill and died.

Ruchay would have been a teenager at the time, and this new information about his past certainly helps to explain—if not to excuse—the grown man's rabid nationalism. It also confirms my hitherto baseless opinion of him as something of a mother's boy.

FRIDAY, JULY 8

An international conference opened a couple of days ago to discuss the Jewish refugee problem. It is taking place in Évian-les-Bains, a small French town on the shore of Lake Geneva, close to the Swiss border. A nice place to visit no doubt, and I'm sure the lucky diplomats involved will enjoy the food and the scenery.

If the German press is to be believed—I have access to no other—the conference is Roosevelt's brainchild, though what he hopes to gain from it is anybody's guess. An optimist might hope he was seeking to persuade his countrymen that they should welcome more Jewish immigrants; a cynic might think he was out to shame others, and so deflect attention from America's niggardly response. Either way, thirty-one other nations have sent delegates. As the primary source of the current problem, Germany has not been invited, and neither it seems have most of the eastern European countries, which have a much longer history of virulent anti-Semitism than Germany does. I hope to be proved wrong, but I can't see anyone rushing to open their borders.

In the meantime, our government shows no sign of relaxing its campaign to drive out the Jews. Ruchay's *Der Stürmer* arrived today—a special edition on Austria's Jews—and over dinner we were treated to a feast of supposedly damning statistics. Eighty percent of Austria's lawyers, 75 percent of its bankers, were Jews. I can't remember all the figures, but there were similar proportions of doctors, dentists, and newspaper magnates. Ruchay read out the lengthy list, then sat there with a nasty smirk on his face, one that said, "Not anymore!"

SATURDAY, JULY 9

I have been stupid. Unusually so, I hope. I had assumed that Otto Tikalsky's obvious distress over the homosexual's death was what he said it was, a natural reaction to the violent loss of someone he knew and liked. I don't know why it never occurred to me that they could have been a lot closer.

Until this afternoon, that is. Catching sight of Otto in town, I followed him down an unfamiliar side street and watched him vanish into a narrow alley. Intrigued, I found shelter in a very convenient café and waited for him to reappear. He didn't for quite some time, but there was a steady procession of men—and only men—into and out of the alley entrance, and it didn't take a genius to work out what sort of establishment was hidden away down there. In the early twenties, when I was last in Germany, *warme Brüder* bars were far from uncommon, and it's clear that one at least has survived into the Nazi era.

With, it seems more than likely, considerable Nazi support. I wasn't shocked by the number of youths and men coming in and out, but I was quite taken aback by their obvious political promiscuity. Half those involved were wearing brown shirts or Nazi badges, and for all I knew, the other half were plainclothes Communists like Otto. I have nothing against the man indulging his sexual inclinations, but the company he's keeping has to rule him out.

MONDAY, JULY 11

The mystery sloganeer remains at large, but there was further news on the three apprentices still in custody. They have allegedly confessed to several of the writings and drawings that still adorn our toilet doors and walls and will face some sort of punishment, but it is not expected to be severe. They're all very young, and all their fathers are party members.

TUESDAY, JULY 12

There was a knock on the front door while we were eating supper, and a few moments later we all caught a glimpse of Anna ushering a tall young man through to her part of the house. He left after staying around twenty minutes, and when Ruchay rudely asked who he was, Anna paused as if weighing her answer, and then said, "A friend of a friend."

Walter was more forthcoming an hour or so later when

he came to my room with his history homework. The young man's name is Eugen Klodt, and he has just been released from Erich's camp. The two of them had met there and discovered they both came from Hamm, and Erich had asked his new friend to let the family know he was fine.

Questioned about the conditions, Eugen had claimed they were not that bad. The hours might have been long, but the work wasn't that hard; the food was awful, but there was usually enough. He wasn't supposed to say what they were doing, but it didn't feel like divulging a state secret to say they were working on the nation's defenses. The camp was close to the Belgian border, and early each morning they were driven to one of several sites to work on various jobs—clearing trees, laying roads, building watchtowers. Erich was in good spirits and doing what his mother had urged him to do—keeping his head down and counting the days.

I suggested to Walter that maybe his brother really had seen the error of his ways.

"Maybe," Walter conceded.

It was good news, though, and Anna must be feeling a little happier.

The history homework posed no problems. An account of the Franco-Prussian War in 1870 had been requested, and Walter had provided a good one, sandwiching a record of the actual fighting between the longer-term causes and consequences. I did fairly well in school, but at Walter's age I would have struggled to write something half as coherent.

After he was gone, I started thinking about something one of my schoolmasters had said years before, that the military is always expecting the next war to echo the last and is, moreover, usually wrong in that expectation. The reason, he explained, was that scientists and technologists spend the time between wars trying to counter what won the last one. The Franco-Prussian War, as Walter had just reminded me, was won by the Germans' superior mobility, so in 1910, my teacher supposed the military scientists would be hard at work trying to slow the enemy down.

I remembered thinking how right he'd been several years later, when both armies on the western front were trapped in mazes of trenches by machine guns and heavy artillery.

Only a few weeks ago the *Frankfurter Zeitung* carried a striking photograph—Hitler on a makeshift podium out on some Pomeranian heath, a throng of tanks stampeding past him, a swarm of the new Stuka bombers whizzing overhead. The next war.

WEDNESDAY, JULY 13

The American millionaire Howard Hughes is apparently trying to establish a new record time for circling the world in an airplane. Needless to say, it was Walter who brought this to my attention, along with a request for all I knew about the man in question. Which wasn't much. That he'd inherited a fortune from his father and proved adept at making it grow. That he'd been involved in making movies—I wasn't sure in what capacity—and loved flying. Walter already knew the details of the airplane, along with Hughes's prospective route and fueling stops, which include Moscow, Omsk, and Yakutsk. I tried to share the boy's enthusiasm, but even at his age the idea of speed for speed's sake always left me cold.

Walter also brought me up to date on our brave Himalayan mountaineers, whom I must admit I'd completely forgotten. The party is apparently still struggling up Nanga Parbat, having recently been resupplied from the air. Keen on a propaganda victory, the regime has dispatched a Junkers Ju 52s to British Kashmir, ready to drop the climbers whatever they need.

And speaking of dropping, the Japanese have resumed their bombing of Canton. Several hundred people who had no interest in risking their lives for a whiff of glory lost them just the same in yesterday's raid. The German papers seemed most excited by the damage done to things—the shattered houseboats on the river, the overturned trains in Wongsha station, the partial destruction of the ancient Laopo bridge.

THURSDAY, JULY 14

According to German radio, a Soviet general named Lyushkov has recently defected to the Japanese. He was serving in Manchuria and apparently took the chance to walk across an unmanned border. Why he did so was not asked—perhaps the Germans assume that leaving the Soviet Union needs no explanation—but Lyushkov's disillusion with Soviet rule was gleefully expounded. According to the defector, Stalin's opponents have only themselves to blame, because instead of grumbling among themselves, they should have taken their case to the rest of the party. Now that history's dustbin has claimed them, all that remains are yes-men blindly following Stalin's lead.

FRIDAY, JULY 15

Despite the prospect of two whole days off, Jakob seemed down in the dumps over supper, so I suggested a drink at the Social Club. Once he'd spent the best part of a minute staring at his untouched beer, I asked him what the matter was.

He gave me a ghost of a smile and said he was sorry. He was just depressed.

"Anything particular?" I asked.

"There's another war coming," he said quietly. "How can they be so stupid? After everything the last one cost us."

I instinctively knew that he wasn't talking about millions of marks or millions of dead. He was thinking about how much it had ended up costing him.

"It was my wedding anniversary today," he said sadly, admitting as much. "It's ridiculous, but I still miss her. If only . . ." He shrugged. "I just couldn't get it all out of my head quickly enough," he went on. "I was always surprised by how other people managed. Or seemed to, at least. How did you?" he asked, almost resentfully.

I took a sip and thought about the question. In my line of work, honest answers are usually too revealing, but in this case I wasn't sure what an honest answer would be. In some ways, I supposed, I'd never shaken it off. I was certainly still fighting a war, one just as vicious, if not quite as visceral, as the one we'd both fought in twenty years earlier. "I got angry," I told Jakob, which was at least partly true. "And I guess the anger carried me until I was able to carry myself. I had no one to go home to, no one who needed me to be the way I'd been before." No one but my parents.

He thought about that. "I don't blame her," he said eventually. "I just wish things had been different."

I asked if he knew where she was.

He didn't. "She married again, a long time ago. Our boy, Martin, never mentions her, but he must know where she is. He got engaged a few weeks ago, so I sent him some money to have a decent celebration. He says he'll come for a visit when he can, but he's so busy at work."

He could invite you to visit him, I thought but had the sense not to say.

I went to the bar for another round, and when I got back, we'd been joined by two of Jakob's colleagues from the engineering department. Both were complaining about their wives, one lamenting several burnt meals in a row, the other his spouse's incessant pleas for a Strength through Joy cruise.

"She thinks you just have to ask and Goebbels turns up at the door with your tickets," he said bitterly.

The two of them were friendly enough, but neither seemed to have noticed that the world's going up in flames, and their ideas grew triter and less forgiving with each passing glass. As my long-dead uncle Berndt was fond of saying, the sort of men "you'd rather share a grave with than a table."

Jakob and I left a while before closing and walked home under a sky slowly filling with stars. As we approached our front door, he apologized for being "so glum" earlier that evening and thanked me for taking him out of himself.

SATURDAY, JULY 16

The Évian Conference ended yesterday, and the obvious lack of any breakthrough must be bitterly disappointing for Germany's Jews. "NOBODY WANTS THEM!" was the gloating front-page headline on Ruchay's *Völkischer Beobachter*, and for once in its life, that rancid rag is only slightly exaggerating. Costa Rica and the Dominican Republic have agreed to take more Jewish immigrants, but the other thirty countries involved have all refused to raise their grossly inadequate current quotas. The United States, Britain, and France, who could and should have been more generous, have not only let themselves down, but offered Hitler a notable victory. To quote the Führer, as Ruchay gleefully did over breakfast, "It is a shameful spectacle to see how the whole democratic world is oozing sympathy for the poor tormented Jewish people, but remains hard-hearted and obdurate when it comes to helping them."

More than a little rich when coming from the tormentor in chief, but hard to dispute.

✦ ✦ ✦

MONDAY, JULY 18

Walter has end-of-year examinations this Friday, and he's enlisted members of the household to help him with his studying. I was first in line this evening with history and spent half an hour testing him on names and dates. His recall was near perfect, and we ended up discussing one of the topics he thinks might come up: the fatal—for Germany—American decision to enter the last war.

Herr Skoumal has apparently told the class that the Americans' main motivation was financial. According to him the Jewish financiers had loaned Britain and France so much money that they couldn't afford a German victory. So when the Russian collapse made that more likely, the financiers persuaded their own government to join the fighting.

Agreeing with Herr Skoumal doesn't come easy, but here he has a point, and I told Walter as much, adding that the Jewish part was probably exaggerated. The only financier I remember handing out huge loans was Jack Morgan, and he belonged to one of the Christian sects.

"One boy asked Herr Skoumal about our U-boat campaign," Walter reported. "He'd read in one of his grandfather's books that the Americans objected to us sinking their ships. Before they were in the war."

"And what did Herr Skoumal say?" I asked.

"He said the Americans might have said that, but the British blockade was killing more innocent people than submarines, so it wasn't a real reason."

Two for Herr Skoumal, I thought. I asked whether he'd mentioned the Zimmermann Telegram.

"No. What was that?"

"It was a telegram sent by one of our government ministers—a man called Zimmermann—to the government of Mexico, offering the return of all the land they'd lost to the

United States—California, Arizona, Texas, I think—if they joined the war on our side. It was in code, but the British intercepted the telegram, decoded it, and told the Americans."

"That must have made them really angry," Walter decided.

It had, I agreed, but if Herr Skoumal didn't think the matter worth mentioning, then Walter should probably stick with evil financiers and brave submariners.

Walter nodded. "I'd like to go to America."

I asked him why.

He said he didn't really know but that it seemed an exciting sort of place.

"It's certainly an interesting one," I said, foolishly forgetting my own fictional history.

"I didn't know you'd been there," Walter said, surprised.

"A long time ago," I improvised. "And only for a few days. I have some relations there, and when I was booking my trip to Argentina, I found it was easy to go via New York."

"So what did you find interesting?"

I thought about that. It was hard to explain, I said eventually. America was such a strange mixture. A country built on slavery and the murder of its natives that thinks itself the finest place on earth. "It feels like it has everything," I told Walter, "from the best to the worst and back again." I pushed back at the memories. "But if you haven't studied it yet, then it won't come up in these exams."

"I know. And I have to do science with Herr Barufka now. You don't know much about science, do you?"

I had to admit I didn't. With Walter gone, I sat by the window for a half hour or more, thinking about him and America. He loves history the way I did when I was his age or perhaps a year or two older; he loves working out why things happened in the way that they did. It's not a useful gift in Hitler's Germany, but despite the Führer's thousand-year prognosis, I suspect his regime will last less than twenty, and the boy will come into his own.

Our talk about America had evoked some memories of my real life there, which began in the summer of 1931 and lasted for almost a year. The months I spent in the Pennsylvania anthracite region were among the most rewarding of my life.

As I told Walter, I docked in New York, spent a few days there, and was indeed impressed by the city's extraordinary vitality. I also received my instructions from the Comintern regional office, which was then housed in an impeccably bourgeois apartment in Queens, overlooking a private flying field that I believe will soon host the city's first public airport. The following morning found me on a train to Scranton, Pennsylvania, where a major miners' strike was several weeks old.

Some necessary background. Since February 1928, the Comintern had been pursuing its new "class against class" policy in which the moderate left was seen as our principal enemy. In the USA, as elsewhere, we had created new unions to both fight the bosses and outflank the older, moderate unions. In the mining sector, the new National Miners Union was taking on, and hoping to replace, the United Mine Workers. The latter, though in our view much more concerned with the interests of its officials than those of the ordinary members, still had a much higher membership, but we had established ourselves and, whenever we got the chance, did our best to show the miners that we would represent their interests better.

The strike in progress was against the Glen Alden company, which owned mines throughout the area and employed around twenty-five thousand miners. The UMW leadership had opposed the strike from the beginning, but the local UMW had called it anyway, and we had then attempted to "capture" it for the NMU. In this we had failed, and the regional Comintern executive had decided that since, in their opinion, the strike was doomed, we should cut our losses. If we could persuade our local people to give up this particular fight, then the UMW would have to own the defeat.

I was the persuader in chief, sent to tell a lot of principled men that they should abandon a fight that wasn't yet lost, and admit that the suffering they had inflicted on their members' families had all been for nothing. I was not expecting the warmest of welcomes, and I won't pretend it was easy. I did the rounds of the towns and mines and talked to as many of our people as I could. Many saw the new direction as a betrayal of our members, and in the short term, of course they were right, but I slowly won most of them over—not just to an acceptance of the new party line, but also to its long-term correctness.

My mission was successful, but that wasn't what made the visit rewarding. During my months in Scranton, I stayed with a quite extraordinary family. Bill Brennan, the husband and father, ran the union branch in the local pit and seemed to be popular with everyone. He constantly put himself out and rarely got enough sleep, yet never seemed to lose his essential affability. The tenth person knocking on his door at the end of an exhausting day would get the same smile as the first one, the same patient listen, the same encouragement. His children got the same, and there were eight of them, ranging in age from two to sixteen.

His wife, Esther, was green-eyed, vivacious, and, if anything, even more openhearted. You might think eight children would have been enough to keep her busy, but their friends, and any stray waif who happened by, were always given the warmest of welcomes. The evening meal was always a dish, such as a casserole or stew, which could be further divided if an extra mouth turned up. While I was there, two orphaned children seemed to be permanent visitors, and if they were treated any differently from Esther's own children, I never saw it. In addition to mothering, she ran the household on next to no money, helped out all over the town, and took an hour each Sunday to write to the local paper about whatever wrong she thought needed righting that week.

She had been brought up a Quaker, and her Communism was infused with pacifism. Yet despite her tenaciously held beliefs, she was one of the least judgmental people I had ever met. I knew she disagreed with what I had come to do, and she argued her case with passion and intelligence, but I never thought she distrusted my motives. She gave me the benefit of the doubt and, as far as I could tell, gave it to everyone else as well. I lived in her house for a little over six months, and I've never been more convinced that this was the sort of life, the sort of relations between human beings, that could and should be our ultimate goal as socialists. I've spent so much of my life dealing with the wrong, but there was something so undeniably right.

A truly remarkable couple. I hope they are still going strong.

TUESDAY, JULY 19

A zookeeper in Munich has been attacked and killed by a four-year-old elephant. The animal in question had been there since birth and was apparently the keeper's favorite.

A sad story, you might think, but the *Beobachter*'s reporter told it with unvarnished relish, as if keen to point out that nothing and no one can ever be trusted.

WEDNESDAY, JULY 20

A twenty-year-old Communist named Helmut Kuhlmann was beheaded in a Berlin prison this morning. He was the seventeenth person to be executed for treason this year, with five months still to go. A few districts still use the hand-wielded ax, but I believe that Berlin employs the more civilized Fallbeil.

I have a horror of being beheaded, which I realize is quite irrational. The Fallbeil is, I believe, always a single-cut job, unlike the ax, which history tells us can take a lot more, depending on sharpness and aim. After the head is severed, consciousness apparently ends within two or three seconds, which may seem long at the time but surely prohibits extended reflection on the fact of one's own demise. No, I'm sure it's short and relatively painless, but I still hate the prospect. My head and torso have been working together in life, and they should rest together in death. I also abhor the thought of dying on my knees, something I believe the Fallbeil requires.

As, indeed, does an NKVD bullet in the back of the head. Whoever said it was better to live on one's feet than die on one's knees knew what he or she was talking about.

I've seen a lot of death in my forty-three years, which is perhaps why the mere prospect of dying doesn't bother me. There are some truly terrible ways to go, and I've seen a lot more of these than I wanted to. The war was bad enough when it came to tearing bodies apart, but there's no sense of cruelty in distant artillery. Most people, on the other hand, can be unbelievably cruel in certain circumstances, and in Russia they were. They say civil wars are the worst, but nothing prepared me for some of the things I saw supposedly normal people do to other normal people's bodies. Witnessing horrors like that, you begin to wonder whether life is worth living, let alone if others are worth dying for.

But then we all die, don't we? And that's why I don't want to do it on my knees, either literally or emotionally. I want to feel my life was worth something, both for myself and for others.

A trifle maudlin, perhaps? Or a way of keeping me on my toes? I'm certainly guilty of treason and could well share

Helmut Kuhlmann's fate. It could happen at any moment—
the sound of a car, a knock on the door. They say the Gestapo
have gotten better at preventing suicides, so I can expect a
great deal of pain before they realize I have nothing to tell
them. The men I deal with in Hamm are mostly ex-Commu-
nists, but the Gestapo already know about them, and none
are currently breaking the law. My only Comintern contact
is Elise, and she's probably out of Germany by now. They'd
want to know where and when the next *treff* is, but by the
time they'd checked out my lie, the truth would be worthless.

Three years ago I would have had an emergency number
to call, but after that practice cost us a couple of men, Moscow decided it was proving too expensive. If I'm unlucky and
have to flee the country at short notice, I shall have to find
my own way out.

THURSDAY, JULY 21

I've shared tables with the driver Artur Zerbe on several occasions during the last seven weeks and have found no reason
to doubt his mental loyalty to the party. I have also contrived
conversations with two male neighbors of his, neither of
whom could contain their envy at the number of women he
entertains. I have to admit I disliked the man from the start,
but having been told on more than one occasion that I nurture a puritanical streak, I gave him the benefit of the doubt.
Not anymore. In the canteen this lunchtime, everyone was
talking about a bloody fight in the locomotive depot, and
I soon discovered that Zerbe had been involved. Two other
drivers had accused him of seducing their wives while they
were away on night duties and had then waded in with their
fists. Zerbe had been rescued by others, but not before needing hospital treatment. A liability if ever I saw one.

Which brings me down to three, as I've also decided not to involve Dariusz Müller. Despite the uncertainties surrounding his recent relations with the Nazi authorities, I instinctively trust the man, but it still seems wiser to err on the side of caution where he's concerned, particularly as involving him would blur the line between my list of relative veterans and the younger Working Group, which I fear includes an informer.

So I have my cell: the Jewess's widower Schulte, the disparate friends Franke and Opatz. They're not aware of their membership yet, and perhaps they never will be. It's for Moscow to set things in motion and then for each of the three to heed the call or betray the caller.

FRIDAY, JULY 22

Walter sat his end-of-year examinations yesterday and today, and he doesn't think he's done too badly. Yesterday's math exam resembled a Wehrmacht entrance exam, requiring the pupils to calculate shell trajectories and how many liters of fuel a plane would need to bomb a target so many kilometers away.

It was history and geography today, the subjects I've been helping with. They're also the ones he likes best, despite the fact that Herr Skoumal teaches them. I was expecting an air of triumph, but what I got was uncertainty—he really wasn't sure how he'd done. Putting dates to events and vice versa had been easy enough, explaining Horst Wessel boring but also straightforward. He had remembered Herr Skoumal's five weaknesses of democracy, and answered that question rather than the alternatives, which were explaining either the Jewish threat to civilization or the socialist betrayal of the German Army in 1918. The final question had asked him to name the three greatest Germans in history and add a few explanatory words. He had chosen Frederick the Great, Bismarck, and Hitler, but had run out of time before he got to the Führer.

I winced.

"I know," he said. But he thought he'd done better in geography. There'd been a mimeographed outline of Europe with the current borders drawn in, and they'd each had to identify all the countries "artificially created" in 1918. He'd known all of them—"even Memel"—and he thought he'd done well with the other map, which had featured all of Germany's lost territories, and on which Herr Skoumal had wanted them to write the things that each had produced for the Second Reich's economy. "Like Silesian coal," Walter explained. There'd been capital cities to name and questions about the expeditions to Nanga Parbat, which they'd talked about in class. The final question had been about canals. They'd been asked to choose three, say where they were, and explain why each was important. "Which was easy."

It sounded to me as if he'd done well, so why was he so unsure?

"You should have seen the look on Herr Skoumal's face when he took my papers," Walter said. "He wants me to fail. And if I've made mistakes, that's what he'll notice."

I'm hoping he's wrong about that, hoping that Skoumal has better things to do than pick on independent-minded twelve-year-olds.

SATURDAY, JULY 23

When Erich was arrested about two months back, Jakob and I hoped that Ruchay's brain would finally succeed in convincing his heart and dick that harnessing the three of them to such a disreputable family was completely out of the question.

Unfortunately, Erich's arrest seems to have had the opposite effect, and Ruchay has mutated into a suitor. "He's decided she's more in need of saving than ever" was Andreas's cynical reading, and I fear he may be right.

After Ruchay took Anna and Walter to that parade in town, all was smiles for several days. Then things soured again—at mealtimes Ruchay was sharp or sulking, and she was bending over backward, trying to appease him. Jakob and I surmised that she'd refused another invitation.

Early this week Ruchay asked her to be his "escort" at a management dinner in town. I know this because she came to me for advice. After confirming our suspicions that she'd refused an earlier date, she told me that fighting him off without earning his undying enmity was wearing her out.

"I can't stand the man," she whispered fiercely, glancing back over her shoulder as she did so, "but spending an evening with him won't kill me. The trouble is, he'll take my going as a hopeful sign, and who will he blame when he finds out the hope is false?"

"Why not just say no?" I asked. "What can he do to you?"

She gave me a look. She didn't know, and she didn't want to find out. He was, she thought, quite capable of turning really nasty.

I wondered out loud how we would tell, which at least raised a smile. The only stratagem I could suggest was the old one of letting him down gently, of blaming everything and everyone but him for the fact that it just wouldn't work. "Make him feel good about being a gentleman," I said. "For once in his life."

That was on Monday. Yesterday evening she went to the dinner, much to Walter's disgust. She looked wonderful—too much so, I thought, observing them leave—and Ruchay looked depressingly happy over breakfast this morning. When I got the chance to ask her how the evening had gone, she told me the meal had been excellent, the conversation disgusting. "But I've won myself a few weeks' reprieve," she added ironically. "When I told him I was too busy bringing up a child to consider a close relationship with any man, he said he was looking forward to Walter's being away in August."

If I were Anna, I think I'd put poison in the bastard's cocoa.

MONDAY, JULY 25

I thought about "Elise" today. She should be back in Moscow by now and facing whatever fate the NKVD have in mind for her. I feel less pessimistic than I did—the purge was already wearing itself out when I left in April, and even at its height, a recall often involved punishments some way short of a death sentence. Some of us have to survive, if only to fill the jobs of those who don't.

TUESDAY, JULY 26

Verena and I had a long chat this evening, sitting out in the sunlit yard while Andreas snored and snuffled in his make-shift wheelchair. She wanted my advice, which seems to be much in demand these days. I'd like to think that a life spent gathering wisdom has turned me into the perfect *Kummer-kastentante*, but I think it's more a case of limited choice. Women have a hard time getting the authorities to take them seriously almost everywhere, and particularly here in Hitler's version of my homeland. Which leaves the men. No woman would want to put herself in debt to Ruchay, or expect Ger-ritzen to see beyond his own concerns. And Jakob, though kindness personified, is no one's idea of a forceful personal-ity. Which left me.

It was of course about Marco. She asked me if I knew what they called "children like him" and supplied the answer before I had time to. "The 'Rhineland bastards,'" she said bitterly. "And do you know why?"

I said that I did.

A lot of women and girls had been raped by the French African soldiers, Verena said, but she had not been one of them. She'd been only eighteen when she'd met this young soldier from Côte d'Ivoire at a dance. His name was Jean, and he hadn't been sure of his age, but he couldn't have been much older than she was. "He was a wonderful dancer and a lovely boy, and I fell in love with him. And I think he fell in love with me."

They would meet in the park after dark and once managed a walk in the nearby countryside. He had talked a lot about Africa, about how much poorer it was in some things and how much richer it seemed to be in other ways. And then, just like that, his unit was on the move, leaving them only minutes to say their goodbyes. He'd promised to write and had kept his word—for almost a year, the letters had arrived, but all without the return address he'd failed to give her before he left. She had written care of the French Colonial Office, the French embassy in Berlin, even the mayor—if there was one—of the biggest town in Côte d'Ivoire, Abidjan. But all to no effect. And then he had stopped writing to her. "I only found I was pregnant after he left, so he never knew about Marco."

A sad story, I thought, wondering where the need for advice came in.

She intuited the question. She was telling me all this because of something she'd overheard in a shop a few days earlier and how that related to something she already knew. Over the last twelve months, some four hundred "Rhineland bastards" living in the Bonn and Cologne areas had been taken from their mothers and sterilized. Verena had known two of the women involved when she lived in Essen, and had kept in touch with them over the years. Both had told her they'd been given no real choice: the authorities had threatened to take their boys away if they refused to sign the permission forms.

Verena paused for a moment, and I could see she was close to tears. She rubbed her eyes, ran both hands through her hair, and shook her head, as if to clear it. Last Friday, she said, she and Marco had been in the grocery store on Ritterstrasse, and two women there had obviously noticed Marco, because a few minutes later she had found herself behind them on the street and heard one say that "they'd better get around to him before he gets much older."

Marco did look old for his age, I thought.

"And of course I don't know whether they were just being, you know, the way some people are or whether they actually know something. I started thinking there might have been something in the papers that I missed, an announcement that the program they ran in Bonn and Cologne was about to be introduced here."

"I haven't seen anything," I said. There might have been something in the Nazi rag that Ruchay reads, but if so, he kept it under his hat.

"And you read the papers, don't you?"

"Not all of them," I had to admit.

She sighed. What she needed, she said, was to find out if there were such plans without bringing herself and Marco to the authorities' attention, and she wondered if I could help. Because if she found out they were coming for Marco, she would have to do something. Move far away; she didn't know what. "Marco may never want a family, but no one should take that choice away from him."

I agreed—what sort of person wouldn't?—and told her

I'd see what I could do. As yet I don't know what that might be. If I pay the Gestapo a visit, and ask why nothing is being done to remove this dreadful stain on German honor, it might just give the local swine ideas. Something more subtle is needed, and soon. Verena seems close to the end of her tether.

WEDNESDAY, JULY 27

There was a new face at the Working Group this evening. The woman arrived with a man named Risse whom I remembered from the last meeting and introduced herself as Ottilie. She said she'd been working in our admin office since leaving a similar post in Hannover a few weeks ago and had always been interested in "workplace issues." She didn't spell out her political creed, but in that regard her attendance was almost self-explanatory. Müller had clearly known she was coming, so some sort of basic checking has presumably been done.

The meeting was less interesting than its predecessor had been. As if keen to avoid a risky clash of ideas, we set ourselves back on the firmer ground of practicalities and discussed how we should counter the ever more frequently floated suggestion that Germany's national interest required our acceptance of lower wages and longer hours. Given that either or both will prove almost universally unpopular, their introduction will be an opportunity for the regime's opponents, but should we try to exploit it from inside or outside the official Labor Front? We argued the matter for almost two hours without reaching a definite conclusion.

As always, Giesemann favored the most confrontational tactics, daring the rest of us to share his contempt for the party in power. When he wasn't waxing indignant, he had trouble taking his eyes off Ottilie. He may have been sizing her up as a possible gift to secret masters, but it was probably only simple desire—she's certainly young and pretty enough.

He wasn't the only one to find her more interesting than the topic at hand. For heirs of Rosa Luxemburg, my comrades seemed absurdly flummoxed by a female presence, trying too hard and not hard enough, often in the same breath. For her part, Ottilie was obviously feeling us out and careful not to say anything too self-revealing.

I have met a lot of women comrades over the years and observed a common pattern: that after years of encountering unspoken expectations and prejudices, they develop a tendency to promote the mind above the heart, at least in their political lives. Ottilie is no exception, but she radiates unused energy, and there's a definite spark in her eyes. She may be another name for my list.

THURSDAY, JULY 28

Herr Skoumal has not exceeded my expectations. Soon after supper I heard feet on the stairs and the usual rap on my door, but it was Anna rather than Walter who accepted my invitation to enter. "Where is he?" I asked, surprised into impoliteness.

"Out playing football," she said, not in the least put out. "He's so angry that he'll probably injure someone. Can I come in?"

She had a sheaf of papers in one hand. "His history and geography exam papers," she explained, handing them over and taking the seat by the window.

"He did badly?" I asked incredulously.

"Take a look," she suggested.

I went through the history paper first, noting the ticks and Skoumal's neatly written comments. Walter had matched every date and event correctly but had "grossly understated Horst Wessel's heroism, almost to the point of belittling it." Reading through what Walter had written, all I saw was a failure to exaggerate it.

When it came to the question on democracy's weakness, Skoumal had made no comment on what Walter had actually written, but was highly critical of what he hadn't done, which was laud the "enduring strength of the Führerprinzip." Skoumal also noted that he would have preferred to see Walter tackle the question concerning the Jews, as "his attitude in racial matters has often left much to be desired."

"This is outrageous," I murmured.

"Isn't it just?" Anna agreed.

Skoumal's final comment on the history paper concerned Walter's "unwillingness" to explain the Führer's greatness as "simply unforgivable."

"He ran out of time," I told Anna.

"I know."

The geography paper was more of the same. According to Skoumal, Walter had forgotten to include the Saarland in his list of the new "artificial states," but even I knew that the Saarland was already back in the Reich. The teacher could find no obvious fault—though not, I suspect, for lack of trying—in Walter's next few answers, but expressed his disappointment that Walter showed so little appreciation of the Nanga Parbat climbers' heroism—"He seems loath to recognize German achievement."

The worst was kept for last. In his account of the Panama Canal, Walter had pointed out the "surprising fact" that the western end was the Atlantic end.

"Is it?" I asked Anna. "The Atlantic end?"

"It is. I went around the corner and asked Herr Hanreiter

if I could look at his atlas. The isthmus runs east—west, the canal north—south, and the Atlantic end at the top is slightly west of the Pacific end at the bottom."

"I didn't know that."

"Neither did I. More to the point, neither did Herr Skoumal. And he still doesn't. He humiliated Walter in front of the whole class. He said that only the most conceited of boys could make up something like that." She shook her head. "Part of me wants to walk in there tomorrow morning and slam Herr Hanreiter's atlas down in front of him and insist that he apologize to Walter in front of the whole damned school."

"But you won't."

"No, I won't. It would make Walter's school life impossible."

I said that Walter just had to know that Skoumal's the fool, not him.

"I think he does," she said. "But today was a bit of a shock. Anyway," she said, getting to her feet, "I thought you should see the papers, and I was afraid Walter would feel too ashamed to bring them up."

I doubted that, and when Walter came up later, I was pleased to see he was much more angry than he was ashamed. "I thought perhaps I'd gotten it wrong," was the first thing he said. "I mean, I knew I hadn't, but . . . And then I thought it might be like Jewish physics. You know, that it wasn't true because a Jew had said it was. So I checked the atlas at school, and the man who drew the maps was Erich Hummel, which isn't a Jewish name."

I told him I doubted there was such a thing as Jewish geography.

He smiled for the first time. "But there is such a thing as Skoumal geography."

"Idiot geography is a better description," I said. I told him I knew it must be difficult, that teachers are not supposed to be idiots, and they're supposed to know more than you do. "But there are always exceptions."

"I got the top score in math," he said. "And I don't even like it."

FRIDAY, JULY 29

The weather on Nanga Parbat has reportedly taken a turn for the worse. I don't know whether the climbers feel like they've been up there forever, but it certainly feels that way to me.

SUNDAY, JULY 31

Yesterday was the last Saturday of the month, so I set off once more to visit my imaginary cousin. This time the *treff* was in Essen, at a café on Frohnhauser Strasse, close to the Krupp works complex. I knew the area well from my time there fifteen years before and thought I remembered the café.

On the two trains it took to get there, and in the half hour between them waiting on the platform at Dortmund, I rehearsed the verbal report I would be giving my new contact and found myself wondering what had happened to the last one when she got back to Moscow. Had they arrested Elise immediately, or allowed her a few days' grace among the other foreign comrades at the Hotel Lux? It was of course possible that she'd talked herself out of whatever mess she was in and been given a new mission. I imagined her walking through the door of the café in Essen later that morning and was surprised by how much I wanted it to happen.

The *treff* was scheduled for noon, the café a fifteen-minute walk from the central station. The town center seemed quieter than I remembered it, but Saturdays in Hitler's Germany are much like other weekdays, now that extra "voluntary" half days and days have become the norm. The industrial area, once I reached it, certainly seemed to be working flat out, the serried ranks of factories throbbing with noise and pouring black smoke into the dark grey sky.

I reached the café ten minutes early and watched the frequent comings and goings from a convenient bench. All the uniforms in evidence were of the less worrying kind—army and Orpo, nothing in black—and no suspicious men in civvies were loitering nearby. If anyone was keeping watch from the windows and roofs, they were keeping their faces well hidden.

I crossed the threshold, carrying the Hamm local paper under my arm, and claimed a seat at a table for two halfway down one wall. It was quite a large establishment—thirty to forty tables—and probably more than half-full, mostly of workers who looked as if they'd just come off the early shift. Half a dozen waitresses were darting this way and that, taking and delivering orders.

I chose the soup over the sausages—a bowl of scalding liquid makes a very good missile—and opened up my newspaper. Like Walter, the local football writer was still, a month later, decrying Schalke's failure to win the German championship.

The soup, when it came, was tasty enough, the accompanying hunks of bread hard as rock until they were dunked. I sipped and chewed, trying not to look up every time someone entered. The minutes went by, ten, fifteen, twenty. I had ten more of nursing the last inch of beer before I had to leave—thirty minutes was the maximum wait allowed.

As the allotted time drew near and there was still no sign of my contact, I realized with a shock that I was actually hoping he or she would fail to show. I say "with a shock" because a nonappearance would signal a serious failure—at the very least, a month's delay in the mission, and quite possibly someone's arrest—and I couldn't remember ever welcoming such a failure before. Why did I feel that? I would have another month of relatively risk-free research, and the danger involved in approaching men of uncertain loyalty would be deferred by at least that length of time, but I knew that wasn't the primary reason. It was the prospect of another month of ordinary life, in an ordinary house, with decent, straightforward people like Anna and Jakob, which made me hope that no one would come, and which sped me on my way the moment the café clock ticked off the half hour. True to my training, I looked neither left nor right all the way back to the station.

And then this evening Walter came to say goodbye. He and Anna are leaving early in the morning for Berlin, where she will hand him over to her cousin for the onward trip to East Prussia. Walter still thinks he's quite capable of delivering himself—"How hard can it be to switch platforms at Silesian Station?"—but the idea of letting him loose in Hitler's Reich was one his mother had refused to contemplate.

He said he would miss our talks and promised to write once a week but couldn't hide his excitement at the prospect of tomorrow's journey, which he expects to be the most interesting part of the entire four weeks away. He is curious about his cousins, but both are several years younger than he is, so he doubts they'll have much in common.

With that in mind, he has a suitcase packed with books, which he brought up to show me. His grandfather has apparently told him that no one can read in East Prussia, and while somewhat skeptical of this information, Walter is determined not to take any chances. We agreed that running out of reading matter was a fate worth avoiding if at all possible.

Before lugging the suitcase back downstairs, he asked if I'd still be here when he got back.

Yes, I told him, unless something terrible happened.

"I'm worried about Herr Ruchay," he said, setting the suitcase down again. "I know he wants to . . . you know, make advances, to Mama, and I think things will end badly."

How? I asked.

"Well, if she tells him no, he'll probably get nasty, and if she says yes, then he'll become my father," Walter said. "He never will be, though," he added defiantly.

Hoping to reassure him, at least on the former count, I rather rashly promised to deal with any nastiness that Ruchay tried to unleash.

"Thank you," Walter said, picking up the suitcase again. As if keen not to leave on a depressing note, he turned at the door for a final word: "By the time I come back, Erich will have served half his sentence."

MONDAY 1 AUGUST

A long day at work. Large military maneuvers are scheduled to start on the twelfth, and the volume and complexity of the traffic involved is huge. All time off has been canceled for the rest of the month, and those who were keenly anticipating a summer break have been given a rude shock. The mood was mutinous, to say the least, but I'm not expecting any concerted attempt to challenge the bosses' decision. Workers' opposition in Nazi Germany rarely expresses itself in anything more than a chronic lack of productivity.

Anna got back from Berlin soon after supper and came up to tell me that Walter had been successfully handed on to the East Prussian side of the family. He apparently spent the entire journey to Berlin in the corridor, staring out of an open window, and arrived in the capital caked in soot. After a visit to the washroom, the two of them had time to take in a few sights—the Tiergarten, Potsdamer Platz, and Wilhelmstrasse. Hitler was not seen leaning out of a Chancellery window, which was probably for the best—they say he loves children, but doubtless not the sort that ask him awkward questions. Then on to Silesian Station, where they lunched in the buffet with the just-arrived Sofie. Walter had been unusually quiet. "Summing her up," Anna guessed. She sighed. "I hope he's not unhappy there."

Her face seemed gaunter than usual, and she admitted to being exhausted. "And now I must run the gauntlet," she added, meaning reach her rooms without bumping into Ruchay. "Wish me luck."

I did but to no avail—I heard his voice a few seconds later, the tone slightly peeved but trying not to sound it.

Outside it was starting to rain, which seemed a suitable augury for a Walter-less August. I sat by the open window for a while watching the water fall through the luminous cone of the streetlight opposite, wondering how I'd let a young boy into my corroded heart. The answer, I fear, would keep the new psychoanalysts busy for quite a long time.

Trying for my own answer, I was ambushed by the phrase "Walter is my salvation." Which sounds ridiculous, but I can't seem to shake the sense that there's more than a grain of truth in it.

To say he's the son I never had might also be true, but would be far too glib. Sometimes Walter feels like the life I never had; sometimes he reminds me of the boy I was before the world and the war hit me for six.

In many ways he's the future I fought for and am still supposedly fighting for: a world of innocence and unending curiosity, of kindness and compassion, of people who think of others as much as they do themselves. In this world of course he's a glorious misfit. He's utterly out of place in Nazi Germany but wouldn't be a much better fit in the muted cruelty of a bourgeois democracy or, though it pains me to say it, in the brutalized realm of my masters.

In that we are alike. I've found a kindred spirit in a twelve-year-old body. Only he has his life before him, whereas mine, I suspect, is nearing its close.

TUESDAY, AUGUST 2

Yesterday Verena was worked off her feet doing Anna's tasks as well as her own, but this evening I got the chance to tell her what I'd found out about Marco's possible futures. On Saturday I'd managed an hour in the town library after work and hastily skimmed through the last few months of the local paper and the national *Beobachter*. I'd found no mention of expanding the geographical extent of the "Rhineland bastard" sterilization program, which was good. There were several mentions of its original introduction in the Bonn-Cologne area, but none was accompanied by any suggestion that it might be exported to other areas, which seemed even better.

I had also talked to Rudolf Faas, who works in our office and who famously has an omnivorous appetite for news. "Ask Faas" is the usual response when anyone else needs to know something, so I did. He knew about the Bonn-Cologne program but had seen nothing about any expansion. As I expected he didn't ask why I wanted to know—like many news addicts, he thinks knowing is all that matters.

I couldn't be certain, I told Verena. Some bright spark might suddenly see raising this issue as a way to get noticed—or, more likely, as a way of distracting attention from something else—but for the time being at least, Marco seemed to be safe.

She was clearly relieved, by both the news and my promise to keep a sharp eye out for any future developments.

"I haven't mentioned any of this to Marco," she told me. "There's no point in worrying him." She offered up one of her wry smiles. "He wants to go to Africa and find his father," she said. She didn't suppose she could blame him, but it was obviously much too late for her and Jean. He would have another family by now.

He probably would, I thought.

"Walter told Marco you've been to America," she said. "Is that true?"

I nodded.

"How do they treat half Negroes over there?" she asked.

I said they were usually treated like full-blown Negroes, who might not be slaves anymore, but weren't considered equals. That it depended to some extent on where you were—things were worse in the southern states—but that generally whites and blacks lived separate lives, with the latter filling all those jobs the former didn't want. A Negro might prosper, but the odds were heavily stacked against him.

"They're not being sterilized, though?"

"No, they aren't."

"And there must be thousands of mixed-race people."

"Hundreds of thousands, I should think."

"I'd like Marco to be somewhere where he's not the only one," she said. "And America seems a much better bet than Africa." Verena's smiles are always brief affairs, and this one was briefer than most. "Dreams, eh?"

FRIDAY, AUGUST 5

A new People's Radio was announced this morning with all the usual fanfare. Two hundred thousand have already been manufactured and are presumably on their way to the shops. They say the new model has better speakers and a purer tone, and perhaps even Goebbels will sound like a nightingale. If Walter were here, I would know the technical specifications by now, but since he isn't, I shall have to remain in ignorance.

I have to say I'm happy with the wireless we have. Jakob and I spent most of this evening listening to it, and for once the chosen music seemed less intent on marching us to glory and more inclined to have us tapping our feet. Jakob fondly reminisced about his former wife's excellent dancing, and from the look on his face, I knew he was seeing her in his mind's eye, dazzling him and everyone else in some Hamburg dancehall before the war. I found myself transported back to Brazil, and a lovely young comrade named Tashia, who loved dancing under the moon on Copacabana Beach and sometimes let me take her home.

SATURDAY, AUGUST 6

Ruchay's mother has been ill, necessitating weekend trips to Hannover. Since, like the rest of us, he's been doing extra shifts at work, Anna has so far been spared the courting offensive that Walter's absence was supposed to enable.

She came up to see me this evening with news from East Prussia. Walter had enjoyed the train journey east from Berlin and, as yet, had no axes to grind with his newfound relatives. He was sharing a bedroom with the younger brother, Stefan, and liked exploring the farm, with its rambling house and myriad outbuildings.

"Have you been there?" I asked Anna.

She had. After her second husband, Ernst, died in 1929, she had even considered moving out to East Prussia, but eight-year-old Erich had hated the idea, and when Anna saw the sort of life the family led, she had felt much the same. There was electricity now, but they hadn't had it then. She'd been there in summer, when the days were mostly work, and the evenings were all spent waiting for darkness to sanction sleep. "I imagined how winter would be and took the train back here."

I said Walter had been wise to take so many books.

Anna laughed. Having discovered that the house contained four books—two Bibles, one reading primer, and a seed catalog—he was rationing himself to fifty pages a day. He was also helping with the farmwork, which was hard but "probably good for me." His aunt Sofie was a good cook but not as good as Verena. "Thank you, by the way, for doing what you did for her," Anna added. "She's very grateful."

I said I was pleased to help.

She got up to go. "I miss him," she said.

"So do I," I told her.

"I know. I'm glad you came here," she said. "Walter needed someone like you."

MONDAY, AUGUST 8

Horror of horrors, the regime's campaign against the Jews is causing problems for the "Aryan" majority. A few weeks ago Berlin women attending the popular summer sales at the surviving Jewish department stores had to fight their way through a cordon of brownshirts to gain entrance. They succeeded, but Goebbels was furious.

Last week we Aryans were informed of new rules when it came to writing our wills. We can no longer leave anything to Jews, to people having "immoral relations," or to any of the churches. Such bequests would apparently run counter to "healthy public sentiment."

And today we've even lost the right to name our children as we wish. Any "typical Jewish name" is forbidden, as are other names that "originate from alien sources of history or thought."

Small problems, you might say, when compared to those facing the Jews. If the latter were depressed after Évian, nothing has happened to cheer them since. It was recently announced that all Jewish doctors' diplomas will be canceled beginning in September, and that henceforth they will be allowed to work only as nurses looking after their fellow Jews. The lawyers will be next, and so on and so on, until the Jews are barred from all professional life. What can they do? They're not allowed to earn an honest living, and now that they have to carry ID cards with photographs and finger-prints, their chances of illegal work aren't that much better. There's nothing for them in Germany, but if no other coun-tries will take them, there's no way they can leave.

According to Dariusz Müller, there are roughly four hundred Jews in Hamm. I've walked past the synagogue, which seems to be still functioning, though after the recent announcement that the big one in Nuremberg is about to be demolished, one wonders for how long. There are a few closed shops bearing faded Jewish names, but the Jews them-selves are harder to spot. I imagine that most are keeping their heads down, living off their savings, and desperately looking for light at the end of their tunnel.

And speaking of ends, the climbers on Nanga Parbat have finally admitted defeat. On their way back down the moun-tain, they stumbled across the corpses of the 1934 expedition and are claiming this as some sort of victory.

There's a moral here somewhere, but I dread to think what it is.

WEDNESDAY, AUGUST 10

When I got home from work today, a letter from Walter was waiting for me, and I read it through while I waited for supper.

He seems to be having an interesting time. He obviously likes his cousins well enough and is suitably equivocal about Uncle Harald, who runs the farm for his elderly mother-in-law: "He knows a lot about soils, but doesn't seem very interested in history." Walter has read two of the three Tom Shark novels already and is saving the third one for later. He has started exploring the Bible and found some bits "hard to believe."

A few days ago Uncle Harald took him into Heilsberg and allowed Walter to explore for an hour while he dealt with some business. Walter seems to have spent most of that time in conversation with someone he met in the town square, an old man who was "interested in history." The Teutonic Knights apparently spent time in Heilsberg, and Walter thought they sounded interesting—when he gets back to Hamm, he plans to look for a book about them at the library. There was a castle not far from the square, and Nicolas Copernicus had been a guest there when he worked out the earth went around the sun. Walter and the old man had walked down to see it—"a big square building with pointed towers on each corner."

After saying goodbye to his new friend, Walter had spent some of his pocket money on a newspaper—"They don't get one at the farm, and there isn't a wireless either"—and finally read about the German seaplane's Atlantic crossing, which had Ruchay gushing superlatives more than a week ago. Walter was almost as enthusiastic, but he's only twelve years old. And he'll no doubt be just as excited when he hears yesterday's news, that a Focke-Wulf Condor owned by Lufthansa is about to make the first nonstop flight from Berlin to New York. All I can think when I read these reports is that Hitler's reach grows longer by the day.

Walter concluded with a reminder that I had promised to write, and I am glad my letter is already in the post. It is much less interesting than his, but then most of the things that fill up my days are things I can't share. I told him everyone here was well and that the railway works have been incredibly busy, leaving Herr Ruchay with less time than usual to make a nuisance of himself.

The item of news hogging the headlines today concerned the street killing of a Sudeten German worker. Every paper but one blamed the Czechs, the *Frankfurter Zeitung* being the odd man out. According to what was once the country's most respected newspaper, the man was killed in a fight between Sudeten German Nazis and Sudeten German Social Democrats. I suspect the editors will pay for this reckless brush with truth.

TUESDAY, AUGUST 16

I think this has probably been the longest interval between entries since I started keeping this diary. The extra hours of work entailed by the Wehrmacht's summer maneuvers over the last few days have left all but the youngest and fittest completely exhausted, and made sleep the sweetest of luxuries. Today was less onerous—the troops and their equipment have now been gathered from all over the Reich and transported to the relevant region south of Berlin. They'll be there for several weeks, and then we must go through it all in reverse, assuming the Führer doesn't decide to send them somewhere else. Into Czechoslovakia, for example.

The all-consuming works schedule has been good news for some. With Ruchay as red-eyed as the rest of us, Anna has had a few days of relative peace and has looked unusually relaxed. All good things come to an end, though, and tonight he insisted on taking her out to dinner. I hope the food was good.

At lunchtime I had a long conversation with Franke and Opatz about the festering mood in the yards, and neither man gave me cause to rethink the role I have planned for them. I have also talked with Schulte on several recent occasions and in any other circumstances would imagine a growing friendship. I won't say I'm a hundred percent certain of any of them, but I think I'm as sure as I could be. Whether or not a committed three-man cell could beget others in the current conditions seems more doubtful, and I can't see it having much of a future on its own. I shall pass on my recommendations at the next *treff*, and Moscow will have the final word.

In the paper this morning, there was a story about a haunted house in the Rhineland, near Koblenz if I remember correctly. For over a year anyone visiting this old, burnt-out house at midnight has been treated to ghostly sighing and creaking floorboards. Then, a few days ago, an intrepid gang of Hitler Youth sifted through blackened stones and found an old clock, still wearily winding itself up at the end of each day.

Just like me, I thought, still working away in the ruins, waiting for Hitler's minions to dig me out.

WEDNESDAY, AUGUST 17

I had a second letter from Walter this morning. He has now heard about the Focke-Wulf Condor flight and thought, correctly, that it should be back in Berlin by the time I read this. It actually landed yesterday in front of a huge cheering crowd, something I'll doubtless be able to watch in next week's cinema newsreel.

Walter has been to the seaside. It was "only forty kilometers away," and on Sunday his Aunt Sofie drove him and his cousins there in the family automobile—"they don't have a wireless but they have a car!" None of the family knew how to swim, so Walter had offered to teach them, but "Aunt Sofie was afraid that someone would be swept away and insisted that we only go in up to our knees." With his usual geographic precision, he pointed out that they were actually paddling in the Vistula Lagoon and not the proper sea. "But at least the water tasted salty."

He has read all the books he took with him and been forced to fall back on the Bible. He liked the book of Esther—"a good story"—but couldn't see why God had needed Mary—"Why not have Jesus grow up in heaven and then send him down to earth?"

This evening's Working Group was canceled, and I was up in my room rereading the letter when Anna knocked on the door. I asked her in and passed it over for her to read, thinking that was why she had come.

She skimmed through it with a distracted air, then handed it back. "God forbid he comes back religious," she said.

I said I didn't think that was likely, that Walter and skepticism were made for each other. I asked her where he'd learned to swim.

"Erich taught him. He learned in the Jungvolk, before he and his friends were expelled." She looked up. "Can you spare a few minutes?"

"As many as you want."

She sighed. "There's something I need to talk about. With a man."

I nodded.

She asked if I knew that Ruchay had taken her out to dinner the previous evening.

I said I did.

"I was running out of excuses, and I thought it would keep him quiet for a while." She laughed, but not with amusement. "The bastard asked me to marry him."

"Oh," I said.

"Yes, oh," she agreed. "And I don't need advice about

whether or not to say yes. What I want to ask you is—why? Why does he want me? I'm not that young, and I'm not that pretty. The only money I have is in this house, and that's worth next to nothing. He surely can't have missed the fact that both my sons loathe him, can he? My father loathes him too, but they've hardly ever spoken, so he probably doesn't think him worth considering. He just seems fixated on me, and I can't for the life of me work out why."

I told her he wanted a woman. He wanted a wife because a wife was a conventional thing to want. He wanted admiration, and whether she knew it or not, people would admire him for winning her. And needless to say, he wanted sex.

"Conventionality, admiration, sex," she repeated. "Three things he'll never get from me, and he should damn well know it by now. Why can't he pick on someone else? There must be women out there who'd think him a catch. He's not that bad looking on the outside. All the women who swoon over Hitler—one of them would do. She'd hang on his every word. Or some of them at least."

I suggested that the thought of approaching a woman he didn't know probably terrified Ruchay. "You're the devil he does know," I said, "and the fact that you're also his housekeeper will make him feel that he's the one with the upper hand. In his mind, he's making a generous offer, a step-up in life in exchange for sex and what he'd consider an appropriate degree of defer-ence. From his point of view, its hard to see why you'd refuse him," I said.

"And because I've done it before, I'll do it again with him," she said, as much to herself as to me. "I actually liked Walter's father," she added.

"That won't have occurred to him."

She grimaced. "No, it won't."

"So what answer did you give him?" I asked.

"Oh, the coward's one. That I had to think about it. It

seemed better to let him down gently, but if you're right about his reasons, he's going to be furious whatever I say. Perhaps I should tell him the real reason, that I find him generally despicable and that the thought of him touching me makes me feel physically sick."

I told her I didn't think that would be prudent.

She laughed. "Oh God, what a mess."

FRIDAY, AUGUST 19

I don't know how many of those who live and work here are aware of Ruchay's offer, but it's hard to believe that anyone could miss the highly charged atmosphere that now pervades the house. Ruchay himself seems both tense and expectant, like someone who thinks the prize is all but his. Sometimes I feel almost sorry for the man, but then I see the way he looks at Anna—covetous seems too clean a word—and the nascent sympathy is instantly stillborn.

Barufka and Gerritzen have gone away for the weekend, the former to his son in Hamburg, the latter to his family in Duisburg. Both trips were arranged some time ago, but each man had the look of an escapee as he left for the station this evening. With Walter away and Verena gone home, only Andreas, Anna, Ruchay, and I are left in the house, which feels more and more like a stage set in waiting.

I thought about going down to the club on my own but decided against it. If the curtain goes up, I want to be here.

SATURDAY, AUGUST 20

I was sitting in the yard with Andreas, enjoying the sunshine and watching the chickens scouring their run for something to eat, when I heard the front door slam. Lifting my eyes above the fence, I saw a hatless Ruchay stalk off down the street and guessed that he'd had the bad news.

A few seconds later Anna came out to confirm it.

"Good," her father said.

I asked how Ruchay had taken the no.

She shook her head. "I don't think he did" was her answer. "He listened, then said he'd allow me a few days to reconsider. When I told him there wasn't any point, that my mind was made up, he said he needed my final answer by Wednesday. And then he just walked out. It was bizarre."

"It'll sink in eventually," Andreas said cheerfully. "And with any luck he'll leave."

I suggested that Ruchay would need a way to save face.

Anna agreed and said she had tried to give him one. She had offered him "all the usual sops"—that she was too set in her ways, that any woman would be lucky to have him, that he was still young and virile enough to have children of his own. "It all went in one ear and straight out the other."

I said that when he cooled down, he might be more sensible. Convince himself that it's her loss rather than his and then save face by withdrawing the offer.

"I hope so," Anna said with feeling. "If he keeps this up, I will have to give him notice."

"Something you should have done months ago," her father muttered.

SUNDAY, AUGUST 21

A strange day. At breakfast, Ruchay was unusually polite to Anna as she served and to me once she had returned to the kitchen. He studied his newspaper, but forbore from reading aloud those items he found most inspiring. He looked like a man who's expecting bad news and is not sure how he will deal with it. Maybe he just needs time to extricate himself. Maybe the threatened storm will not arrive.

The world outside shows little sign of coming to its senses. On the contrary, the news these days sounds like a surrealist manifesto. Some institute in Rome has discovered that Italians are getting taller, and the Duce's government has claimed the credit—its racial improvement campaign must be working. Jews in Germany are now allowed to open their bank strongboxes only in the presence of a policeman, though what exactly the policeman is there for hasn't been stated. And following the recent injunction on gentiles using traditional Jewish names, all Jews with "non-Jewish" names are now required to take either Israel or Sara as their second names. Why not take things to their logical conclusion and insist on "Jew" or "Jewess"?

Meanwhile, the Börse is slumping, reflecting the fact that the only way up for the German economy is a high-risk war. The regime is reaching for its usual scapegoats—according to Reich Minister Walther Funk, the slump is wholly down to Jews and foreigners. How this riffraff is proving so damningly effective in a country lit up by the Führer's genius is yet to be explained.

And the *Frankfurter Zeitung* has received its punishment for confusing reportage with telling the truth. It was the last newspaper printing Jewish births, marriages, and deaths, and has now been forbidden from doing so. There's no limit to the pettiness of the men who rule this country; nothing escapes their meanness or stands in the way of the pleasure they get from hurting others.

I tried to escape it all by taking a long walk beside the canal, but the sense of dejection stayed with me. Out in the country, the first signs of autumn are easy to spot, and perhaps we humans are emotionally tuned to lament the passing of summer. Or maybe it's just that the winter ahead seems to belong to the Nazis.

MONDAY, AUGUST 22

Barufka and Gerritzen both arrived back late last night, so breakfast felt more or less normal. Ruchay was quiet, but for once Jakob was not—he'd had a better-than-expected two days with his son and proudly announced he would soon be a grandfather. Gerritzen slapped him jovially on the shoulder, and Ruchay lifted his gaze from the *Beobachter* to offer congratulations. He wasn't, I realized after several minutes' surreptitious observation, actually reading the paper, merely holding it up like a prop or a shield. And the worry in his eyes looked close to panic. I assume that Anna is waiting till Wednesday before she rejects him again, and I wonder if Ruchay will find some relief in the final crushing of his hopes. He isn't enjoying the wait.

This evening the principal news on the wireless was of Admiral Horthy's arrival. Hungary's leader of almost twenty years—another Fascist in all but name—is here for a week and is currently heading to Kiel to watch the latest naval maneuvers on Hitler's yacht. An admiral running a country without a coastline must surely deserve a place in my surrealist manifesto.

In 1928 I was almost an unwelcome guest of his regime. The Hungarian Communist party, the KMP, had been decimated in the White Terror that followed the short-lived Soviet Republic of 1919, with thousands killed and hundreds more decamping to the safety of Moscow. Those still at liberty in Hungary were mostly inexperienced cadres whose ambitions extended little further than mere survival. Through alternating periods of semilegal operation and a perilous underground existence, they followed the orders of the leadership headed by Béla Kun in Moscow, orders that were handed on by people like myself.

My cover on that trip was that of a German literary editor in Budapest to explore the cultural scene, so much of my time was spent in those cafés haunted by local writers, actors, and filmmakers. The fact that most of these establishments were also frequented by Communists was not lost on the authorities, and it was only a swift and somewhat unnerving departure across a succession of high roofs that saved me from one particular police raid.

An occupational hazard, of course, and once across the border, the closeness of the shave swiftly lost its sting. Which is more than I can say for the other abiding memory of that summer I spent in Budapest—the conversations I shared with a young poet named Attila Jószef.

He was in his early twenties and already famous in local circles for the brilliance of his verse. One short poem, which opened with a cheerful announcement that he considered himself fatherless, motherless, godless, and stateless, hadn't gone down well with the authorities, and had led to his expulsion from university. But his reputation as a poet had kept on rising. He was as poor as famous poets often are and would sit for hours with the same cup of coffee in one of the cafés I frequented, the one most popular with my party contacts. This was not a coincidence—Jószef was also a Communist and enjoyed nothing more than arguing the finer points of theory with comrades like me. His own beliefs were hard to pin down, but he clearly felt closer to Trotsky's notion of Bolshevism than Stalin's, and in 1928, that was already a dangerous space to inhabit. More interestingly, he was fascinated by psychoanalysis and often spoke of synthesizing Marx and Freud. I had several friendly arguments with him and never came out on top.

I felt dim in his presence, and looking back now, I can

see that I retreated into a sense of "correctness"; I told myself that while he talked and wrote poetry, I was actually getting things done.

But how he could talk, and how he could write.

We were on the same side, but the revolution he envisaged seemed cleaner and much more romantic than mine, and probably not attainable with the methods the Comintern favored at the time. Talking to him, I felt both inspired and depressed, and for months afterward my memories of that café—his face in that amber light, the food odors and the endless clatter—were profoundly bittersweet. And every time I told myself that I was the one doing the work that mattered, another voice within would raise a hollow laugh.

I remember talking to Esther Brennan about Attila one lovely summer evening on her Scranton porch. She told me that she had always believed that we all have our parts to play, that some must learn to be hard in order to force through change, and some must nurture their kindness so that when the change comes, there are people to lead who haven't been hardened.

There's a line in one of Brecht's recent poems that says much the same thing, that "we who desired to prepare the soil for kindness could not ourselves be kind." My life in a nutshell, at least until now.

In March this year, I learned from an exiled Hungarian comrade in a Greenwich Village bar that Attila had died a few months earlier. He had thrown himself under one of the freight trains he so often described in his verse.

TUESDAY, AUGUST 23

It was unusually hot today, and we worked with both doors open and the fan at maximum speed. We were also extremely busy, and for a somewhat ominous reason—the Wehrmacht maneuvers are still underway, and new contingency plans have been requested for moving the troops involved south to the Czechoslovak border. Plans, it was stressed, that we must not discuss in public.

I didn't get home until past eight and ate my reheated dinner alone. Afterward, as I headed for my room, I came across Ruchay in the hallway. He looked in all sorts of torment but just managed a curt "Good evening" in passing.

About fifteen minutes later Anna knocked on my door. "He told me couldn't wait any longer," she said, perching herself on the edge of the bed. "And I told him I was sorry, but I hadn't changed my mind. I had no idea how he'd react, whether he'd rant and rave and hit me or even get down on his knees and beg, but what he actually did was nothing. He just stood there looking at me, as if he couldn't quite take in what I'd said." She smiled to herself. "So I raised the stakes. I told him he'd been a model lodger but that given the circumstances it was clearly impossible for the two of us to carry on living under the same roof. And he agreed! Just like that. He said he'd be gone as soon as he finds new accommodation, and then he just turned and walked away. What do you think of that?"

I said he wouldn't be missed.

Only his money, Anna said—she would have to find someone else to take the bastard's room.

I said I would pass the word around. "One thing's for sure," I told her, "Walter will be delighted."

WEDNESDAY, AUGUST 24

This morning Ruchay was at breakfast, but Verena did the serving. This evening Anna did the honors, but he wasn't there. Out hunting for somewhere to live perhaps, or simply avoiding her. She took the opportunity to inform the rest of us that Ruchay was leaving and that his room would be relet. Gerritzen said he had a colleague at work who might be interested.

I had a letter from Walter, who didn't have much to say. The only event he mentioned was the weekly trip into town, and that with a singular lack of enthusiasm—"There's nothing there really." With nothing to read and no one to talk to who shares his interests, he is clearly bored stiff and can hardly wait to board the train for home. Anna will collect him in Berlin next Monday.

This evening's Working Group was hosted by Risse and poorly attended, with two of the regulars ill and one, Paul Giesemann, on a Strength through Joy week on the North Sea coast. The eight of us present talked for a while about how little the younger workers knew of traditional union methods and how we might put that right without unduly upsetting the local Labor Front leaders. But it was dreadfully hot in the small apartment, and no one objected when Müller suggested adjourning to the Social Club, where we sat outside and drank and played skat by the light of the yard lamps. With some livelier-than-usual music playing on the club wireless and a wonderfully dramatic sunset to look at, it turned into a very pleasant evening, and walking home I felt a rare sense of contentment. Walter was coming home; Ruchay would soon be gone. Things were looking up.

THURSDAY, AUGUST 25

Verena was waiting on the doorstep when Jakob and I arrived home this evening. She looked in shock, and there was a dark contusion on one side of her face. "They took Anna," she said.

She didn't need to say who. "When?" I asked stupidly, as if the hour could be important.

She shook her head. "This morning. Late this morning. I tried to tell her father, but he was having one of his bad days. You know what he's like—he seems to take things in, but then you find he hasn't. But this afternoon he seemed better. 'Wait for Josef,' he said. 'He'll know what to do.'"

I didn't. I felt in shock myself. "What happened to you?" I asked Verena.

"Oh, I was a fool. I tried to stop them, and one of them hit me. It's nothing."

I asked her where the other lodgers were.

Herr Ruchay was in his room, Herr Gerritzen not yet home.

"Does Ruchay know?"

"I told him. He looked . . . I don't know . . . sad, I suppose. But he said there was nothing he could do. That the law must take its course."

As I realized that I hadn't asked the obvious question, Jakob beat me to it. Why had they taken her?

"They wouldn't say. She asked them twice, and they just kept saying she had to come with them."

There was only one thing to do. "I think Jakob and I should go down to the Gestapo office and find out," I said, looking to him for agreement.

"Of course," he said.

I asked Verena if she would stay and look after Andreas and received the same answer. I hesitated for a moment, then said that I doubted Anna would be back by morning, so perhaps she and Marco could sleep here tonight. She nodded.

I went to see Andreas in his room and found him at his lucid best. When I told him where Jakob and I were going, he looked almost hopeful.

I asked if he knew why his daughter had been arrested.

He shook his head rather too vigorously. "She promised she wouldn't get involved again. Not while she still had Walter to care for. And my Anna always keeps her word."

"All right," I said, suspicions confirmed and fears not exactly allayed.

Jakob and I started off. It was still light, but the air was terribly humid, as if a storm was about to break. "It must be a mistake," Jakob said more than once as we walked, and I hoped he was right.

But if he was, no one at the Gestapo office was prepared to admit it. We patiently explained that we were there on behalf of Anna's disabled father, but the duty officer refused to tell us why she'd been arrested or where she was being held. He said, "Come back in the morning" so many times that he sounded like a gramophone record on which the needle had stuck.

We argued, but it was like talking to a stone wall. Eventually I noticed that Jakob seemed about to explode—like most men who rarely lose their temper, he isn't very good at it—and I managed to usher him out before things got ugly. "They can't do this," he said once we were back on the street, but of course they can. And do.

Back at the lodging house, I gave Verena and Andreas the bad news and agreed to go back in the morning—Jakob would have to tell Dariusz Müller why I was late for work. Gerritzen came bouncing in while we were talking, pleased with himself for finding Anna the lodger she'd said she needed. The news that his landlady had been arrested sobered him somewhat, but like Barufka he swiftly took refuge in assuming it was all a mistake.

There was nothing else we could do, and I came up to sit by my open window. The air still feels close, but there are flashes of lightning far to the west and the faintest rumblings of thunder. I hope Jakob's right, and it is a mistake or something so trivial that Anna will soon be released. But what if it isn't? What if Walter has now lost his mother as well as his brother? If there's no one to look after him, will the state take him too?

FRIDAY, AUGUST 26

I slept badly last night and woke up early this morning. The sky was barely starting to lighten, and rain was falling in a steady drizzle. I dressed and went down to talk to Verena, who was already at work in the kitchen. Was she willing to keep things going until we knew when—I didn't dare think "if"— Anna was coming home? I said I would help with the meals and other jobs and was sure Barufka would do the same.

She said of course she would.

The Gestapo office opened at eight—I had noticed their hours on my earlier visit with Anna—so there seemed no point in delaying. I ate my jam-filled rolls as I walked, then briefly stopped for a coffee on the way in the probably mistaken belief that my mental alertness would be thereby enhanced.

The office opened on time, but it was more than half an hour before I was seen. I just about managed to keep my temper in check—something of a must for undercover agents in Gestapo anterooms.

When I was eventually seen, it was by the same Kriminalsekretär who had interviewed Anna and me two months ago. And this time he had a name: Gunther Appel, according to the shiny new sign on his desk. At our previous meeting, he had been surprisingly reasonable but not very helpful and today offered more of the same.

Appel told me Anna was under arrest for making several seditious statements. These statements, which he wouldn't repeat, were of an extremely serious nature, and she would remain in custody until her trial. No date had yet been set for the latter, but when one was fixed, Herr Biesinger would be informed. She was being held in the local prison—the one where Erich had spent his pretrial weeks—but neither letters nor visits would be permitted.

I tried to explain the family situation—the invalid father in need of round-the-clock care, the twelve-year-old son who would soon be back from visiting relations.

Appel leaned back in his chair and asked if I thought the father and son would be better off in institutions.

I said no, of course not.

"Then I suggest you make your own arrangements," he said.

Was he trying to be helpful? Or just being dismissive? I couldn't tell. "What sort of arrangements?" I asked, not really expecting an answer.

He shrugged and said that was hardly a matter for the Gestapo, though I might have to satisfy the local block warden that any new arrangements were in the interests of all.

"Of course," I agreed, silently thanking God that Andreas was on good terms with ours.

"Then I think that concludes our business," Appel announced.

Not quite, I thought. As I got to my feet, I asked him whether we were talking days or weeks. "It will help the boy to know," I added.

"Weeks or months," he said tersely.

I risked one more question. "I don't suppose you'll tell me who informed on Frau Gersdorff?"

He smiled at that. "You suppose correctly."

I thanked him for his time and left, wondering why I'd bothered to ask. There were no prizes for guessing who had informed on Anna. The only question was what—if anything—to do about it.

I was already two hours late for work but felt obligated

to drop in at the lodging house and share what I'd discovered with Andreas and Verena. Both were shocked, and both thought the same man responsible. "That worm Ruchay," as Andreas put it.

"She might have said something," Verena thought out loud, "but who hasn't?"

I said he might just as well have made something up, but what did it matter? He couldn't prove anything, and we could all testify that she had just turned him down and that this was his way of paying her back.

Andreas looked at me sadly. "You don't understand how it works. When people are denounced, the Gestapo go to their records. If there's nothing in the accused person's past, then they get away with a slap on the wrist. But if there's something there, then they see the new offence as simple confirmation. The accused has proved himself—or herself—an inveterate enemy. Why would they let such a person go?"

I knew he was right, but my heart still sank. "And I assume there is something there?"

Andreas sank his chin on two clenched fists. "Of course there is. She was an active member of the KPD before she met Erich's father, and he was one of Liebknecht's golden boys—you know who Liebknecht was?"

I said I did.

"Well, her Karl was one of those daredevil sorts whom everyone loves. Except his enemies, of course. The Freikorps kept trying to kill him, and eventually they succeeded. He'll certainly feature in the Gestapo's records, and Anna's name will be there beside his. He wasn't good to her, but he got himself killed before she realized it. And now his reputation will do her in. The Gestapo won't care that she hasn't been active since their precious boss took over."

Seeing the distraught expression on Verena's face, I tried to sound more hopeful than I felt. "Maybe they're not as

efficient as people think they are," I said. "And they still have
to prove she said whatever she's accused of saying."

"Maybe," Andreas conceded.

For the moment we just had to keep the house going, I
said. For Anna's sake and Walter's. And our own. And no
matter how ridiculous it sounded in the circumstances, I had
to get to work.

Which is what I did. Müller had covered for my late arrival
and was clearly upset by Anna's arrest. I told him what the
Gestapo had told me, and he said he'd try to find out more
from some "useful friends" he had. The prospect of learning anything new was encouraging; the fact that he had such
contacts could only revive those suspicions I thought I'd
abandoned.

The next few hours at my desk were less than productive:
every few minutes, it seemed, my mind would wander off on
its own. Toward the end of my shift, I realized that Jakob
might be planning a confrontation with Ruchay, and when
the clock chimed, I made sure I was out at the gate before
Jakob was. I needn't have bothered—we got home to find
Ruchay already gone. He had told Verena he was spending
the weekend at his mother's, but Verena had then checked
his room and found all his belongings in boxes and bags. We
guessed that someone else would be around to pick them up.

Which was something of a relief, because I wanted emo-
tions to cool before I talked to him again. I felt like hitting
him as much as Jakob did, but that wouldn't help Anna. As
far as I could see, persuading the bastard to withdraw his
accusations was the only thing that would.

Verena also had some better news. The block warden had
paid an official visit, and Andreas, having one of his better
mornings, had convinced his old comrade that the lodging
house could function without Anna for a while and that with
Verena as a live-in surrogate mother, and Jakob and me as

surrogate uncles, Walter would not lack for carers when he returned.

First, of course, he has to be met in Berlin, and since Andreas can't travel and Verena is needed at home, I am the one who must do it. Being the bearer of this bad news will be unpleasant, hearing it a whole lot worse, but that moment is still almost three days away.

Tomorrow I must go back to Barmen for the monthly *treff,* and I can't say I've ever felt less interested in what my superiors have to tell me.

SATURDAY, AUGUST 27

I took an early train this morning—when one or both parties fail to turn up at a monthly *treff,* the next one is held where the last successful rendezvous took place, two hours ahead of the previous time.

My contact was one table down from where Elise had sat, the telltale book beside the half-drunk cup of coffee. Once we had gone through the prearranged greetings, and warmly shaken hands, the two of us left the buffet loudly discussing the weather and headed, as Elise and I had two months before, down toward the river.

He was young for the job, not much more than thirty, and I thought his suit was too well cut for the anonymity he was presumably seeking. He was obviously German, with an accent acquired in Bremen or Wilhelmshaven. He called himself Dieter, and he seemed very keen.

The weather was kinder than it had been on my last visit, sunny and fresh with barely a cloud to be seen. Once we were out on the open path above the river, he gave me Moscow's replies to the questions I'd sent through Elise. Of the seven names I'd put forward, only Müller's had set off alarm bells, which was good as far as it went. One or two peals would have shown they knew something and been more reassuring. When I explained that I'd since met Schulte and chosen him, Franke and Opatz for my putative cell, Dieter seemed impressed, which suggested a worrying lack of experience.

Trains went by in each direction, scraping rather than rattling on the underslung rails, and once the noise had faded, Dieter told me that Moscow had high hopes for the Working Group. The only problem was Dariusz Müller, whose party record displayed an unfortunate fondness for sectarian solutions, and whom I should seek to expel. When asked for details, Dieter told me that Müller had initially championed this incorrect line at the KPD Congress of November 1928 and, despite admonishment then, had persisted in his error for several more years. I was tempted to point out that the sectarian approach was then CPSU and Comintern policy, endorsed by Stalin himself, but if the young man didn't know that already, he surely wouldn't want to. I told myself that, smart suit or not, he was risking his life for the cause, and to let him have his illusions.

Another train went by. Off to our left, a large group of boys a few years older than Walter were lining up for a football match, and I found myself thinking that within three years they'd all be wearing Wehrmacht grey.

"You seem pessimistic," Dieter said, picking up on my mood, which of course had much more to do with events back in Hamm than the perilous state of Europe.

I said another war was coming and that there seemed no reason to believe it would be short.

"But perhaps that's what we need," he said blithely, as only someone too young for the last war could. "The last war sparked a revolution in Russia and almost another one here in Germany. Next time we can finish the job."

I told him he might be right and tried not to look too

depressed at the prospect. If each new revolution requires forty million human sacrifices, I think I'd rather wait for ordinary people to catch up with Marx and find some less corrosive way of bringing their exploiters down.

We parted on friendly terms, and I rode the train back to Hamm feeling relieved that I have another month to try and sort things out at home. To do all I can to get Anna released and, in the event that I can't, to leave the rest of the household able to ride out the time it takes for Erich or her to return.

SUNDAY, AUGUST 28

Given the circumstances, today was almost pleasant. Verena and Marco collected most of their belongings from the room they rent a ten minute walk away—until we know how long Anna will be gone, Verena is understandably loath to give it up. Marco seems to have taken it all in stride and is looking forward to sharing a room with Walter. Marco gets on well with Jakob, and this afternoon I even saw Gerritzen taking an avuncular interest. Sometimes racial prejudice seems so easy to turn on and off.

Tomorrow morning I'm taking the first train to Berlin. A search of Anna's room failed to turn up any details of the prospective rendezvous with her cousin, so I've been forced to rely on Reichsbahn timetables and guesswork. As far as I can judge, there are only two obvious trains she and Walter might take, and I intend to be there when the first one pulls into Silesian Station. If by any chance we fail to meet up, then I assume Sofie will take her nephew back to East Prussia. She might want to do that anyway when she finds out what's happened to Anna from a man she's never met.

Much as I've been looking forward to Walter's return, I

have been asking myself whether it might be kinder and safer to leave him where he is. But when I suggested as much to Andreas, he almost bit my head off. This was where Walter's friends were; this was where he'd hear news of his mother; this was the house his brother would soon come back to. This was where he belonged.

MONDAY, AUGUST 29

A long and heartbreaking day.

The sun was just climbing over the skyline as I walked to Hamm station, and the half-empty streets had that air of promise a fine morning always brings, but my heart felt heavy as I boarded the train and grew no lighter as the journey unfurled. I spent much of my time imagining the meeting to come and wondering how I could soften the blow. Nothing came to mind.

The view through the window was hardly uplifting—stretches of rain-swept plain interspersed with small stations and towns where almost everyone was in a uniform and every last pole and roof was wearing the same evil flag. The newspapers I'd brought to read were full of aggressive nationalism, most of it aimed at the government in Prague. Anyone reading—and believing—the German press is forced to conclude that Czechs are all sadistic bastards, and that all Sudeten Germans are either unsung heroes or maidens about to be raped.

The journey time was just over five hours, and as we approached Berlin, I found myself wondering how much the city had changed in the fifteen years since I'd seen it. I went there only once before the war—a trip with my father to wind up an uncle's estate—and I was still in Russia when the uprising failed in 1919, but I lived there for almost a year in 1922, working for the KPD as a political instructor. Now, staring out of the carriage window, I saw the same vista of grey monolithic blocks interspersed with the occasional spire. Hitler's grandiose plans for the place are frequently in the papers, but so far the only change I could see was in the number and size of the flags.

I had more than two hours to wait before the first train arrived at Silesian Station, so I got off mine at Friedrichstrasse for a walk around. After taking a look at the Tiergarten, I strolled down Unter der Linden and crossed the two bridges over the Spree. The old town looked much as I remembered it, the area around Alexanderplatz much less lively. One boarded-up former dancehall brought back a night I'd long since forgotten of dancing to a visiting American jazz band with a comrade from party HQ named Hilde. Where was she now? I wondered. She might still be there, married with children out in the suburbs, praying that her past stays hidden; she might be one of a thousand exiles in Russia, all biding their time until it's safe to come home. She could of course be dead. Working for the KPD in the 1920s hadn't come with a high life expectancy.

I thought of the person I'd been then. So young, so angry, so certain.

With less than a half hour to spare, I took an S-Bahn train to Silesian Station and, after checking which platform the train was due to arrive at, climbed the appropriate steps. I was slightly worried that Anna and her cousin had arranged the handover for either Friedrichstrasse or Zoo Station, but since they had met at Silesian a month before, there seemed no obvious reason for them not to do so again.

I needn't have worried, at least about that. When the train pulled in a few minutes late, Walter was one of the first to get off. Then, clutching his suitcase with one hand, he offered the other to help his aunt Sofie across the gap.

They were about thirty meters away. Scanning the platform

for his mother, Walter failed at first to see me, and I was only ten meters away when his eyes lit up, first with pleasure and then with the sudden realization that something must be wrong.

"Anna couldn't come," I said, fighting to be heard above a new arrival on the adjoining platform. "I'm Josef Hofmann, one of her lodgers," I informed Sofie, who looked like a plumper, less harassed version of her cousin. I suggested we all go downstairs, away from the noise, and received a nod of assent.

The cafeteria on the concourse below was not much quieter, but there wasn't anywhere else. "I'm afraid she's been arrested," I told them once we'd sat down.

Walter looked stunned.

"Why? What for?" Sofie wanted to know.

I went through what we knew, that she'd been denounced to the Gestapo for saying things she shouldn't have. I also said what we suspected, that another lodger named Ruchay had done the denouncing, in revenge for her refusing his offer of marriage.

"So she's innocent?" Sofie said hopefully.

"She may have spoken unwisely, or he may have made something up. But she's in custody, and no one can see her until the trial, which is probably several weeks away."

Walter looked torn between exploding with anger and bursting into tears. "I never liked Herr Ruchay," he almost stammered, "but I didn't think he would ever do something so . . ."

"None of us did," I said.

"So will they take me away now?" Walter wanted to know.

"No, why should they?" Sofie asked.

Walter said he'd had a friend at school whose mother was dead, and that when his father was arrested, they'd put the friend in an orphanage.

"You have a grandfather," I reminded him.

"And you also have a whole other family at the farm," Sofie said. "And I think you should come back with me now, until things are sorted out."

The look of panic that flashed across Walter's face would have been comic in less serious circumstances. "I think I ought to be at home," he said solemnly, looking to me for support.

I told Sofie her uncle Andreas thought that would be best, and went through his reasons one by one.

She looked doubtful but didn't argue further. "Very well," she said. "But you know you're always welcome," she told Walter. "And tell my uncle I want to know what's happening," she said, turning to me. "I know he can't write himself, but he can always ask someone like you."

That settled, we agreed to have some lunch, mostly, I suspect, because it gave us something to do before our journeys home. We ate in silence, and only Sofie cleaned her plate. Walter had lost his appetite, and I hadn't had one to begin with.

When the time came, we took Sofie up to her train and waved her goodbye as it steamed away. As the last coach cleared the platform, Walter finally burst into tears and, much to his own despair, was unable to stop crying for several minutes. I held him and let him sob into my chest, telling him over and over what my mother had often told me as a boy, that there was no shame in crying when something or someone was worth crying over.

Our journey back to Hamm seemed endless, especially after darkness fell. Walter was mostly silent, his face against the window, staring blankly out at the country that won't let his family alone.

Finally home, I watched him engulfed by Verena's warm and tearful embrace and found myself thinking that bad as things are, they could be worse.

✦ ✦ ✦

FRIDAY, SEPTEMBER 2

It's almost midnight, and the rest of the house is quiet. The days since I brought Walter back have been overly full, not to mention exhausting, but we seem to have survived them.

Walter, of course, has been our main concern, but none of us are finding him easy to read. He hasn't retreated into silence or weeping or anger, but at least around us adults, he does seem more self-contained. He doesn't come up to my room the way he used to, and Verena says she hasn't been able to get him to talk. He's happy playing football with Marco and his other friends, apparently at ease with his nose buried deep in an old Tom Shark, and always his usual polite self, but there's no denying that he hasn't yet come to terms with what's happened. School begins again on Monday, and I'm hoping that will help the process, but it might just as easily have the opposite effect.

At least the house is functioning smoothly. Verena has worked her socks off, and Jakob and I are doing what we can to help in our off-work hours. As someone who's lived most of his life in hotels and other people's houses, I can't say I've much experience of cleaning, and after the last four days, I have a keener understanding of what many of my female comrades have long been saying on the subject of domestic slavery.

One definite improvement is that we've all started eating together—lodgers, children, and Verena once she's served the food up. The Nazis might be rampant outside, but socialism thrives at our mealtimes! Even Andreas joined us on one occasion and treated all and sundry to some stomach-churning memories of what passed for food in the trenches.

The new lodger arrived on Monday, only minutes after a

moving company had come for Ruchay's belongings. His name is Thomas Buchloh, and like Gerritzen, he works for Islacker Wire and Cable, albeit in a more scientific capacity. For someone in his midtwenties, he seems very serious-minded. He has a fiancée named Ella in Dortmund, whom he travels to see every Sunday and plans to marry next summer.

If I had to sum up Buchloh's politics, I'd probably say he has none. He neither supports the regime nor opposes it—as far as he's concerned, it's just there. Which doesn't mean he's stupid. We still gather around the wireless in the evening—now without Ruchay's running commentary—and some of Jakob's and my more critical asides have clearly surprised Buchloh. And on more than one occasion, I've seen a smile slip out.

Speaking of Ruchay, he now has a room on the far side of town and a lengthy walk to work. I've run into him twice at the office, and on both occasions he has refused to meet my eye. The man looks haggard and several years older, which strengthens my suspicion that he hadn't intended his revenge to prove so brutal. Jakob and I have agreed to let him stew for another week before we appeal to his conscience.

Given that I'd already taken some unauthorized time off, it was Jakob who went back to the Gestapo yesterday, seeking more information about Anna's case and well-being. He came back with nothing where that was concerned but did get confirmation that Erich would be home in early December after serving his six-month sentence. The Gestapo officer was apparently indignant that there should be any doubt, telling Jakob that his organization was "scrupulous to a fault" when it came to such matters.

All of which might prove moot if the papers are any guide. The ongoing campaign against Czechoslovakia is growing more strident each day, presumably at Hitler's behest and Goebbels's direction. It feels like a playground bully taunting his unfortunate victim until the latter, out of sheer desperation, throws the first punch, thereby sanctioning his own destruction. Some sort of war, whether local or general, seems almost inevitable, and if it's the latter, then everything else—Walter's heartache, Buchloh's marriage, my own political scheming—will be swept away in its wake.

SUNDAY, SEPTEMBER 4

With the new school year beginning tomorrow, this afternoon I took it upon myself to make sure Walter was ready. He demurred at first, but without much conviction, and together we checked that he had all he needed when it came to stationery supplies (Verena having already dealt with his clothes). We also went through the various tasks he'd been set for the summer, some of which he'd completed before going away. Given his mother's arrest, it's more than ever imperative that Walter keeps to the current political script.

But he knows this as well as I do and seemed slightly vexed that I felt the need to remind him. I'd been putting off raising his promise to join the Jungvolk, thinking that he might dig his heels in—what child wants to laud those who locked up his mother?—but today he brought up the matter himself. He has already persuaded his grandfather to sign the application form—"He wasn't keen, but I told him he had to"—and asked me if I would take him shopping for the uniform and other regalia once his membership was confirmed.

MONDAY, SEPTEMBER 5

Walter's first day back at school seems to have gone well. Herr Skoumal is no longer one of his teachers, which certainly bodes well, and according to Walter none of the new ones are anything like as "stupid." Of course we have only Walter's word on this, and he does seem newly determined to keep any problems he has to himself. Sometimes I think the Nazis will make liars of us all.

Speaking of which, the latest Nuremberg Rally began today with what I assume is the usual bombast. Having missed the previous fifteen, I must admit to an interest in what sort of show they put on over the next seven days. This year's extravaganza is dubbed the "Rally of Greater Germany," in commemoration of Austria's accession to the Reich. Other states with German populations will no doubt be wondering—and worrying—just how much "greater" Hitler wants it to be.

TUESDAY, SEPTEMBER 6

When I got back to the house tonight, I found Verena bathing Walter's left eye and Marco already wearing a dressing on his left cheek. The boys' initial claim that these were football injuries had already fallen apart under Verena's cross-examination, and the twosome had now conceded that their injures had been sustained in a playground fight. "But it was really nothing," Walter insisted, and his friend backed him up.

"It was just one of the boys who likes to throw his weight around," Marco said. "His brother's in the SS, and the whole family thinks they're better than anyone else."

I asked why this boy had picked on them and received one of Walter's "you must be kidding" looks for my pains. When I asked how the fight had ended, he said one of the new teachers had pulled them apart. "And he didn't just blame me and Marco," Walter said, as if that was a hopeful sign.

Verena and I exchanged rueful looks—both of us know that any complaint to the school would probably make things worse—and reached an unspoken agreement not to pursue the matter. "I have some better news," I told them. With Müller's permission I had left work half an hour early and gone to see the Gestapo again, in the probably mistaken belief that the more we showed our faces the more attention they'd pay to Anna's fate. I wasn't expecting news, but the Kriminalsekretär actually had some—her hearing has been scheduled for October 5. Four weeks is a long time to wait, but any timescale is better than none.

One last thing I should note down today, because I fear it will prove significant. The German wireless and newspapers have been quoting an editorial in the London *Times,* a newspaper which often acts as a semiofficial mouthpiece for the British government. "The Czechs," the editorial argues, "will gain in homogeneity if the Sudetenland is allowed to secede." Having finally realized what sort of hook they're on, the men in London are seeking to wriggle themselves off it.

THURSDAY, SEPTEMBER 8

The last two school days have been uneventful, at least as far as we adults know. The house arrangements are still working well, but the extra work and longer hours were clearly taking a toll on Verena, so something had to be done. Jakob and I managed to persuade Gerritzen and Buchloh that she deserved some time off, and from now on we lodgers will feed ourselves between Saturday's breakfast and Sunday's supper. Jakob's further suggestion that he and I should cook Sunday breakfast was also accepted, though with more relief than enthusiasm. I can't remember the last time I cooked a meal.

The wretched Nuremberg Rally has taken over the wireless: speech after speech full of bile and self-congratulation, breathless descriptions of how amazing everything looks. I can hardly wait for the newsreel.

No doubt encouraged by the bloodcurdling threats every speaker seems honor bound to issue, the Sudeten Germans have broken off talks with their government in Prague.

FRIDAY, SEPTEMBER 9

After agreeing tactics with Andreas and Jakob, I caught up with Ruchay this evening. Having followed him half the way back to his lodgings a few days ago, it wasn't hard to appear at his side as he hurried on home. As I intended, this abrupt reunion came as a shock.

His first reaction was a quick step backward, his second to splutter: "What do you want?"

When I said I just wanted to talk, he said he was late for a meeting. I told him I'd walk along with him.

I'm sure he expected me to accuse him of denouncing Anna, but Andreas, Jakob, and I had decided that the chances of him making an official retraction were negligible—whatever we threatened, the Gestapo would still scare him more, and he wasn't about to admit he'd made it all up. I thought a less aggressive approach might prove equally futile, but if Ruchay was feeling as guilty as I hoped he was, it offered at least some chance of success.

"I need your help," I said, much to his obvious surprise. "I know you and Frau Gersdorff had your differences. Political ones and personal ones. But given how much you esteemed her, I can't believe you want to see her spend years in prison over a few intemperate remarks."

"No, of course not," he agreed, not even attempting to

deny his role in reporting her. "But what can I do?" he asked almost pathetically.

"You could put in a good word," I told him. "Explain the situation, the emotional stress that both of you were under at the time. Tell them that it wasn't like her, that if that was who she normally was, you would never have asked her to marry you. You're a member of the party—they'll listen to you."

He stopped and looked at me, and I thought—fancifully, perhaps—that I could see the inner struggle in his eyes. "I will give it some thought," he said. "Now leave me alone."

I watched him walk away, half of me wanting to push him under a tram, the better half wishing his mother had done something right.

Back here at the house, Jakob and Andreas were waiting to hear how things had gone. I told them I didn't know, that Ruchay's guilt and fear were well-matched opponents, and that predicting the outcome was beyond me.

After supper Gerritzen and Buchloh both went out, and once the boys were in their room, the rest of us took a kerosene lamp out to the yard and sat there for over an hour, enjoying the warmth of the evening and nursing glasses of beer. There wasn't much in the way of conversation, but just being there together felt good to me. And as far as I could tell, the other three felt the same.

Back in my room, as I wrote the above, I couldn't help noticing how little attention I'm paying to the job I was sent here to do. In my not-so humble opinion, Dieter's instruction to somehow force Müller out of the group is completely wrongheaded, a classic example of those far removed from events believing they know better than the people they have on the spot. This is far from the first time I've run into this problem, and lives are usually lost as a result of it. This time I shall do what I think is right, even though the feeling this decision evokes is that of a small boy defying his father. Or perhaps young Oliver Twist demanding "more."

What I must now do as a matter of urgency is investigate Paul Giesemann. Until I know whether he is or isn't an agent provocateur, there is no way I can approach the group on Moscow's behalf.

SUNDAY, SEPTEMBER 11

The sky was blue and clear this morning, and Verena decided that she and I should take the boys out for a picnic. After a short ride on a local train we took what was clearly a popular walk along the Ems. It was pleasant enough, but Anna's absence cast a long shadow. Some days I'm amazed by how well we've adapted to her not being here; on others I'm aware of how thin the pretense is.

Walter was clearly making an effort not to spoil it for the rest of us, but I could see how hard it was. Yesterday we went to collect his Jungvolk uniform, and he stood there in the brand-new outfit, staring at himself in the tall shop mirror as if he couldn't quite believe what he was seeing. "Think of it as a disguise," I told him quietly, and received a wan smile in return.

MONDAY, SEPTEMBER 12

Today was the final day of the Nuremberg Rally. I missed last week's cinema newsreel, but there's been no shortage of pictures in the papers and magazines, most of them showing either our glorious leaders or long columns of tanks and marching troops. I shouldn't be thinking it, let alone writing it, but swap the hooked crosses for hammers and sickles, and you could be looking at May Day in Moscow.

This evening we adults all gathered around the wireless for Hitler's closing speech. I suppose there was an air of foreboding. For weeks now the government has been using every opportunity to put pressure on the Czechs and their ever-more-reluctant allies—would this be the moment that Hitler threw caution aside?

The answer was no, not quite. The Czechs are worse than scum, and enemies forever, but Hitler's not quite ready to fire the starting pistol. He's waving it around, finger on the trigger, but he'll wait a while longer because he's such a peace-loving man. And the horror of it is, the man's blend of fiction and fact can sound so believable. There's just enough truth there to cover the lies. When he says that democracy is little more than the manipulation of public opinion by money and the press, he's telling the truth, and everyone knows it. When he accuses the Western democracies of gross hypocrisy for supporting cruel regimes and doing virtually nothing to help the Jews, he can hardly be gainsaid. When he claims that Czechoslovakia demeans the idea of self-determination, he has a point. And so it goes on. I'm sure that most of my countrymen and women are lapping it up. They're as angry as he is at all the hypocrites who stand between their country and the fairer deal Hitler claims it deserves.

Most people are inclined to hear what they want to hear, and Hitler knows that only too well. He also has a genius for helping them set aside any doubts.

Coming back to the rally and May Day, there is, I suspect, one huge difference. When Comrade Stalin looks down from his Red Square podium at all his military hardware, the question uppermost in his mind is probably: Will this suffice to keep our enemies out? When Hitler looks down from his podium, I'd lay a bet he's wondering: How far will this lot take me?

Given the situation Hitler has put himself and Germany

in, he doesn't have a great deal of choice. Only war can prevent—or mask—the collapse of the economy he's created, so it's all about timing, about choosing the moment to strike. If he thinks that's now, then he'll use the Sudeten Germans to provoke a general showdown. If, as seems more likely, he's not convinced that the odds have swung far enough in his favor, he'll simply bide his time. The man is drunk on success and as such has no reason to think enough is enough. Eventually someone will have to stop him, and no one seems keen to put themselves forward.

It was a strange feeling, sitting in our parlor, listening to that voice for over an hour, watching the faces around me, serious, worried, trying to work out what the man really means and whether it's what they want him to mean. Trying not to acknowledge what they already know in their hearts— that his is the voice that will take them to war.

TUESDAY, SEPTEMBER 13

Despite the rain, there was good attendance at this evening's group meeting—all who had come since June were there, and the Woszes' porch was thick with umbrellas. Ottilie came for only the second time and, no doubt aware how distracting some had found her prettiness on that first occasion, was even more soberly dressed. She flashed me a smile across the room, which I happily returned—we've shared a canteen table a couple of times in the last few weeks, and I enjoy her company. For herself, of course, but also because she reminds me of the old days, when comrades could speak their minds with each other, and wry asides about the party's shortcomings were not considered grounds for suspicion.

Unsurprisingly, Hitler's speech last night was still on everyone's mind, and most of those present had bones to pick. We have all learned to voice our criticisms constructively—anyone reading a transcript might be forgiven for thinking we really were trying to help out our Führer—but the tone was mostly contemptuous, the angry frustration beneath it impossible to miss.

As people had their say, I kept my eye on Giesemann. Yesterday I followed him home and then to the bar where he met up with friends. None of the latter looked like Gestapo or, indeed, like anything other than single young men out for a drink. As I watched him this evening, I wondered if my intuition had failed me for once. He wore a look of rapt concentration throughout the discussion, but that was no crime. He might have been storing up others' treasonous words for a report he meant to write later; he might have just been showing a youth's fierce commitment.

If the former, he must have been disappointed. The anger was palpable, but so was the sense that the group is marking time. Someone needs to push them over the edge, and Moscow's expecting that to be me. I don't think the time is ripe, but I'm very aware that I may be letting other considerations warp my judgment.

In the meantime the group just keeps talking. We confine ourselves to workplace issues—toilet breaks took up much of this evening's agenda—occasionally straying across the invisible border that separates these from their political context. Giesemann always seems keen to press the wider connections, but young people often have a weakness for righteous generalizations. Provocation or exuberance? I still don't know.

Before the meeting broke up, Müller surprised me by bringing up Anna's arrest. It was clear from the facial expressions that most of those present knew who she was, but Müller didn't mention her being a former comrade. He said Frau Gersdorff was a local widow whom the Gestapo had recently arrested for making seditious statements, purely on the word of an informer. It was, he said, a matter for our group, because the denouncer concerned was her lodger Aksel Ruchay, a fellow Reichsbahn employee whom many of us knew. "We don't know what she's accused of saying," Müller told the room, "but we do know that she had only just turned down his offer of marriage." Some sort of action was required, and he asked for suggestions.

The only one offered that seemed practical—making life hell for Ruchay at work—was not about to help Anna, and after explaining that I was also one of Frau Gersdorff's lodgers, I got up and explained the rather less punitive strategy the family favored, at least in the short run. The general consensus was that appealing to Ruchay's better nature was like looking for mercy in one of the Führer's speeches, but all conceded that treating the man like a leper could wait a few weeks.

Müller walked part of the way home with me and seemed eager to tell me how upset he was about Anna's continued detention. He sounded genuine, and again I considered raising my concerns about Giesemann. So why didn't I? I'm already as sure as I can be that Müller isn't a traitor, so the risk of revealing myself is not going to get any smaller.

It might be age and experience making me more averse to any sort of gamble, but I don't think that's the reason. If Anna or Erich were here to look after Walter, I think I'd have spoken up by now.

WEDNESDAY, SEPTEMBER 14

Walter came up to see me this evening, the first time he's done so in quite a while. I've missed his visits, but I haven't taken the decline in their frequency personally—he spends more time with his grandfather now that Anna can't, and with Marco living here, he has someone roughly his own age for company.

Yesterday evening, while I was out, he had attended his first Jungvolk meeting. I asked him how it had gone.

He sighed the Walter sigh. "All right, I suppose."

I asked him what they had done.

A lot of physical exercises, he said. Climbing ropes, vaulting horses, "like PE at school, except that we have to carry things."

Military training for twelve-year-olds, I thought.

An outdoor exercise is scheduled for the weekend after next, and they've all been assigned to competing teams. Last night his team was studying maps and working out how to reach their objectives ahead of the others.

With the future in mind, they have also all been asked to think about which of the three special groups—ground transport, ships, or planes—they want to join when they turn fourteen.

"You'll say planes," I guessed.

"Of course."

The meeting had concluded with a game of "trappers and Indians," which from Walter's account was a brawl by another name. "One boy fell on his wrist and broke it," he reported, "so the troop leader had to take him to the hospital, and the rest of us were all sent home."

Seeing my grimace, he insisted it hadn't been that bad. He'd even enjoyed the map reading.

A silence ensued, which I filled by asking him how he was feeling.

He took the question seriously, which was probably more than it deserved. "Useless," he said. "I feel useless. Mama's in prison, and there's nothing I can do. I worry about her all the time. All except when I'm playing football and some-times when I'm reading—then I forget for a while. But then I remember, and there's nothing I can do. I can't put things right the way Tom Shark could. I couldn't even if I was grown-up." He looked at me. "I can't tell them how much I hate their Führer."

That shocked me, though God knows why. I told him he could tell me. And Verena, and Jakob, and his grandfather. "We have to stick together," I said. "And we have to keep hoping for the best."

"I know," he said in a very small voice.

I asked if he liked having Marco here.

He said he did. "He's a good friend. He looks out for me. And I want to get him a Hitler dagger, but we're only allowed one each."

I was about to say I'd look out for one when he asked if I knew where Herr Ruchay had gone to live.

"Why?" I asked him. "Are you planning on sending a Christmas card?"

He smiled at that and didn't ask again. "It just feels like he's escaped," Walter explained, as much to himself as me.

"He hasn't," I promised, probably falsely.

Walter smiled again. "In class today we all had to stand up and say what we want to be when we grow up. Most boys said scientists or soldiers or pilots, but Emil Wollheim said he wanted to be the Führer's barber. A few boys laughed, and the teacher thought Emil was making a joke. But he wasn't. He's just not very clever."

I asked Walter what future he had chosen for himself.

"The thing that came into my head was what I didn't want to be, and that's an orphan. But I couldn't say that, so I said an airplane designer—it pleased the teacher."

That reminded me of the day's headline news—the maiden flight of the new *Graf Zeppelin* airship. We had passed around the picture in the evening paper at supper, and Walter had barely given it a glance. I asked him what he thought of it. What had the engineers done to improve on the ill-fated Hindenburg? I expected the old Walter's head full of technical detail; what I got was an older boy's interest in moral dilemmas.

He asked if I knew why they were filling the gas cells with hydrogen instead of what they now know is the much safer helium, and when I said no, he told me the reason. Apparently helium's available in large quantities only in America, and the American government has reneged on a promise to supply it because of the Anschluss with Austria. How, Walter asked me, could making an airship less safe help anyone?

I agreed that it couldn't. Seeing him so downcast, I searched my brain for some way to cheer him up and actually came up with something that did. When I suggested that the two of us and Marco could go to a Schalke game, his eyes truly lit up. And when I added that I'd have to ask Verena about Marco, he happily replied that she'd love a few hours without him. I thought that a trifle cruel for Walter, but thinking about it later, I realized that he was actually being perceptive. Over the years how many neighbors can Verena have had who would willingly babysit a mixed-race boy? Finding any time for herself can't have been easy.

Walter took his leave—it was almost his bedtime, and he wanted to check his fixture list for Schalke's next home game. He would tell me at breakfast.

I listened to his usual thunderous descent of the stairs and wondered what he'll eventually make of this life he's been given. Something worthwhile, I decided, because anything else would be a terrible waste.

THURSDAY, SEPTEMBER 15

The last two days have been really busy at work. Keeping the Reich's normal trains running, while simultaneously preparing to launch a possible invasion on one side of the country and delivering the wherewithal to build a huge defensive wall on the other, is proving more than a little challenging.

One piece of good news I have for Hitler's future targets—the Wehrmacht may have tanks and bombers to spare, but Germany's railways are in no shape to fight a war.

But as our work gets harder, the workplace grows more beautiful! All our buildings are again being painted inside and out, mostly by "volunteers" from the local Hitler Youth. A new sports field is being laid out on the land beyond the loco works, and a lorry load of shiny white goalposts has already been delivered. A number of saplings have been planted in the pots around our office to replace the ones planted six months ago, which all wilted and died in the smoke drifting across from the sheds.

FRIDAY, SEPTEMBER 16

We learned today that Prime Minister Chamberlain has visited Hitler in Berchtesgaden; the desire to see the Führer was apparently so overwhelming that the sixty-nine-year-old British leader took to the sky for the first time in his life! And for seven hours each way! If he also laid flowers at Hitler's feet, that hasn't been reported.

And neither has any outcome to their talks. Since Hitler's speech on Monday, the German press has ramped up its outrage at the Czechs' treatment of the Sudeten Germans, but the government in Berlin has not moved a muscle. Perhaps Hitler has now persuaded Chamberlain to do his dirty work for him and pull the rug out from under Beneš's feet.

SUNDAY, SEPTEMBER 18

I took Walter and Marco to the cinema this afternoon. There was a lengthy queue, but we were in our seats in time for the newsreel, which was mostly about last week's rally. Whoever organizes these events, he or she certainly knows how to make them dramatic, and for those who believe in the message, I imagine they leave a lasting impression.

The feature was the latest spy thriller *Secret Code LB 17*. The story concerned a terrorist plot to assassinate the war minister, which almost succeeded because of a traitor in the authorities' ranks. Like most bourgeois escapism, it wasn't very realistic, but it distracted Walter for a couple of hours.

This evening I sat with Andreas, who talked a lot about Anna: what she was like as a child, how angry her mother's early death had made her. Andreas had loved his two sons—both of whom died in the war—and like most fathers had seen them as his personal legacy, but he'd always known that his daughter was something special, cleverer than either of her brothers, more determined, bigger hearted. Not to mention a lot more stubborn.

I came away feeling more hopeful that she will return.

MONDAY, SEPTEMBER 19

Jakob and I got home from work this evening just before Walter and Marco. They're usually back at least an hour before us, but on this occasion they'd clearly wanted to put their homecoming off as long as possible.

There'd been another fight at school. Our boys were showing no visible wounds, and for a moment I wondered why they weren't leaving us adults in blissful ignorance, but the answer soon emerged—one of their foes had lost a tooth. And he wasn't just any foe—Kurt Pietzch was the only son of a local block warden.

"We didn't start it," Marco told his mother, who looked close to tears.

Walter just shook his head. He knew it didn't matter who had started it.

"So what happened?" I asked.

Walter described what had happened. Several other boys had cornered him in the toilet and started pushing and shoving him. "They were calling me names, but I didn't hit back . . ."

"What names?" I asked.

"Oh, 'son of a traitor,' 'secret Jew,' lots of stupid stuff. And then Marco came in and saved me. He hit Kurt in the mouth and knocked his front tooth out, and then they all left us alone."

Verena asked what had happened after that.

Nothing, her son said. Nothing yet, Walter corrected him. It had happened after classes, and there weren't any teachers around. "It all depends on what Kurt tells his father," Walter explained. "He won't want to admit he lost a fight."

Especially not to someone with Marco's ancestry, I thought.

"So maybe we're in the clear," Walter said, sounding like someone from one of his Tom Shark novels. Maybe they are, but even if this one blows over, we seem set for many more such crises. As targets for Nazi bullying, Walter and Marco are made-to-measure.

Rather like Czechoslovakia, which is still being pummeled in the press. Ordinary people all over Europe have no idea what's going on above their heads, and there's a general feeling of helplessness in the air. We don't know who's talking to whom, let alone about what. Are the English and French telling the Poles to talk to Moscow? Because there's no way Soviet troops can come to the aid of Czechoslovakia without crossing Polish soil. Are London and Paris trying to convince each other to support the Czechs? Or pleading with the Czechs to be "reasonable," stressing the blessings of "homogeneity"? I can't see Beneš buying that one.

⚊ ⚊ ⚊

TUESDAY, SEPTEMBER 20

Walter's faith in Kurt Pietzch's pride has proved misplaced. He did tell his father how the tooth got broken, and the father has made his displeasure known to the school. The principal spoke to each boy involved today—according to Walter and Marco, he just listened to their stories and said very little. But he did send them home with a letter asking Verena to see him first thing tomorrow. I said I'd go with her.

WEDNESDAY, SEPTEMBER 21

Walter's school principal confounded most of my expectations. An athletic-looking man of around thirty-five with wavy blond hair and keen blue eyes, Herr Huelse invited Verena and me into his office with an almost apologetic smile and thanked us for coming. After sitting us down in two of the three seats facing his desk, he looked at his watch and said that Kurt's father should arrive soon. While we waited I let my eyes wander and was encouraged by the placing of the Führer's portrait on the wall beside the only window, where it was hard to make out.

Herr Pietzch arrived around five minutes later and looked almost too like the man I expected—running to fat, red nosed, and piggy eyed. He had a swastika badge pinned to the lapel of his too-tight dark grey suit, and a block warden's armband wound around one sleeve. After shaking hands with the principal and treating Verena and me to looks of disdain, he moved his chair another half meter away from us and heavily sat down.

The principal introduced us, and I had to spend the next

few minutes defending my right to be there as Walter's representative. Once that had been sorted out, Verena and I both said how sorry we were that Kurt had been injured.

"How are you going to punish these boys?" Pietzch asked the principal, ignoring us completely.

The principal smiled at him, and there was something in the way he did it that made me feel a lot less anxious. It was beginning to look as if Huelse was as combative as he was decent. Which certainly made sense—a decent man doing his job in Nazi Germany would always have a fight on his hands. "After talking to Kurt, Marco, and Walter, I have two very different accounts of what happened," Huelse said, "and since I cannot be sure who is telling the truth . . ." He shrugged.

Pietzch looked dumbfounded. "You're not going to—"

"I can only punish a boy I know to be guilty," Huelse told him. "And there's no conclusive evidence either way."

"What about my son's lost tooth?"

That, Huelse agreed, was certainly evidence, but all it proved was that Kurt had lost. It threw no light on who had started the fight.

By this time Pietzch was not so much incredulous as furious. "Let me get this straight," he said, pointing a chubby index finger across the desk. "You are refusing to take my son's word over that of a Rhineland bastard and a boy whose mother and brother are both in prison?"

"Neither Marco nor Walter are responsible for their parentage," Herr Huelse said coldly.

"I think you've just said goodbye to your job," Pietzch responded in kind. "I shall be reporting you to the governors. And the local party."

"You must do what you think is right. But be warned: they will look at your son's record and note the many occasions on which he has been caught bullying others. By several different teachers. If I were you, Herr Pietzch, I would talk to your son. He is clearly a bright boy, but he is damaging his prospects with such behavior."

Pietzch looked at him and then at us. "So you won't be taking any further action."

"I think things are best left as they are. Don't you?"

Pietzch didn't, but he suspected he'd met his match. The block warden got to his feet, opened his mouth to speak, and then thought better of whatever he was going to say. Rather to my surprise, he left without slamming the door.

Huelse shook his head. "Politics, I'm afraid," he said. "I believe your boys' account of what happened, but it would be pushing my luck to say that to Herr Pietzch." He smiled wryly. "And of course Karl has been punished already. I'd like to prevent its happening again, but that's easier said than done. All I can say to you is that Walter and Marco must make every effort not to give boys like Karl an excuse."

"I think they already do," Verena said.

"That may be true, and I know it's not fair to put the onus on them. But short of transforming the national mood there's not much else I can do. These are challenging times."

They are indeed, but Verena and I walked back to the house with a spring in our step. In Hitler's Germany, meeting one decent man in authority feels like winning the jackpot.

THURSDAY, SEPTEMBER 22

Czechoslovakia is beginning to look like a bull awaiting the matador's coup de grâce. The Poles stuck a stick in yesterday, demanding a plebiscite in the Teschen area; today it was Hungary's turn to weaken the bull, with strident demands for more pieces of territorial flesh. The Slovaks—or at least the Slovak Fascists—say they want independence, and the

Sudeten Freikorps claim to have "liberated" several predomi-
nantly German towns in the Czech Sudetenland. The German
matador is yet to enter the ring, but I imagine his hooves are
pawing the ground. Hardly surprisingly, the mood at home
and work grows darker by the day.

Another of today's news items had a special resonance for
me. The Spanish Republican government has announced
that the International Brigades are being taken out of the
front line prior to their disbandment. The Brigades haven't
proved a great success in military terms—most of the men
recruited were amateurs, after all—but the fact that they exist
at all has been a mighty symbol of resistance. Their demise
feels like the end of an era.

FRIDAY, SEPTEMBER 23

The worst possible news. This afternoon a letter arrived for
Andreas. It was an Orpo officer who delivered it, but the letter was on Gestapo notepaper.

Anna has been moved to the Lichtenburg concentration
camp, which we think is south of Berlin. Her trial for sedition
"will no longer be necessary" because now she is detained as
an enemy of the state, "in accordance with the Decree of
the Reich President for the Protection of People and State
(1933)." There was no mention of a sentence and therefore
no clue as to when she might be released.

The letter was typed, but Kriminalsekretär Appel had
added a note in pencil. Should we need further clarification,
he would be in his office on Monday morning.

I thought we probably had all the clarity we could take but
knew it would be unwise to cut off contact.

The immediate issue—which Andreas, Verena, and I
then discussed—was whether or not to tell Walter. Verena

was doubtful, but Andreas and I both thought Walter would want to know. As he's going to be out all tomorrow with the Jungvolk, we decided to postpone the telling till Sunday—letting him carry such news around on his own all day didn't seem like a good idea.

After that the three of us just sat around the table for a while, not knowing what else to say. Andreas and Verena both looked stricken, and I'm sure that I did too. Three hours have passed since then, but if I had a mirror in front of me now, I imagine I'd see the same.

SATURDAY, SEPTEMBER 24

When I woke up this morning, Anna was there in my mind. It was all too easy to imagine her despair now that she's been torn away from the father and child who need her. I pushed back the thought that the place they've sent her is one from which she might not return.

If I hadn't had the monthly *treff* to attend, I might have just stayed in bed. As it was, Walter had left by the time I got downstairs. Verena had seen him studying his uniformed self in the parlor mirror. "He just stood there shaking his head," she told me.

I ate breakfast with Gerritzen and Buchloh—Jakob was doing an early shift at work—and listened to them chatting on about where they were taking their girlfriends tonight. Some people still lead ordinary lives, I thought. The realization was almost shocking.

It was a bright autumn day outside, cool but decidedly sunny, ideal weather for Walter's day in the country fighting imaginary foes. My *treff* was in Essen at the lakeside café in the Stadtgarten.

I walked to Hamm station and took a train that would get

me to Essen with almost an hour to spare. The journey was uneventful, the train only two minutes late, and I sat in the station buffet watching other ordinary lives go by until it was time to walk to the park.

Dieter was there ahead of me, absorbed in reading the latest news of the current crisis. "Do you think the threat of war will wake up the German proletariat?" was the first thing he asked once I'd sat down. The previous month he'd been hoping a war would bring forth the revolution; now he was hoping that maybe the threat would suffice.

I said that probably depended on what sort of war and how it went but that I wasn't expecting too much.

He seemed disappointed by my estimation, which suggested that Comrade Stalin has seen something different in his crystal ball. I waited for further enlightenment, but was kept in suspense while the waiter brought us the cups of hot chocolate that Dieter had already ordered.

"The committee have decided that further delay would be ill-advised," he told me, after taking an appreciative sip. "Which means that risks must be taken," he added superfluously. "You must activate the three-man cell at once and subordinate the Working Group to one of the three. What progress have you made with neutralizing Dariusz Müller?"

I said I was proceeding carefully, rather than admitting that I wasn't proceeding at all.

"Caution often leads to paralysis," Dieter warned, which sounded vaguely Buddhist but was probably a catchphrase coined at the last party conference. I forbore from listing the times I'd seen a lack of caution cost the party and its members dear. If the committee wanted caution thrown to the winds—and me to the dogs—then who was I to complain? I'd thrown enough comrades to the dogs myself.

"Müller must be removed," Dieter was insisting. "And the man you believe to be an informer."

"Understood," I said.

"Once that is done and the cell is operational, you will return to Moscow for reassignment."

"How?" I asked, my voice commendably steady. My time in Germany was clearly coming to a close, and I wasn't sure which I dreaded most, whatever was waiting in Moscow or the thought of leaving Hamm.

When Dieter gave me a Duisburg number to call, I deduced that the Rhine was my likely escape route. He repeated the number and password until sure I'd memorized both and, after passing on the time and place of next month's *treff*, dropped his second bombshell—not I, but a member of my putative cell would be joining him in Bochum on October 29, because by then I would be gone. I had less than five weeks left with Walter and his family.

"Soon you'll be home in Moscow," Dieter said cheerfully, rubbing it in.

On the train back to Hamm, I felt strangely calm. The moment I'd dreaded had come—I had to decide whether or not I was still a Comintern rep. Activate the cell, and if I've misread any one of the three, I'll be under arrest within twenty-four hours. Link the cell and group, and the risk of exposure will more than triple for everyone concerned. I was already fairly certain that I wouldn't be taking the latter course, but I did feel confident about my chosen three. I had the strange thought that I owed it to Anna, that if she'd been condemned for doing nothing, I should at least be doing something in her name. Which sounds, and probably is, absurd.

I was still weighing risks when I got back home and received the latest ill tidings. Andreas has had a cold for several days, but this morning it took a marked turn for the worse, and Verena decided he needed professional help. We've been as lucky with our doctor as we have with our block warden—Dr.

Offner, the sprightly young man I first met back in May, actually cares for his patients. He's also fond of Andreas, who he says reminds him of his late uncle.

After examining Andreas, Offner had said that the cold had gone to the old man's chest and might turn into something much more serious. He had given Verena a list of symptoms to watch out for and promised to return tomorrow morning.

"He didn't sound very hopeful," Verena lamented. She looked as if she'd suffered a blow too many, and I felt much the same. We were both worried for Andreas but probably even more anxious for Walter, whose entire family seems in danger of disappearing.

He arrived home early this evening looking exhausted but also slightly elated. I guessed he'd enjoyed himself despite the unfortunate context.

Everything changed when he heard how ill his grandfather is—Walter looked utterly desolate and refused to talk about his day. And tomorrow we have to give him the news of his mother.

Once the boys had gone to bed, Jakob suggested a drink at the Social, but I told him I had a headache and he should go on his own. Once he had left, I sat downstairs with the wireless, trying and failing to lose my sense of impending disaster in Berlioz and Brahms. The news, when it came, felt like a release. For the last few days, it's been all about Czechoslovakia, and this evening offered more of the same. Chamberlain has visited the Führer again, this time at Bad Godesberg, where Chamberlain apparently stayed two nights. If an agreement has been reached, no one is saying what it amounts to. Chamberlain traveled back home this morning, but whether to muster troops or stand them down remains a mystery.

How would we know? The German press can't be relied

on to tell the truth or indeed anything like it, and these days it's next to impossible to find a foreign newspaper—I tried in Berlin the day I met Walter. German wireless is the same, and it's strictly forbidden to tune in to foreign stations. People still do it, though, and many try to spread the news they've gleaned without admitting where they've gleaned it. One of Jakob's friends—a man who lives alone some way out of town—is an ardent trawler of foreign airwaves, and when their paths crossed by chance this afternoon, he filled Jakob in on the latest news. According to this friend, the British and French have persuaded the Czechs to give up the Sudetenland without a fight, and Chamberlain arrived at Bad Godesberg on Thursday expecting smiles of gratitude. What he got was Hitler fuming that it wasn't enough, that his troops were about to march in, and that Chamberlain had only a couple of days to persuade the Czechs that their utter humiliation has to be part of the deal.

If this is all true—and it sounds convincing—has Hitler gone too far? Will this prove too much for the British and the French? The next few days will tell.

SUNDAY, SEPTEMBER 25

Last night I dreamt I was playing with my brother in our house in Offenbach—hide-and-seek, I think, though it wasn't clear. I must have been happy, because my first thoughts on waking were of what we had to tell Walter, and the emotional jolt was severe.

I lay there wondering what we could say, what crumb of comfort we might be able to offer. That one day she would be home? We didn't know that she would. That the camp might not be so bad? We knew it would be.

Remembering our conversation last week, I wondered

if Walter would seek revenge on the man who'd informed on his mother. I told myself I was being fanciful—that the boy's only twelve, and what could he actually do? And then I remembered his brand-new Jungvolk knife.

Ruchay may have already withdrawn or altered his testimony, or been planning to do so at the now-canceled hearing. We have no way of knowing, and the Gestapo are extremely unlikely to tell us. But whether he sticks to his story or not is irrelevant now, and I'm inclined to leave him stewing in his obvious guilt. Walter may not see it like that. He's grown up in a country where taking an eye for an eye is the standard response, and turning the other cheek is for failures. And what other outlets does he have for his anger?

Verena and I talked to Walter just before noon, after the doctor had visited Andreas and pronounced him no better, no worse. Walter knew from the summons and the looks on our faces that something was wrong. "It's bad news, isn't it?" he said before we had a chance to open our mouths.

"Yes, it is," Verena said. "Your mother—"

"She's dead, isn't she?"

"No," I told him. "It's not that. She's been moved to a camp."

"What sort of camp?" he asked, noticing I hadn't said.

"A KZ," I admitted. "The one at Lichtenburg."

"But that must be four hundred kilometers away," Walter protested.

"Yes," I agreed, surprised that he knew where Lichtenburg was.

"But what about the trial?"

"There won't be one." I explained the situation, the law they'd used to put her in the camp, the absence of a finite sentence. It felt as if I were hammering nails into his twelve-year-old heart.

I waited for shock, for anger, but all he did was nod, tears welling in his eyes. Verena pulled his head onto her shoulder, and I thought he would sob his heart out, but after a few seconds he gently drew himself away. "I want to say, I can't bear it," he said quietly, "but I have to, don't I?"

"Yes," I told him. "And hope." I almost added "and pray," but Verena beat me to it.

He nodded again and asked if there was anything else he should know. When we told him no, he gave us both a tearstained hug and left the room.

That was this morning, and I've been thinking about little else all day. One thing I know for certain—at this particular moment in time, Walter's need is greater than Comrade Stalin's.

MONDAY, SEPTEMBER 26

Walter went off to school this morning without any fuss but without much sign of life in his eyes. He came back this evening in much the same state, which is probably the best we can hope for. I know how hard accepting such loss is for even the strongest adult, let alone a twelve-year-old child who's already lost a father and brother and might soon lose his grandfather.

Dr. Offner came again and left the same prognosis. Andreas is wheezing a lot and eating little, and I don't like the color of his skin. The more I think about it, the more I'm sure that it was the news of Anna's transfer that turned the cold into something that may prove lethal.

As if we didn't have enough to concern us, there was a much-heralded speech from Hitler on the wireless tonight. I imagine he had a big audience—most Germans want to know what's in store, whether it's peace or war. He was speaking at the Sportpalast in Berlin in front of the usual baying crowd, but our household—like, I suspect, millions of others—mostly listened in anxious silence.

He started off as usual, listing his many contributions to European peace—the pact with Poland, the naval treaty with Britain, the renunciation of Alsace-Lorraine. There was just this one last problem, and once it was resolved, he'd be done. And resolve it he would! It was really quite simple— all he asked was that the British and French should apply their own principle of self-determination. Czechoslovakia was founded on "a single lie." There was no such thing as a Czechoslovak. It was the Czechs who ran this mongrel state, cruelly lording it over the Slovaks, Magyars, Poles, and Sudeten Germans.

Even the Czechs knew their rule was intolerable and, at British and French behest, had agreed to transfer those territories inhabited by Sudeten Germans. But now the Czechs were objecting to an immediate German occupation. What did they imagine a transfer entailed?

Written down like this, it all sounds so reasonable; when the words were being spoken, shouted, sometimes screamed, it was quite another matter. I've known a lot of political figures but never another one whose self-control seemed so fragile. There was excitement in his voice from the start, and as the speech wore on, he sounded increasingly manic; by the end he was close to hysteria.

Seconds after he finished speaking, the familiar voice of Goebbels was heard, shouting, "Nineteen eighteen will not be repeated!"

There was a bang, as if someone had hit something, and then Hitler's voice screeching, "Yes!" like a man possessed.

That "yes!" was probably audible on the moon, not to mention in Prague, where it will be taken as a declaration of war. As Hitler said earlier in the speech: "The time has come when one must mince matters no longer."

What does this mean for me and my mission? Two things, I think—one good, one bad. If war breaks out and we attack Belgium and Holland, I'll be cut off from my controllers for an indefinite period. And Erich might well be released straight into war work of one kind or another, in which case he won't be coming home to look after Walter.

TUESDAY, SEPTEMBER 27

Everyone's waiting. There hasn't been a word in the press about an actual ultimatum, but every person I talked to today was convinced that one has been given and that Hitler is awaiting the reply. One thing we do know at work: the trains have been waiting to roll for several days, and if something doesn't happen soon, the whole network will begin to seize up.

According to the wireless Hitler and Roosevelt have been exchanging telegrams, though the contents have not been divulged. I doubt the messages have been congratulatory—arrogance seems the only thing the two men have in common. And if FDR is lecturing Hitler on a leader's moral duty to preserve the peace, he's wasting his breath.

We also learned that the British have launched a new ocean liner named after their current queen. According to Walter it's not only the biggest liner ever built; it's also the biggest ship. Which reminded me of something someone said of the Roman Empire—that as the buildings grew bigger, the spirit eroded. The world will certainly breathe a sigh of relief if the British betray the Czechs, but Britain's reputation will still be in tatters.

Here in Germany, war might be imminent, but the Jews have not been forgotten. Today it was announced that Jewish lawyers will not be permitted to practice from November 30.

This in itself was no surprise, but I found myself hoping that the Nazi obsession with Jews, if not sufficiently distracting in itself, does represent a wider denial of rationality that may in the end cost them dear.

Here in the house, Andreas has shown no sign of recovery, but neither has he taken an obvious turn for the worse.

WEDNESDAY, SEPTEMBER 28

And still we wait. The government keeps up its usual blustering, but neither war nor peace is announced. The British and French are silent, the Czechs apparently waiting like everyone else for some sort of decision. The mood at work today was one of resignation—most people now believe it's a matter of when, not if. But nobody's pleased; the difference between now and 1914 could hardly be more marked.

I remember those days in August 1914 all too well: the crazy joy and camaraderie, the sense of destiny, the pure excitement. When I look back now, we seem like fools, but there were excuses. There hadn't been a major war in nearly half a century, and no one knew—not even the professionals, as it turned out—how the latest weapons had changed things. But that's not the case these days—anyone over forty has either first- or secondhand experience of what modern war is like, and most over twenty will have read or seen cinematic accounts of what men endured in the trenches. There's no glory in literally losing your head to a long-range shell. No glory in firing it either. Most adults know this, and according to Walter most of his fellow Jungvolk do too, despite all the regime's efforts.

But it's not just the horrors of war that make my fellow Germans reluctant warriors. Few are actually pacifists, but most want a decent reason to risk their own or their children's lives, and the Czech treatment of the Sudeten Germans falls somewhat short in that regard. They'll fight if they have to, but not with any enthusiasm.

Thinking about my fellow Germans today, I decided that they're a people who've lost confidence in themselves and their choices. They embraced war in 1914 and went down to defeat and economic ruin. They turned to the Nazis to put things right, and I suspect that many now regret doing so, partly because Hitler and his cronies make them ashamed to be German, mostly because of where it all seems to be leading.

FRIDAY, SEPTEMBER 30

We are saved, at least for the moment. Agreement has been reached at an international conference in Munich, and the threat of war has been lifted. This has been Chamberlain's third visit to Germany in as many weeks, and it looks at first sight as if the English saying "Third time lucky" reflects his efforts. The Czechs have been sold down the river, but that was a price everyone else thought worth paying. They are spared a violent incursion, the rest of us a European war.

It was all smiles at work as we started the job of putting the Reichsbahn back on a peacetime footing. All those old enough to fight themselves, all those with sons, brothers, husbands, or fathers in the same situation, could hardly keep their toes from tapping, so great was the sudden relief. I wasn't immune myself. Despite what my Comintern contact Dieter thinks, wars between nations are bloody and pointless, and I felt as pleased as the next man that one had been avoided.

Which is not to say that I think the reprieve will last. If Hitler knows that sooner or later the German economy must have a war, he should also be aware that adding the Sudetenland to the Reich will not provide much of a military or economic boost. What it will do, by stripping the Czechs of their mountain defense lines, is make it that much easier to seize the real prize—the Škoda armaments industry in western Bohemia. Easier militarily, that is, but still hard politically, because the lack of Germans in that part of Czechoslovakia means Hitler won't be able to use self-determination as an excuse.

But that potential crisis is, I hope, some way off. At home I found the same relieved faces I'd seen at work and an extra cause for celebration—Andreas was better. Had he been buoyed by the news, or was that just coincidence? According to Verena the doctor was surprised by the old man's recovery, but I am not. Andreas has a will of iron, and he knows his grandsons have never needed him more.

Walter was pleased, but thoughtful as well. "This is better for Mama, isn't it?" he asked me after supper. I said I thought it was, though in truth I'm not at all sure it will make any difference.

The mood on the wireless was suitably self-congratulatory—another three million Germans have come home to the Reich, all thanks to our peace-loving Führer. Listening, I felt the sense of relief start to fade. According to Monday's Sportpalast speech, the Sudetenland had been his last territorial claim, but what of the Germans living in Poland, Danzig, and Memel? How long will they have to wait for their homecoming?

It's probably only a matter of time, but why waste the time that we have? As I sit by my open window, I can hear more than the usual Friday night revelry—it may just be a reprieve, but people are making the most of the moment. Live for the day, I tell myself, but when you've devoted your life to the future, that's not something that comes naturally.

SUNDAY, OCTOBER 2

I took Walter and Marco to the cinema again; our Sunday afternoon entertainments are fast becoming a ritual—something to hang on to among the buffetings of personal and political fate. It was a comedy this time—not a very good one, but the audience greeted each comic situation with semi-hysterical howls of laughter. The tension of the last few weeks has taken a toll.

Marco laughed more than Walter did, which didn't surprise me. Marco hasn't suffered the emotional blows that Walter has, and his temperament is much more happy-go-lucky. I'm sure he's well aware of the disadvantages of being black in Nazi Germany, but he seems to see them as something to overcome if and when he can. A practical challenge rather than an existential one.

And he may be right. Marco's fate does seem, for the moment at least, beyond his control. So why worry about it?

Walter worried before his brother and mother were taken away, and now he worries a great deal more. Since he got the news of Anna's transfer a week ago, he's been living very much inside himself, and it's hard to tell what he's thinking and feeling. Verena says he cried himself to sleep for the first couple of nights but hasn't since. And even though he's holding the outside world at bay, he's managing to function within it, which is probably the best we can expect for quite a while.

Jakob arrived back from Hamburg soon after supper, having spent another enjoyable weekend with his son and pregnant daughter-in-law. What has caused the improvement in family relations is far from clear—Jakob himself seems mystified—but I hope it continues. On our way to the Social Club, Jakob was wondering out loud about moving to Hamburg once the child is born—he says it's due in February. "They're family," he said apologetically, as if I might take umbrage at being abandoned.

The post-Munich mood at the club was probably typical. Everyone's relieved, but only the dimmest are optimistic. Time has been gained, nothing more.

TUESDAY, OCTOBER 4

I was going to write that things are getting back to normal, but the personal situations in this house are such that the word hardly seems appropriate. Things are calmer at least, less fraught than they were a week ago. There haven't been any fresh incidents at school, or none of which Verena and I are aware. I'm sure the boys are being careful, but I suspect that Herr Huelse has also been active in their defense.

Since it seems unlikely that Anna will return anytime soon, Verena has given up the other room she rents and fully moved in. She had her doubts about doing so—mostly because she feared that Walter would make the same connection—but Andreas and I persuaded her. Walter no longer has a room of his own and no doubt sometimes misses the privacy, but having Marco around all the time does take his mind off his troubles.

The burden was also lightened somewhat this evening. Another Dude arrested and sentenced with Erich—a boy named Werner—arrived back in Hamm today and this evening came to the house with a verbal message. Erich is not only well but also "fitter than he's ever been," and looking forward to being home in a couple of months.

Werner was distressed to hear that Erich's mother had been arrested and glad that Erich didn't know—"He talks about her a lot."

And might well go after Ruchay, I thought. Or do something equally rash.

Andreas was cheered by the news that Erich was well and that the boy has done nothing silly to delay his release. Sometimes it feels as if the old man is just hanging on until his older grandson comes back to look after the younger. I know he likes me, but he's not convinced that I'll always be here to step into the breach. He suspects I have other, undisclosed loyalties, and in that of course he's right.

He doesn't know how strong those loyalties are, and these days neither do I. Since receiving Moscow's orders ten days ago, I have done absolutely nothing to carry them out. I haven't made a firm decision to either ignore or defy them, but my chosen three remain in ignorance of the putative cell, and the Working Group—which meets tomorrow—still includes Dariusz Müller. I also seem to have dropped the ball when it comes to proving that Giesemann is an informer.

All of which can be put right. Dieter's orders were clear, but I am the man on the spot, and if something comes up that persuades me that activation should wait, then my superiors in Moscow will allow me a few weeks' grace. I am an experienced rep, and any doubts concerning my political loyalty will probably not extend to my competence in the field. But of course they won't wait forever—if I wish to remain a Comintern agent, I must get things moving before too long.

And I think I do. For one thing, I find it hard to envisage a different life. For another, I'm still a believer, at least in the foulness of the enemy. I can't imagine a higher calling than putting spokes in Hitler's wheels.

That, after all, is why I am here. And it's what I intend to do when Erich or Anna comes home.

⚊ ⚊ ⚊

WEDNESDAY, OCTOBER 5

We were worked off our feet at the office today. A derailment early this morning between Gelsenkirchen and Wanne caused serious disruption across the Ruhr, and by noon the ripples were reaching up and down the Rhine. Rumor has it that a broken rail was responsible, which would come as no surprise—the money the government's spending on arms is not being spent on the railways, something Hitler might come to regret if he finds his conquering armies can't be supplied.

The weather has also turned: on my way to this evening's Working Group meeting, I had my hands firmly wedged in my pockets for the first time this year. I would have sooner stayed home, but duty called, and I actually enjoyed the walk. Provincial German towns after dark look much the same as each other, and I found myself reliving similar walks through the town where I grew up. Friends I'd long forgotten came to mind, a girl I'd dearly wanted to kiss but never had.

The meeting at Heinrich's apartment was well attended— of the regulars, only my bugbear Giesemann was missing. The relief that most Germans felt at the avoidance of war is still palpable, and even these comrades—who know in their hearts it will be only temporary—seemed lulled into thinking that time is on our side. The lion's share of the evening was given over to the latest management directives on increasing productivity, which needless to say involve either more hours, less pay, or both. Several tactical responses were suggested, all of them worthy of further consideration—as discussions go, it was a good one.

I did more watching than speaking. I studied these men and this woman, all so relieved that they weren't now at war with England and France. Would they be any more willing to take up arms against Hitler? Their hearts would doubtless be more engaged, their chances of survival that much less.

I also watched how they were with Dariusz Müller, and there was no mistaking the fact that they trust him. Most of them have known him longer than I have, and the notion that he's managed to fool them all simply beggars belief. And if anyone in the group is a natural leader, it's him.

I found myself thinking ahead, rehearsing what I would say to them: That they would have to source their own weapons and explosives, but that money would be provided. That what I was really offering was a sense of purpose and an end to isolation, the chance to be true to themselves and part of something much bigger than Hamm or Germany and, last but not least, access to the party's escape routes if and when the shit hit the fan.

And how did they react to my imaginary speech? With grim faces but also a glint in the eyes. Those are the faces I've seen in the past, and I expect to see them again. For better or for worse.

Looking at Müller, I thought about Moscow's order to exclude him, the order I intend to ignore. When the time comes, I can tell my superiors that I believe their concerns are unjustified, that he's by far the best man to lead the group. But what will I say to Müller himself? All I can do is repeat what Dieter told me and leave Müller to work out how he can bring himself back into favor.

And then there is Giesemann, absent this evening but unforgotten. My instincts still say that he's an informer, but the other members of the group show no sign of thinking so, and I haven't found any real evidence. I need to be certain one way or the other before I take the risk of approaching anyone.

As I walked home alone, I tried to bring back the town of

my childhood, but all I could see was Hamm and its modern streetlights, the host of bloodred flags shivering in the wind.

THURSDAY, OCTOBER 6

Last night I dreamt I was in Sofia, walking down Maria Luiza Boulevard with Vyara and Yasen. I could see the Saint Nedelya Church up ahead, but no matter how far we walked it never seemed to get any nearer. And then a tram went past, ringing its bell like an ambulance, so loud it woke me up. And as I lay in my bed here in Hamm, feeling the tendrils of sadness twine around my heart, I knew I had to tell the story, if only to exorcise the ghosts.

Grozdan Bozhidarov and I arrived in the Bulgarian capital in the dying days of 1924. We had been traveling for more than a week, having taken a long and circuitous route from Moscow: a train to Odessa, a boat to Constantinople, and another train to Sofia. According to our papers, I was a German businessman, my Bulgarian comrade an expatriate from Thessaloníki visiting distant relatives, but these identities were only for travel—once ensconced in Sofia we would not be walking the streets in daylight.

We were met at the station by two party members masquerading as members of Bozhidarov's fictional family and swiftly taken to our separate lodgings. Mine were only a short walk away, in a block of flats just north of the Slivnitsa Boulevard. My hosts were a young married couple, Yasen and Vyara Marinov, both rank-and-file party members. Staying with such comrades, rather than a better-known senior figure, was considered safer for me.

I took to them both immediately and felt slightly guilty about occupying half of their flat, but they couldn't have been more welcoming, and looking back now, I know I enjoyed the glamour that went with the role of a Comintern rep. I was only a few years older than them, but I'd seen a lot more of the world, and I'd fought in the two revolutions that mattered most, those in Russia and Germany. I came from the party of Luxemburg and Liebknecht; I had breathed the same air as Lenin, Trotsky, and Bukharin. In Sofia I was a celebrity, albeit one who could leave home only after dark.

The background to our mission was this: Two years after the war, in which Bulgaria had been one of the losers, the peasant party had won elections and formed a government. Despite violent opposition, some reforms favoring the poor were introduced, and our party supported these as a first step toward the wider transformation it championed. But when the nationalist right violently overthrew the BZNS government in 1923, the Bulgarian comrades decided not to offer the latter any active support but to stand aside and let the other two forces fight it out. This proved a serious error of judgment, because the moment the right was in power it came after our party with all guns blazing. And when, too late, the Bulgarian comrades rose in their own defense, the cost was terrible. The leadership was virtually wiped out by arrests and executions, leaving those they had led arguing over how best to respond, with some insisting that a strategic retreat was unavoidable if the party wished to survive, others insisting, with equal fervor, that attack was the only form of defense with any chance of success, that fire must be fought with fire.

This was the argument that Bozhidarov and I stepped into in January 1925, the one that was rehearsed again and again over subsequent months in unlit back rooms and shuttered cafés, every ear half-cocked for the sound of a warning whistle outside. And we weren't just another two comrades—we were the envoys from Moscow, the voice of the Comintern, and we had come armed with Zinoviev's instructions. I don't remember the precise wording, but I do recall the confusion they created—Zinoviev was a great orator, but he was never the brightest of sparks, and most of the comrades I've met who worked with him had trouble understanding how he had reached the positions he had. He urged the Bulgarian comrades not to repeat the "opportunism" of 1923, which our more fiery members took to mean the spineless abandonment of the peasant party and our more moderate members assumed was a reference to the doomed rising that had followed a few weeks later. The former option was given more credence by the instructions to construct an underground organization, establish ties with the more revolutionary peasants, and counter police persecution through armed resistance. The party was ordered to prepare itself for—in a favorite phrase of the times—"the inevitably maturing revolutionary situation."

As a blueprint this was all utterly useless, but of course no one dared say so. Our underground organization was constantly being undone by arrests, the revolutionary peasants were mostly already in jail, and anyone thinking he'd stumbled across a "maturing revolutionary situation" was deluding himself. In this situation the ideological response—working out which of our choices was theoretically correct—seemed less and less relevant. The Bulgarian comrades were literally fighting for their lives, and if they didn't kill the enemy, the enemy was going to kill them. After each new meeting to discuss what Zinoviev actually meant, more became convinced that he was in favor of action.

In hindsight, this was when I should have intervened. Because of what we represented, Bozhidarov and I had influence, I more than he because he was just another Bulgarian. But I was torn. The action in prospect involved the killing of someone high enough in the government or army to warrant a state funeral, and then an attack on the funeral itself, which many other political and military leaders would perforce be attending. This scheme felt nihilistic, anarchistic, anything indeed but Bolshevist. Assassination had never been a Bolshevik tactic and neither had mass murder. Added to which, in the likely absence of Zinoviev's "maturing situation," a lot more people on our side were going to die for little if any gain. But—and it was a big but—the authorities were running riot, arresting and executing comrades on what felt like an hourly basis. The situation was certainly desperate, and I didn't feel sure enough of my doubts to veto the only response we had planned. I did communicate my misgivings to Zinoviev, but his dismissive reply felt almost instant given the distance involved, and I didn't press the argument any further. I doubt it would have made any difference if I had, but I should have tried. It was my first major mission abroad, and Zinoviev was the head of the Comintern. I say this to explain, not to excuse.

Life went on, winter turning to early spring. I spent many an evening with Vyara and Yasen, answering their questions about the world beyond Bulgaria and, to my shame, rarely asking any in return. Vyara was expecting a child in the summer, and was working only half days as a typist, so the two of us would talk away the afternoons until Yasen came home from his job as an office clerk. With her sleek blonde hair, catlike face, and shapely curves, Vyara was extremely attractive, but they were both such lovely people, and such a well-matched couple, that I made sure to keep my desire to myself. I may have killed them in the end, but I didn't insult their hospitality.

Outside the war continued. More arrests, more rumors of torture, the latter often confirmed when a comrade's mutilated body was found in some field or forest outside the city. Our plans were made, discussed, remade. A sexton at Saint Nedelya cathedral had already been recruited, and with his help the twenty-five kilograms of explosive were smuggled inside and carried up to the rafters. The bait was selected—a high-ranking policeman named Nachev whose funeral would prove a magnet to his senior colleagues. Nachev was killed, but on the day of the ceremony, there were so many guards around the cathedral that the attack had to be called off.

Another victim was chosen, General Konstantin Georgiev. He was gunned down in front of another church sometime in mid-April, and two days later his funeral took place at Saint Nedelya. Many government ministers were in attendance, along with most of the highest-ranked officers from the police and armed forces. And this time, for reasons that were never explained, there was hardly any security.

The service had barely begun when two comrades lit the fifteen-meter fuse and made their escape. The explosion brought down much of the roof on the mourners, killing a hundred and fifty, and injuring five hundred more.

Across the city, having taken the risk of a short trip outside in daylight, I heard the crack and the thunder, saw the cloud of smoke and dust smudging the clear blue sky. I should have been elated, but all I felt was dread.

It's late now, and if I am to sleep, I must leave the rest of this story for another day.

FRIDAY, OCTOBER 7

Over dinner we learned that Buchloh's younger brother has joined the SS and that his parents are less than pleased. Buchloh didn't explain the latter, but from things he's said in the past, I would guess that Social Democrat sympathies are a more likely reason than bourgeois snobbery.

Gerritzen, meanwhile, has bought a new car, which he keeps at his new fiancée's house, partly because it's less likely to be vandalized on her middle-class street, mostly, I suspect, to impress her father.

According to the wireless this evening, the occupation of the Sudetenland is almost complete. The next victim is yet to be announced, and the ugly, strident tone of September's editorials has noticeably softened. The beast is resting between hunts, temporarily sated.

SUNDAY, OCTOBER 9

Today I took Walter and Marco to see Walter's beloved Schalke 04 play Rot-Weiss Essen. The train trip to Gelsenkirchen took almost two hours, and we were inside the ground with more than one to spare, which at least ensured an excellent spot at the front close to the halfway line. Neither Walter nor Marco had been to a professional game before, and I hadn't seen one for more than fifteen years, so it was a journey of discovery for all of us.

The boys took the wait in their stride, taking in the atmosphere as the stadium slowly filled up. The visibility was poor, and I spent most of the hour silently begging the fog not to thicken and cause a postponement. My prayer was eventually answered just before kickoff when a pale lemony sun forced its way through the mist.

I've rarely seen Walter look happier than he did when his heroes ran out. He recognized all the Schalke players from the album of pictures he has at home, and gleefully shared their identities with Marco and me, along with potted histories and sundry statistics. Most of the Schalke players had also played for the national team at some point, and one, Fritz Szepan, was the current national captain.

Even I could see Szepan was a special player, but the muddy pitch clearly favored powerful players over skillful ones, and the Essen team seemed full of young giants. One of these scored early in the second half, and we were bracing ourselves for defeat when Walter's other favorite, Ernst Kuzorra, scored a dramatic last-minute equalizer. Given the circumstances, the draw felt like a win, and our walk back to the station verged on the triumphant.

We had stepped outside our troubles for an afternoon, and on the train coming back, I saw the look on Walter's face that I'd been half-expecting—part confused, wholly guilty.

It was okay to enjoy things, I told him. His mother would want him to.

"I know that," he said. "It's just hard to do."

MONDAY, OCTOBER 10

Andreas has given me a shock this evening. He has known for quite a while that my political leanings are, like Anna's, the sort best kept under one's hat in National Socialist Germany. And since, unlike Anna, I have no children to care for, Andreas might well have suspected that I was still actively involved in some way or other. But nothing was said, no questions asked, until this evening.

When I took him a cup of what passes for chocolate these days, he asked if I had a few minutes to talk, and when I said yes, he suggested I close the door.

"Josef," he began, "I've been doing some thinking." He said that during the week he'd been really ill, he hadn't been able to stop worrying about what would happen to Walter if he died. Who would look after the boy? He knew that Verena would be willing, but she would have no legal standing, and he doubted the state would provide her with one, given her son's unfortunate ancestry. Erich should be back soon, but it was far from certain—the boy might do something stupid again, or the regime might simply decide they liked his forced labor. And if war came, they'd put him in uniform and take him off to fight. As for Anna, it would probably be years before she came back. If she ever did.

He looked at me, or at least turned his milky eyes in my direction.

I didn't know how to reply. I wanted to say I'd look after Walter but knew I'd be making a promise I might not be able to keep.

And that was when Andreas surprised me.

"I may be wrong," he said, "but I think there may come a day when you will have to leave us. And Germany too," he added pointedly. "And I'm hoping you might consider taking Walter with you."

I was stunned.

"He likes you," Andreas continued. "He trusts you. And I trust you to bring him back to his family if and when that becomes possible. If he stays, and I die, and Erich isn't here, then the bastards will take him. He'll end up in an orphanage, alone and at anyone's mercy until he's old enough to wear a uniform." He gave me the blind man's stare. "Well, say something."

I laughed, which made him do the same. "Andreas," I said, "I like Walter. I love Walter." I hesitated, but only out of habit. "And you're right—I may have to leave in a hurry. But I don't know where I'd be going," I added with rather less candor, "and I'm not at all sure—"

"Wherever it is," he said, cutting me off, "he'll be better off with you than on his own. But I realize it's a lot to ask."

I told him it wasn't. That being asked was an honor. But that I'd have to think about it.

And I have been now for a couple of hours. I would love to believe that Walter would be better off with me, but when I leave here, it will probably be for Moscow, where prison, death, or another Comintern mission awaits. All would involve leaving Walter, and I can't persuade myself that a Moscow orphanage would be any improvement on one in Hamm. At least he speaks the language here.

I could of course refuse Moscow's recall. But that would mean spending the rest of my years one step ahead of Yezhov's assassins. Which is not a life I would want to inflict on anyone else, let alone a twelve-year-old boy.

TUESDAY, OCTOBER 11

With a heavy heart, I must complete my account of events in Sofia.

Our bombing of the cathedral killed a lot of prominent people—a former minister of war, an army commander, mayors and governors, the chief of police—but nowhere near enough of the ones that mattered. Too many of those we were after were pulled alive from the rubble, in some cases with barely a scratch. We had wounded the beast badly enough to enrage it, scared it enough to invite a terrible vengeance.

For twenty-four hours the city seemed stunned by the enormity of what had happened. But this wasn't the calm before a revolutionary storm. There was no popular uprising, no waves of strikes or demonstrations. Zinoviev's "maturing situation" was nowhere to be seen.

The forces of reaction showed no such reluctance to assert their strength, and soon the streets were full of police and soldiers, the cells filling with comrades. I was smuggled out of Sofia in a farmer's cart and three night marches later was safe in Yugoslavia. But there was no escape for most of those comrades I'd come to know during my four-month stay. Those shot on the spot were often the lucky ones; torture and slow hanging were meted out to many who were captured alive.

By the time I got back to Moscow, the Bulgarian party was all but extinct in Bulgaria, and the Russians were asking why. I was lucky—before the catastrophe, Zinoviev had shown others my letter advising caution, claiming it exemplified a less than wholehearted approach, so he could hardly use me as a scapegoat for his own rash adventurism. I found myself on the same side as Comrade Stalin, which then as now was the safest place to be.

It was only much later that a comrade I met in Moscow told me what had happened to Yasen and Vyara. The Bulgarian authorities, in their determination to prove that the Soviet Union had been behind the cathedral bombing, had tortured their way to learning that a Comintern rep had indeed been present in Sofia and then tortured their way to finding out which locals had harbored him. Yasen they hanged with wire; Vyara they raped and burned, before cutting out her unborn child.

When I consider abandoning my Comintern duty to take care of one German boy, it's people like them who give me pause. I owe them, every last one of them over the years, who suffered and died for a world not run by the rich and the powerful. I owe it to them to continue the struggle.

THURSDAY, OCTOBER 13

Ruchay and I passed each other on the street today. He hesitated when he saw me, as if he had something he wanted to say, but then lowered his head and hurried on.

SUNDAY, OCTOBER 16

Setting down my memories of Sofia cured me of wanting to write for several days. Not that there's been much to write about—the house has been ticking over, adults and children alike seeing to their daily duties at work and school. The only bad news has been a lack of good news.

This morning, while the boys were playing football outside, Andreas, Verena, and I had a conversation about Walter. We agreed that all things considered he's bearing up well and that expecting anything more would be foolish. Verena has her son as an unwitting informant, and according to Marco, Walter is keeping very much to himself at school, keeping old friends at a distance, and refusing to be provoked by his enemies. But "he's still Walter," as Marco puts it. Out of the mouths of babes.

We talked about my taking another trip downtown to see the Gestapo, but agreed that if Kriminalsekretär Appel had any news, he would let us know, and that pestering him would be counterproductive. I felt relieved, then guilty for feeling it. If we don't hear anything by the end of the month, I will pay them a visit.

I have of course been thinking about what Andreas said last week, that if I have to leave, I should consider taking Walter with me. And since writing about Bulgaria, I've also been agonizing over my mission. Neither requires an instant decision, and I realize I'm letting things drift until circumstances force my hand. Andreas may fall ill again and die. He may not. With each passing week, the day set for Erich's release grows closer, and I can only hope that they actually let him go.

As far as my work for the party's concerned, there's much less chance of a calamitous surprise. If no one turns up at the next *treff* in two weeks' time, the liaison people in Amsterdam will assume that something unforeseen has occurred—I could have broken an ankle or already been tortured to death—and they will wait at least another month before sending someone else in to find out.

Over the last few days, I have had long conversations with

Franke and Opatz, two of the three whom I should have already invited to form a cell. Neither man gave me reason to doubt him, and once Erich returns I shall take that step. The two-month delay will mean much more to Walter than Hitler.

One thing I asked both Franke and Opatz—something I should have asked them before—was why they weren't in Müller's Working Group. They both gave me the same answer: that in the current situation, talking felt like a waste of time.

I neither agree nor disagree—in my experience it depends on who you are. Some comrades rely on the sense of solidarity that "talking" builds to fortify their commitment. Others don't. They will be true as long as they believe in themselves.

THURSDAY, OCTOBER 20

The Czech bourgeoisie has wasted no time in turning the loss of the Sudetenland to its advantage. With Beneš gone, the new government has banned the Communist Party and started persecuting the country's Jews in earnest. All Jewish teachers have been suspended, and the confiscation of all Jewish-owned businesses is underway.

I expected better of the Czechs. God knows why.

SATURDAY, OCTOBER 22

Walter and I went to the barber's this morning and took turns waiting for each other to be sheared. I had offered to bring Marco as well, but should have realized that Verena takes care of her son's crinkly hair. An average German barber wouldn't know how to deal with it, and she's probably rightly afraid of the comments Marco might get from the man and his other customers.

Walter and I had only football talk and several bad jokes to contend with, as the Führer looked on disapprovingly from his place on the wall. Most of the barber's creams and lotions are now imprinted with swastikas, and I found myself wondering if the barber himself should have one tattooed on his forehead.

We finally emerged into the cold grey morning, and I was about to offer coffee and cake when Walter preempted me. "It's Mama's birthday today," he said, almost aggressively, as if everyone else were deliberately ignoring the fact. "She's thirty-seven," he added. "I want to buy some flowers and a box of Mohrenköpfe. It's her favorite cake, and I thought we could all have one for supper. And think of her." He looked up at me and probably saw the surprise in my face. "Does that sound silly?"

I said it most certainly didn't.

We went to the confectioner's first, where Walter picked the most expensive-looking Mohrenköpfe on display. He had obviously been saving the pocket money Verena gives him on Anna's behalf, but watching him counting out his coins, I realized he was coming up short and insisted on sharing the cost. He tried to protest but relented when I pointed out he'd have more to spend on the flowers.

With it being almost November, the choice at the stall was limited, but there were more than enough dark red roses for a decent bunch. Either the florist was having a generous day, or she saw the feeling in Walter's eyes, because she gave him the lot at a vastly reduced rate.

When we got home, Verena brought out a vase, and the roses took pride of place on the dining room sideboard. This evening we each had one of the cream-filled, chocolate-glazed cakes and sang the birthday song for Anna. I found myself shedding tears for the first time in twenty years, and I wasn't alone—both boys, Jakob, Verena, and Andreas, all of them were crying. Even Gerritzen seemed close to tears, leaving Buchloh just looking stunned, as if he'd stumbled into a mass nervous breakdown.

If an Indian I met in Peru is right, and feelings cross countries like radio waves, then Anna will have had a lump in her throat.

MONDAY, OCTOBER 24

An unexpected development at work. There are one or more noticeboards in most of the buildings that make up the Reichsbahn complex in Hamm, and when the morning shift clocked on this morning, a copy of the same exposé was pinned to each and every one of them. The man accused is Dietmar Hefelmann, who's in charge of the depot's Labor Front section. The accusation, spelled out in exquisite detail, and with an abundance of damning statistics, is that a substantial proportion of our Labor Front dues over the last three years have disappeared into his pockets. There was even a list of his purchases, which include a Frisian Islands beach house, the latest Adler Trumpf motorcar, and a flat in Dortmund for a woman named Lulu.

Now, hardly anyone of my acquaintance has ever believed that his or her Labor Front subscription ended up benefitting laborers, but seeing what they really were being spent on spelled out like this in black and white was still a bit of a shock. Not to mention enraging.

I read only half of the piece myself. The sheet was ripped from the board in front of my eyes by one of Hefelmann's minions. Many didn't see it at all, because every copy was found and removed before an hour had gone by. But enough had read it for word of mouth to do the rest, and by midmorning there were few who remained in ignorance of either the gist or the details. In our dispatch office, the only men wearing smiles were the cynics—even some of the regime's staunchest supporters were incandescent with rage.

I took frequent glances through the window, half expecting a visit from the Gestapo, but no cars pulled into the lot. It looked as if no one had reported the outrage—were Hefelmann and his cronies more afraid of an investigation than they were of their angry members? If so, we members had a pretty strong hand.

In the old days, when the unions actually meant something, the stewards would have come around with the time and place of a meeting. In 1938 it's more like Chinese whispers, with the word getting around by something akin to osmosis. Noon in the canteen was what filtered through, and when the time came, the place was packed. Hefelmann's minions had tried to block the entrance, but had been beaten back by sheer weight of numbers and were now stuck in the middle of the crowd, nervously eyeing their neighbors.

Several men got up on one of the tables to speak, the canteen women behind them offering vocal encouragement. Müller was one of the speakers and, like all the others, refused to condemn the Labor Front. It was rotten apples like Hefelmann whom they objected to, men whose venal ways brought the whole organization into disrepute. "The Führer will be furious!" Müller concluded, not even bothering to conceal his smile. Half his audience grimly applauded; the other half laughed as they did so.

It was agreed that a three-man delegation—Müller, Joachim Wosz and an engineer I didn't know—would visit the works director and demand Hefelmann's dismissal and prosecution. It duly did so and, as we learned within the hour, were duly fobbed off. The bosses were either fighting each other or waiting for party instructions. I was still keeping one eye on the window, but by the time our shift ended, the Gestapo remained conspicuous by their absence.

So what will happen next? Given the wealth of detail in the original accusation, I presume that the author won't be that hard to catch. There can't be that many men with access to that sort of information. So are Hefelmann and co. now wondering what to do with the author? Handing him over to the police will bring the whole business into the open and enrage his fellow workers. Dealing with him themselves might keep the matter under wraps for a while, but having a workmate fished out of the canal will make the rest of us even angrier.

The other option for those in power is to cut their losses and toss Hefelmann overboard, hoping thereby to nip the business in the bud. Could they do that and keep face?

A cold look at the facts suggests that neither side is in a good position. If the Nazis don't dare call the workers' bluff, they will either be tarred with Hefelmann's sordid brush or look like people who abandon their own. But if they do call that bluff, then the workers will have a problem. Strikes of any kind are illegal, and the way things are going stopping to catch your breath will soon be considered sabotage. How many KZ consignments will it take to bring the workforce back into line?

There is of course another explanation for what happened today—that it's all a provocation, designed to bring troublemakers into the open. But that doesn't seem likely. I can imagine Hefelmann having enemies on his own side who would consider his downfall a collateral bonus, but such a scheme seems far too subtle for the people involved. These are men who adore boots and whips.

TUESDAY, OCTOBER 25

The unmasking of Hefelmann's corruption was not a provocation. This morning word spread through the works that a

man named Wilhelm Spoerl has been arrested and is helping
the Gestapo with their inquiries. He's an accountant in the
Labor Front office, which makes Hefelmann's guilt more or
less certain, because who could be better placed to know?

With the management saying nothing, another workers'
meeting was called for noon in the canteen. We arrived to
find widely separate parts of the ceiling were being painted,
a ploy about as subtle as a *Der Stürmer* editorial. Everyone
just moved outside, ignoring demands from Hefelmann's
men that we all return to work. The meeting was held in
the parking lot, and after several angry speeches, an almost
unanimous vote sent our delegation back to the bosses for
some sort of clear response.

One was promised but has still not been given. Management is taking care not to exacerbate matters—the Gestapo
was noticeably missing in action again—hoping that soon it
will all blow away and that things will get back to normal.

If the mood at this evening's Working Group was anything
to go by, I think they'll have a long wait. Müller and Wosz
had invited the third member of the delegation to join us,
and the only thing on the agenda was what our next move
should be. It felt like the twenties all over again. Here we
were, a bunch of comrades gnawing away at a juicy political
bone, working out ways to strengthen ourselves and weaken
the opposition.

As usual, Giesemann pushed the more extreme options—
working to rule, wildcat walkouts, a full-on strike. He had a few
supporters for once, but wiser heads prevailed. Most people
knew that pushing too hard would be a mistake; it was better
to tell the bosses that we sought a resolution that suited both
them and us. Our threats would need to be regretful—that we
were holding the wilder ones back, that a failure to meet our
demands would result in a potentially crippling lack of cooper-
ation, an epidemic of absenteeism, slow working, and holdups

caused by accidents. That the very last thing the Reichsbahn needed in times like these was a collapse in morale.

And to avoid these deeply unpleasant results, all that management needed to do was sack the man who had brought disgrace on their organization and reinstate the one who had bravely exposed him. Heil Hitler!

Whether or not our tactics will work remains to be seen, but I walked back home from the meeting feeling more than a little exhilarated.

WEDNESDAY, OCTOBER 26

Walter's history teacher has been replaced, and as far as Walter's aware, no explanation has been offered to any of his classes. If the man has been sacked or even arrested, no one is saying why or what for. But rumors abound. According to Walter, Herr Scheringer was one of his better teachers. He had tried to be fair to everyone—not supporting one point of view and dismissing others, but encouraging his pupils to look at them all and make up their own minds. He hadn't expressed any criticism of current developments in Walter's class, but he had often asked the more fanatical boys to justify their viewpoints, and their attempts to do so had sometimes been embarrassingly stupid.

"He sounds like a good teacher," I said, pleased that Walter had come up to my room to discuss the matter. Since Anna's transfer, he hasn't shared as much as he used to.

"His replacement arrived today," Walter told me. Herr Bodenschatz was young and very nervous, "as if he's afraid of making mistakes." And the very first homework he'd set was an essay on the Führer's genius.

"So what should I say?" Walter asked.

"Say that he's brought ten million Germans back to the fatherland without starting a war," I began.

"But the Austrians were never part of the fatherland," Walter protested.

I shook my head. "I don't think you need to point that out. Say that he's made Germany strong and feared and made our enemies look weak and divided."

"Which is true. But . . ."

I told him the English had a phrase: "the truth, the whole truth, and nothing but the truth."

"So what you just said is the truth, but not the whole truth."

"Exactly. I don't expect this teacher will want to hear the whole truth."

"No, I'm sure he won't. But what do you think? Is the Führer a genius, at least in part?"

"Time will tell. If he's a genius, he'll know when to stop."

Walter thought about that. "Maybe he's an evil genius," he said. "Like Fu Manchu."

I said I didn't think Herr Bodenschatz would like that comparison.

The grin was pure Walter.

THURSDAY, OCTOBER 27

It has taken us two days to prevail, but the authorities have finally conceded defeat. The mood at work over those forty-eight hours has been sufficiently mutinous—several quarrels that turned into fights, a rash of accidents and time-consuming breakdowns, a veritable deluge of sick notes—that they must have felt they had no choice. Our heroic accountant has been released and was back at work this afternoon, moving rather gingerly but without any obvious bruising where it shows. Dietmar Hefelmann has been removed from his position, and the police will "consider the possibility" of bringing charges. I'll believe that when I see it—the more likely outcome is that he'll just swap places with another official who's had his hand in the jar somewhere else.

The victory isn't complete, but it certainly has been a victory. The workers have shown their solidarity and consequent power for the first time in years, and the enemy looks more vulnerable than it did. A spell has been broken, and things that seemed out of the question seem possible again. Hope is contagious. When I take the plunge and ask my chosen men to do the same, it won't just feel, to them or me, as if I'm looking for sacrificial lambs.

FRIDAY, OCTOBER 28

Those Jews with Polish citizenship who currently live in Germany are facing a crisis. Yesterday our government announced its decision to deport them, and today the Poles announced their refusal to take them back. Around fifteen thousand Jews have been shoved across the border—or, more accurately, into the no-man's-land between the two countries—and are stuck there with no food or shelter until either Berlin or Warsaw backs down.

What's even more depressing is my strong suspicion that large majorities of the German and Polish populations think their government should stick to its guns. It's hard to believe how much better people might be when they seem so determined to show you what they are.

SATURDAY, OCTOBER 29

It's two in the morning, and the house is wrapped in silence. Jakob and I spent the evening at the Social Club, and after drinking as much as we did, I didn't foresee any problem falling asleep. But for once too much alcohol had the opposite effect, and after tossing in bed for a couple of hours, I got myself up again, retrieved this journal from its hiding place in the window frame, and sat down by my window to write.

Today—yesterday now—was the last Saturday of the month, and I didn't turn up for the *treff* in Bochum. Instead I took a very long walk into the countryside, and slowly put aside the mental picture of Dieter waiting in vain for those thirty minutes our protocol dictates. To say I felt guilty would be to overstate, but I will admit to that sense of unease that goes with behaving uncharacteristically. I reminded myself that Dieter wouldn't be risking a few days in Germany to see only me. I told myself that I had given the Comintern fifteen years of my life and that it could spare a few weeks in return. And I enjoyed my walk.

Immersion in the natural world has always brought me peace, and as a boy my favored futures included exploring, foresting, and plant gathering. At Walter's age I had a near-encyclopedic knowledge of trees, now mostly forgotten after twenty years living not just in cities but in those neighborhoods less blessed with space and greenery. Would I have been happier as a botanist? Perhaps. But happiness and fulfillment are different things, and I have often felt fulfilled in the life I chose. If someone had asked me a few months ago, I would have denied I had any lasting regrets gnawing away at my heart, and that remains more true than not. But if I had to pick one, it would be the lack of closeness in my life. I have not been a monk, but Lin was the first and last woman I know I loved, and leaving her that night was the greatest mistake of my life.

I suppose everyone has regrets. There are always choices to be made, and who can choose right each and every time? Esther Brennan used to quote me a line from one of the women detective writers she loves—as usual I can't remember the name—to the effect that people always have the defects of their qualities. And of course vice versa.

I imagine lives are much the same.

MONDAY, OCTOBER 31

A momentary respite from our national woes. This evening's extraordinary news concerned an American radio adaption of H. G. Wells's *The War of the Worlds*, a book I read in a Ukrainian trench with more amusement than fright, having used up all my reserves of the latter on the war going on around me. This new American adaptation, which went on the air yesterday evening, was apparently too realistic, and succeeded in convincing large numbers of Americans that beings from Mars had invaded their country. The authorities were swamped with alarm calls, frightened mobs roamed the streets, and emergency rooms filled up with people displaying serious symptoms of shock.

Given that the broadcast supposedly offered live coverage of a full-scale war—from the initial landings all the way to the Martians' ultimate victory—in under forty-five minutes, one has to wonder just how gullible many Americans are.

But then I remember the millions of Germans who voted for Hitler, most of whom are still insisting they were right.

TUESDAY, NOVEMBER 1

Gelnhausen in Hesse is the latest small town to declare itself "free of Jews." The choice of phrase is interesting as well as repugnant, evoking, as it does, something medical. The Aryan residents of Gelnhausen have ejected more than a group of people—like a medieval town casting out those stricken with plague, they believe they have saved themselves from future infection.

People seem indifferent to this ludicrous cruelty. At work, in town, wherever I go, I never hear anyone speak against it. I know most people prefer to keep their heads down, and I know that minority groups, religious and racial, have always made for convenient scapegoats. There's usually some small grain of truth in the accusations, and it's true that the Jews, for historical reasons, had come to wield a disproportionate influence in German financial and professional circles.

But a disease?

It's only twenty years since tens of thousands of Jews were fighting in the trenches for the old Germany. I had several Jewish brothers-in-arms, some of whom I discovered were Jews only after long acquaintances. When everyone's living that close to death, nobody cares very much about ancestry.

But now it seems that nothing matters more. The Nazis are truly obsessive where the Jews are concerned—so much so that it's hard to believe they're using them as scapegoats. It isn't cynicism at work here; it's unadulterated loathing, a hatred so devoid of reason that only a psychiatrist could hope to unravel it.

WEDNESDAY, NOVEMBER 2

The projected Rhine-Main-Danube Canal was in the news again today, and I remembered the map Walter drew for his homework back in June. Only a few months have passed, but it feels like so much longer.

THURSDAY, NOVEMBER 3

I visited the Gestapo office after work. I wasn't expecting any fresh news but felt an obligation to check. Kriminalsekretär

Appel was as considerate as could be expected, reminding me almost apologetically that no release date is set for those imprisoned as enemies of the state. I came away wondering what the man is doing in the Gestapo, but as Jakob later reminded me, the political police have been around much longer than the Nazis, and many men recruited before the change of government are still in their posts.

SATURDAY, NOVEMBER 5

More executions were announced on the wireless this evening between pieces of classical music. One minute we were listening to a Beethoven piano concerto, the next to a voice that could barely contain its joy in slaughter, then to some playful piece by Mozart. These people are hardly sentient.

Their victims were all convicted of treason, which has always struck me as a fairly strange notion. When I was about Walter's age, I remember asking my father why one's country should demand more loyalty than friends, family, or conscience, and seeing the look of surprise on his face when he found he lacked a convincing answer.

There's no doubt I'm betraying my country, if by country you mean its government. I don't consider myself a traitor to the German people—quite the contrary. Those who work for the Comintern see themselves as serving humanity as a whole.

There are layers and layers. The Nazis—and any other capitalist regime—would say I betray my country by working for a foreign power. The Comintern would say I'm betraying the international proletariat by allowing my involvement with a single family to distract me from political work.

I would be betraying my conscience if I acted any other way.

✦ ✦ ✦

MONDAY, NOVEMBER 7

At lunchtime today, the news went around the canteen that a diplomat had been shot at the German embassy in Paris. The evening news added more detail—the diplomat's name is Ernst vom Rath, and he's now fighting for his life in a Paris hospital. More to the point as far as the world is concerned, his assailant, now under French lock and key, is a Polish Jew.

By what might seem an extraordinary coincidence, the editors of our two evening papers used identical words—"an attack by world Jewry on the Third Reich"—to describe the attempted murder, and the exact same phrase—"the heaviest consequences for Germany's Jews"—to promise retribution.

Hitler—or someone in his circle—has seen an opportunity.

TUESDAY, NOVEMBER 8

Several synagogues have been destroyed today, all apparently in Hesse and Hannover. There's no reason to think that the people of these two provinces have a particular hatred of Jews, so I suspect that the local parties were following Berlin's orders. Trial balloons, perhaps, to see how far they can go without risking a public backlash. Quite a long way, I should think.

The Polish Jew's act has been used to justify further restrictions. The Jews are no longer allowed to publish any papers or magazines, and their children are henceforth barred from attending state elementary schools. It's hard to see how the Nazis could make Jewish life more difficult, but if there is a way, I'm sure they'll find it.

At the end of the wireless news, Jakob suggested, without a great deal of conviction, that today's excesses might be enough to satisfy the bastards. I hope he's right, but I doubt it. Vom Rath remains critically injured in his hospital bed, and if he dies they'll have a brand-new hook on which to hang their bloodlust.

As if to rub salt in the wound, today the Führer chose to bring up last week's American broadcast of "The War of the Worlds." According to Hitler, the show offered proof of the "corrupt condition" and "decadent state of affairs" that characterizes the Western democracies.

WEDNESDAY, NOVEMBER 9

The press is attributing yesterday's destruction of synagogues, homes, and shops in Hesse and Hannover to "the spontaneous rage of the German people." If so, we Germans are not so angry today, because there haven't been many new incidents. Perhaps we're over the worst, at least for a while.

THURSDAY, NOVEMBER 10

How wrong can you be? The last twenty-fours have been terrible.

I went to bed last night thinking the worst might be over, and was woken an hour or so later by what sounded like a woman's scream. I got up and went to the window, but all I could see at first was our empty street. And then, over the roofs, I noticed a bank of dark smoke smudging the starless sky and a faint orange glow that lined the horizon. With the window open, I could hear distant shouts from what sounded like several directions.

I got dressed and went downstairs, intent on investigation. Given that I'm a foreign agent, given that I'm needed here in this house, it would have been wiser to stay in bed, and read about it all in the morning paper. Which, of course, is what most of my fellow Germans did. Not Jakob, though—he was already buttoning up his coat when I reached the hall. Armed only with curiosity, we let ourselves out and started walking.

The noise grew louder as we made our way into the center of town, and I didn't think it was just the narrowing distance. The further we got the surer we were that the town synagogue was the source of much of the din, and in that we weren't mistaken. When we reached the old building, we found it was being demolished. All the windows had already been smashed, and a brownshirt with a sledgehammer was dementedly swinging it against the heavy doors. All this was lit by the bonfire in front of the building, which other storm troopers kept refueling with stuff they brought out from within. Off to one side, three men whom I took to be Jewish elders were being held under guard by another two brownshirts, and each time a new trove of holy effects was consigned to the flames one of them let out a desperate wail. Until one of the brownshirts jabbed a rifle butt hard in the man's face.

I remembered what Dariusz Müller had told me, that there were more than four hundred Jews living in Hamm, that the Jewish presence in the town went back to the thirteenth century. Time enough, you'd think, for some mutual understanding.

Considering the hour, quite a crowd had gathered—a hundred or more, some of them children. Examining the faces in the bonfire glow, I saw few looks of disgust and many of grim satisfaction. Each time a brownshirt brought out more books or scrolls for the flames most of the children and some adults wildly clapped. "Burn the whole place down!" one woman shouted, but I could see why they wouldn't—the adjoining buildings were much too close.

Jakob noticed more activity further up the street, and we went to see what was happening there. As we approached a man came literally flying out of a doorway, swiftly followed by what looked like his wife and children and rather more slowly by two grinning brownshirts. From inside came the sounds of a home—a life—being ripped to shreds.

Our instinctive move toward the man's prone figure was not to the brownshirts' liking. "You two—get lost!" one of them said.

We stopped but stood our ground and might have been in trouble if an open lorry hadn't driven up a few seconds later. The driver and his companion were both wearing black, and so were the two who got down from the already crowded back. They pulled the man to his feet; half dragged, half carried him to their vehicle; and bundled him over the tail-gate. The woman's wail was cut short by another rifle butt, and the children threw themselves across her body like a human shield.

"What can we do?" Jakob said, his tone of resignation an answer in itself.

Two choices, I thought. We could do nothing, or we could get ourselves arrested. There was shock and sympathy on the faces of quite a few onlookers, but the most opposition any-one offered was a woman shouting, "What have they done to you?" and a man muttering, "Fucking bullies."

The two of us walked home, hearing cries in the distance, watching the sky turn slowly redder as fires blazed and mul-tiplied. And shutting our door behind us, far from shutting it out, merely gave free rein to our shame and sense of impo-tence.

I slept badly and was awake an hour ahead of my usual

time. Taking the opportunity, I went for a walk in the gathering light, retracing our steps from last night. The synagogue was a ruin, two of the outer walls leaning drunkenly inward, like paralyzed supplicants. Charred fragments of holy scrolls were visible in the smoldering bonfire embers.

I bought a morning paper—as I'd suspected, vom Rath died yesterday.

Walking on I saw several homes badly damaged by fire but no sign of former occupants. The two Jewish shops I knew about were both burnt out, shards from their large front windows littering the pavement. Scavengers in school uniforms were sifting through the embers.

I saw no Jews, alive or dead.

Almost everyone I did see looked stunned, but I talked only to those who also looked saddened. I was sometimes mistaken—as one woman put it, "If they murder our diplomats, what do they expect?"—but usually correct. From one person after another, I got the sense that their deepest fears had come true. What they had long suspected, but hadn't allowed themselves to believe, was staring them full in the face.

Back home, our breakfast table seemed as punch-drunk as the town. Walter was eager for information, and although I saw no reason to hold anything back, I also warned him that today would not be a day for speaking one's mind—that feelings would be running high, that people would be keener than usual to emphasize their loyalty.

Work was much the same, a collective sigh and shake of the head. There were exceptions—on one side some with self-satisfied smirks, on the other a few having obvious trouble repressing their anger. Could this be the end of Germany's infatuation with the Nazis and their lunatic leader? Probably not, but I suspect quite a few are telling themselves that enough is enough.

This evening's papers are sparse on details, but the list of towns and cities in which the people have expressed their "spontaneous rage" is quite exhaustive. The river of hatred has finally burst its banks, and where we go from here is anyone's guess. If nothing else, this exhibition of barbarism is a gauntlet thrown at the feet of the bourgeois democracies, but if Évian was anything to go by, it's not one they'll want to pick up.

SATURDAY, NOVEMBER 12

Like a drunk with a truly awful hangover, the country is slowly coming to terms with what it saw of itself in the mirror three long nights ago. Denial is one popular cure, anger another. The regime's press and wireless are still immersed in self-congratulation.

Thousands of Jews have been arrested and taken away, presumably to camps. Four perished here in Hamm, which probably means that hundreds died across the country. Those left free are mostly clinging together for safety, although it must be said that some have been taken in by goyish friends and neighbors. I imagine the queues for exit visas are longer than ever.

All I know of the foreign reaction is what the regime tells us, which isn't very much. Mussolini has apparently been inspired to start his own anti-Jewish crusade. He must have been swayed by the sadistic violence that made up so much of the newsreel footage.

Göring, meanwhile, has been talking up Madagascar as a future home for Europe's Jews. His atlas must have fallen open at that particular page, because I can't think of any other reason for choosing a French-owned tropical island as a possible home for the people of Mendelssohn, Einstein, and Marx.

More chilling, for those with the slightest regard for truth or justice, is the regime's announcement that the Jews should pay for the damage done by its own murderous rampage, with each individual or family obliged to surrender a fifth of all assets.

MONDAY, NOVEMBER 14

The next Working Group was scheduled for Wednesday, but Müller and Wosz brought it forward a couple of days, and once the meeting was underway, I understood why. The "Night of Broken Glass"—as some callous wit in Berlin has dubbed last week's assault on the Jews—might have persuaded most Germans to push their heads even farther into the sand, but it seems to have had the opposite effect on those who already despised the regime. The sort of resistance that everyone thought both futile and reckless is suddenly back on the table.

Müller and Wosz had obviously thought things through. For the first fifteen minutes, they let everyone else pour out their feelings—how appalled and ashamed each person felt, how sitting back and doing nothing was no longer an option he or she could live with. I was one of the few to counsel caution, mostly because I didn't want people to go too far in front of Paul Giesemann. He, of course, was the one most angered, the one who could hardly wait to take the bastards on.

Müller then calmed things down. He said he could see that most of those present were keen to step things up and that he and Wosz had been thinking about how we could do that. But as everyone there knew, there would be risks involved, and he understood why some would be unwilling to take them. Those comrades should feel free to opt out and not attend the next meeting, which would take place on November 30. In the meantime, those who opted in should set down ideas of their own for the group to discuss.

I walked home feeling both intrigued and apprehensive, and as I write I'm aware that one ear is cocked for a car in the street or a knock on the outside door. Müller and Wosz didn't cross the line into illegality, but they more or less announced their intention of doing so, and if I am right about Giese-mann, the Gestapo may be picking us up one by one. But I doubt it. Everything I know about the Gestapo—and all the other similar organizations I've had the misfortune to deal with—tells me that they'll wait, let plots unfold and damning evidence gather, before they tighten their net. My late uncle Berndt once told me that expectation always satisfies more than achievement, and where security police are concerned, I think he might have been right.

So what should I do about Giesemann in the meantime? Share my suspicions with Müller is the obvious answer, but he'll want to know why I suspect the young man, and that will be hard to explain without revealing my previous expe-rience in this sort of situation. I could take a leaf out of the Nazis' book and denounce him by anonymous letter, but that seems no way to deliver what could well be a death sentence. If Giesemann really is an informer, then he does need to die, or some of us will surely die instead. But if he's just an impa-tient young man . . .

I remember when another comrade had to be killed in similar circumstances. It was in Essen in 1923, just before the rising was called off. We all felt bad about it, because we knew he'd done it only to ward off a police threat to arrest his handicapped sister. Or thought we knew. We felt a whole lot worse later on, when we found out the traitor was some-body else.

❧ ❧ ❧

WEDNESDAY, NOVEMBER 16

When I came home from work this evening, Andreas, Walter, and Erich were sitting around the kitchen table. Erich leapt to his feet and warmly shook my hand—clearly Andreas or Walter had told him that I've been doing my best to help out.

Andreas explained that the authorities had been short of places for all the Jews arrested last week, so Erich had been let out three weeks early. "Him and a lot of others," he added, managing to sound both pleased and disgusted.

The old man did look remarkably happy, though, and Walter's eyes were as bright as I'd seen them in months. Erich, by contrast, seemed more than a little distracted, and I assumed that he'd only just found out that his mother was in a KZ. He looked thinner than I remembered but also fitter—five months' hard labor had clearly not beaten him down.

I left the family to their reunion and walked up to my room thinking how astonishing it was that something as black as the "Night of Broken Glass" could have a silver lining.

I expected to see Erich at supper, but according to Walter, Erich had walked across town to deliver a fellow inmate's message. Erich must know that Ruchay is gone, and if Andreas has told him that Ruchay was largely responsible for his mother's arrest, then I trust Andreas has also impressed on his older grandson that looking after a brother requires him to stay out of prison.

If, as I expect, Erich rises to the occasion and does what his mother would want him to do, that will be good news for all concerned. Including, of course, myself. No longer indispensable here, I can get back to my real work. A state of affairs that finds me relieved, but feeling somewhat diminished.

✦ ✦ ✦

THURSDAY, NOVEMBER 17

Andreas was not at his best today, and after supper Jakob and I had a long talk with Erich. The months in prison have either changed the boy or—Jakob's view—brought out the one who was already there. He certainly looks different with an ordinary haircut and ordinary clothes—up until yesterday I'd only ever seen him in uniform, the one worn for work or the one he donned as a Traveling Dude. But that's just on the surface. There's also a stillness about him that's new; all the old restless evasion is gone. The youth has turned into a man.

He thanked us for helping to look after his family and said he hoped he'd manage half as well. He's assuming, probably rightly—the labor shortage gets worse each year—that they'll give him his old job back and plans to apply at the office first thing tomorrow, with a view to starting on Monday. The doctor is going to visit Andreas tomorrow, and Erich intends to ask him how the old man really is.

I didn't want to give the young man any more worries than he already had, but I felt I had to ask—what would happen if there was a war and he was called up?

He said he didn't know but that he hoped Verena would look after Walter. When I pointed out her lack of legal status where Walter was concerned, he looked surprised. "Surely if war breaks out, they'll have more important things to worry about. And maybe our mother will be back before then."

I shrugged.

He sighed. "All I can do is play it by ear," he admitted. "Sometimes that's all you can do."

Which was true enough. Andreas obviously hadn't told

Erich about asking me to take Walter out of the Reich—
either Andreas is protecting my secrets, or he no longer sees
it as relevant now that Erich is back. Which it isn't.

After the talk, Jakob and I went out for a beer and agreed
that we felt reassured. "Anna would be proud of him," Jakob
said, wiping away what looked like a tear.

She would. She will be.

I have decided to see Müller this weekend. I will say what
I feel about Giesemann and see where the conversation
goes from there. If that doesn't take me to prison, next
week I will start to put my resistance cell together. First
Schulte, then Franke, then Opatz. Three pieces. Three
gambles.

FRIDAY, NOVEMBER 18

This afternoon I contrived a few private moments with
Dariusz Müller and asked if he'd meet me tomorrow. He
seemed unsurprised by the request and readily agreed to
the time and place I suggested. I was left with the suspicion
that if I hadn't come to him, he would have come to me.

On a more exalted plane, our idiot foreign minister has
been bitterly complaining that we Germans inhabit a hostile
world. One, he might care to think how responsible he and
his puppet master are for provoking all the hostility—did he
really think the rest of the world would not be disgusted and
enraged by last week's pogrom and its aftermath? Two, he
might put himself in the place of people who really are up
against it, such as the Spanish Republicans whom his bombers are battering into submission. This week has seen more
Fascist victories in Spain, and it feels as if the end is near. It's
the left that's living in a hostile world, not evil buffoons like
Ribbentrop.

→ → →

SATURDAY, NOVEMBER 19

It was bitterly cold this morning but mercifully dry, given that I had decided Müller and I should meet in the open. He was sitting on the open lock gate when I got there, and we greeted each other like people well met by chance. There were other walkers strung out along the towpath, and several warmly wrapped fisherman exhaling clouds of breath in the frigid air. A kilometer or so to the south our workplace sprawled beneath its usual canopy of smoke.

I suggested we walk, and we did so in companionable silence for most of a minute.

"So why did you want to meet?" he finally asked.

I said that I wanted to explain why I'd been so cautious at Monday's meeting. That I believed Paul Giesemann was a Gestapo informer.

"And what makes you think so?" Müller asked in an unruffled tone.

"I have no definite proof," I admitted. "And I have tried to find some," I added, bending over backward on Giesemann's behalf.

"How?"

"I've followed him on several occasions, seen who he's spent time with. I've brought him up in conversations, listened to what others have to say about him."

"And?"

"And nothing."

"But you're still convinced."

"Ninety-five percent."

Müller gave me a sideways glance and waited until we had passed an angler and his tin of writhing maggots. "Just a layman's hunch?" he asked. "Or one based on experience?"

I told him the latter.

He smiled at that and pointedly asked me why had I come home to Germany.

The moment of truth. Or something close to it. I told him that watching events from afar, I'd begun to feel like a soldier gone AWOL, a man who'd left others to do his fighting for him.

"You were in the party," Müller said. It wasn't a question.

"And so were you," I countered, thinking it was time. "Anna told me they arrested you in '33," I added. She hadn't, but I had to know it from someone, and I wasn't yet willing to reveal my real employer.

"I was," Müller admitted.

"Why did they let you go?" I asked.

Another smile, thinner than the last. "Why do you think? Because I agreed to work for them."

"And have you? Do you?"

"Of course. But I have never knowingly put a comrade's life at risk. I have reported on waverers, on those not displaying enough enthusiasm. I've gotten people fired, but the way things there are, they soon get another job. I've strung the bastards along, and I've used them as much as they've used me. Knowing who they are and what they know will be important one of these days. Soon, I hope."

"A dangerous game," I said, somewhat superfluously.

Müller agreed that it was. But it was one he chose to play. "At the beginning I could have said no, taken some beatings, served my five years, and come home to the family and just kept my head down. It didn't appeal. I believe in the party. I always have."

It didn't seem the moment to mention that the party had rather less faith in him.

"And I'm serious about taking things to another level," he went on.

"Then you'll have to be certain of Giesemann."

"We are," he said, surprising me. "Wosz and I have been suspicious for a while. We searched his locker a few weeks ago and didn't find anything incriminating, but this week we went through his room and found a report he'd compiled on the group that was clearly intended for other eyes." Müller smiled. "He described you as 'probably harmless.'"

I allowed myself a moment of professional pride and then asked Müller whether Giesemann knew that both of them reported to the Gestapo. Because if so, Giesemann could use the knowledge to counteraccuse.

Müller said Giesemann might know. "They haven't told me about him, but they may trust him more than me. But it doesn't matter. Wosz and several of the others already know about me—I told them from the start—and they trust me."

"Do you know what you're going to do?"

Müller's brief scan of the heavens might have been a search for mercy. If so, he came up empty. "We have no choice, do we? We thought about forming another group, a secret one without Giesemann, and keeping the present one going to put him off the scent, but we'd spend more time and energy keeping up the deception than we would fighting the Nazis. And if we try and warn him off with threats, he'll take fright and have us all arrested. No, we have to kill him."

I could see the logic.

"Are you with us in this?" Müller asked.

"Yes," I told him.

He nodded. "Good. I'll let you know when and where."

We walked back separately, Müller a minute ahead of me. As I followed him up the towpath, I trawled back through our conversation, reaffirming my conviction that he was telling the truth. Twelve hours have passed since then, and I've had no reason to change my mind. No car has screeched to a halt outside, disgorging men in leather coats.

I doubt he believed me completely, but if he's who he says he is, and I'm who he thinks I am, then he'll know I can't be more open. The webs we weave.

That said, I think and hope we understand each other. Our new partnership may be a short one, but I hope it will give birth to something that lasts. If I don't feel like breaking out in carefree whistling or dancing with joy, it's because I've reached that familiar moment, the one where a singular secret existence gives way to reliance on another's discretion. Someone else knows, and—rationally or not—I'm suddenly feeling vulnerable.

SUNDAY, NOVEMBER 20

Gerritzen brought his new car over to show us. It's a small Mercedes convertible, which must have been expensive— how he afforded it, God only knows. He took Verena, Walter, and Marco out for a drive, which made me like him more—I can't see his Nazi friends or prospective father-in-law offering someone of mixed race a ride.

MONDAY, NOVEMBER 21

Anna is dead.

I heard the news from Verena, whose face looked raw from crying. She told me the letter had come in the late-morning post—*"Anna Gersdorff, died 14 November 1938, aged 37. Cause of death: pneumonia."*

I asked where the family was, and she said they were all in the kitchen.

I walked through with a heavy heart, the ache of loss held at bay by the thought of what I would find there. Over the years, I've seen hundreds of people struck down by sudden grief, and the faces came as no surprise. Andreas looked stunned and, for the first time since I'd met him, truly blind. Walter had his head on his grandfather's shoulder, and the tearstained face he turned toward me was utterly bereft.

I said how sorry I was, the words sounding trite and inadequate, the way they always do.

Andreas gave no sign that he'd heard, and Walter, polite to the last, whispered, "Thank you."

"Where's Erich?" I asked, after suddenly realizing where he might be.

Walter shook his head as if wondering why I cared.

"Does he know about Ruchay?" I asked Andreas.

The old man looked blank for a moment; then realization dawned. "Go after him, Josef," he said. "Please."

I took the first few streets at a run, the rest as fast as my shortage of breath and a stitch in my side would allow. There was no sign of police outside Ruchay's lodgings and no sounds of mayhem coming from within. When I knocked on the door and demanded to see him, the woman who answered gave me a look and told me to wait on the step.

Ruchay appeared, napkin in hand—I'd interrupted his dinner. He looked more than a little apprehensive, but not as if he'd just been beaten up.

"Anna Gersdorff is dead," I said bluntly, and he took a step backward as if he'd been hit.

"I didn't kill her," he said automatically, but the look on his face told a different story.

"Others think you did," I said, "so if I were you, I'd go away for a while. A couple of weeks looking after your mother, perhaps."

His face twisted into a smile. "Why would you care what happens to me?"

"I don't," I said coldly. "But I will be really upset if someone else gets punished for giving you what you deserve. So make yourself scarce."

I wanted to hit him myself, so I turned on my heel and recrossed the street, hearing the door close behind me. It seemed prudent to keep the house under observation—for all I knew, Erich was still coming—and I paced to and fro on the opposite sidewalk for a face-numbing hour before giving up. Hoping to find him at home, I ran into him on the way, sitting on a bench in the square, gazing across at the giant swastika which hangs on the Rathaus facade.

I sat down beside him, wondering what sort of reception I'd get.

He nodded in the flag's direction. "This country is fucked," he said. "Fucked beyond repair." He turned toward me. "We knew that in the Dudes," he said. "We all did. But then it felt like a joke. A really bad one, but still a joke."

I told him how sorry I was about his mother.

He nodded.

"I was looking for you," I said. "I was afraid you'd gone to see Ruchay."

The smile was bitter. "The idea did occur to me. In fact I got as far as the place where he lives now. And I stood there, thinking that Walter only has me and Granddad, and Granddad . . ." He shrugged.

"Did the doctor tell you anything?"

"Not much. That Granddad might live for years. The 'might not' bit was left unsaid." He offered a wry smile. "We can only hope."

"Yes," I said sadly. The thought crossed my mind that Erich would be a good recruit for my cell, but this family has already given far too much.

The two of us walked home together, and Erich insisted on shaking my hand when we parted. I came up to my room, sat down in my chair, and suddenly felt the wave of personal loss that the family's greater grief had kept in check. Anna and I weren't close—there was always that unspoken wall between us, which we each had good reason to keep in place. But I admired her enormously, as a mother, as a person. She was honest and brave; she made her choices in life and accepted their consequences with precious little complaint.

I have missed her since her arrest, and now the loss is forever. A shock but not a surprise. I am used to people not coming back.

TUESDAY, NOVEMBER 22

First thing this morning Verena conveyed a message from Andreas that he wanted to see me, and after saying I should shut the door behind me, he asked if I'd visit the Gestapo office in town and inquire about bringing his daughter's body back for burial. He was, he said, afraid to ask Erich. "I know he wants to act responsibly, but that might be too much to ask."

I agreed, of course, and was there when the building opened. Kriminalsekretär Appel arrived a few minutes later and rather brusquely said he had no news. When I showed him the notification of death, his face turned red, and he actually said he was sorry.

My explaining why I was there had him sadly shaking his head. "The remains are never returned," he said, in a tone that suggested the reason should be obvious. And I supposed that it was—the numbers would be prohibitive. Half of the Reichsbahn's trains would have to include a mortuary carriage.

"They have to process fatalities quickly," Appel was saying. "There's typhoid in the camps; it's in everyone's interest." If he was trying to soften the blow, he wasn't succeeding.

"The letter said she died of pneumonia," I pointed out coldly. Not that I believed that either.

Knowing there was no point in pressing the matter, I managed a cursory thank you and left. Andreas took the news better than I expected and agreed we could still have some sort of ceremony, giving people a chance to say goodbye.

"Like in the war," he said. "When collecting all the pieces would take too long."

I nodded, sharing the memory.

"What life has become," he murmured.

I set off to work, where an official warning awaited me for being two hours late. This afternoon at home, insult was added to injury—Anna's effects came back in a parcel. Verena brought it in and had the sense to open it on her own. "There are just a few clothes," she told me, "no ring, no watch. And the blouse she was wearing when she left is covered in bloodstains. I don't think they should see that," she added, meaning the family.

I agreed, and carried it up to my room for later disposal. Verena said she would give the rest to Erich, and by now I expect she has.

The family ate apart in Andreas's room, Verena flitting between them and us lodgers. Our mood was somber, and we all ate quickly, keen to escape.

I've hardly seen Walter since the terrible news. Erich and Verena thought it better he go to school than stay home alone with his grief, and they may have been right, but I doubt he took anything in. When our paths crossed down in the hall, it felt like it took all he had to remember who I was.

What life has become, as Andreas said. And the only answer I have to that—the only one I've ever had—is what life could be.

I have to admit: I'm no longer holding my breath.

✦ ✦ ✦

THURSDAY, NOVEMBER 24

We killed Paul Giesemann this evening. Earlier in the day Müller had told me where and when we should meet: in the rarely used storeroom adjoining the depot roundhouse at 7:30 P.M. Giesemann would be there half an hour later, expecting a hastily rearranged meeting to discuss the group's subversive future.

There were four of us lying in ambush and two more I didn't yet know about, waiting to play their part. It was quick and humane as killing can be, one man hitting him over the head with a heavy spanner as he came through the door, another slipping a blade through his rib cage as he lay there unconscious. We rolled him up in a sheet of tarpaulin, and three of us shouldered the bundle out into the night, the fourth man a few steps ahead, acting as our lookout.

Two of the yard lamps above our route had been disabled, and we stumbled down the dark and clinker-strewn path to the front of the engine shed, where two other comrades were waiting on the footplate of a hissing locomotive. Once the tarp had been hoisted and unrolled, one of the crew hooked a fire iron through Giesemann's belt and patiently maneuvered him through the open grate and onto the glowing coals. A fresh layer of fuel was shoveled on top of the corpse.

We stared at one another for a moment or two, our firelit faces all looking slightly crazed. Killing someone does that to you, at least the first few times. With the smell of burning flesh now filling our nostrils, we left the crew to go and pick up their train. The reek was bringing back too many long-buried memories, and I didn't envy them their first few miles.

Back in the storeroom, Müller told us he will see his

Gestapo contact tomorrow, say that Giesemann did not turn up for work that day, and ask if he's been arrested. An obvious diversionary ploy, perhaps, but better than none at all. Before the four of us started leaving at five-minute intervals, he also offered absolution. "We had no choice," he insisted, looking at each of us in turn. "Now we can go forward."

I hope so, although it seems unlikely that I will still be here.

When my turn came, I made my way back from one violent death to a house still mourning another. The common spaces were empty, everyone shut in their own little worlds. I climbed up to mine and sat in the dark, trying and failing to sort out my feelings about what we had done.

Why had Giesemann worked for them? Shared beliefs? It seems unlikely. Ambition? Perhaps. The cost of refusing? We might never know.

It no longer matters, for us or for him.

So why do I feel that it does?

FRIDAY, NOVEMBER 25

As this entry attests, I am still a free man, and until I arrived home this evening, I thought the day had gone well. The two comrades who crewed last night's loco returned without mishap, having dumped the ash from their boiler in one of the Hannover shed pits. If someone at our depot saw or reported anything suspicious, I would have expected to see the Gestapo, but so far that organization has shown no sign of knowing that one of its men has gone missing.

All good news, but as so often of late, bad news came close on its heels. Fate and the Nazis aren't done with these people I live with. As I discovered on reaching the house, today had brought two more bolts from the blue.

One was Marco's suspension from school—a suspension

that sounds very much like expulsion. Verena will get the full picture on Monday. He got onto another fight, and while it's unclear what the fight was about—even Marco doesn't seem to know—the extent of the damage he inflicted before a teacher could intervene appears to have been considerable. The other boy's parents are party members and were dissuaded from calling the police only by the principal's promise of drastic action.

Verena is frantic, and with good reason. It's hard to imagine another school eager to take Marco on, and seeking one out is bound to bring her son to the authorities' attention, with what might well be dreadful consequences. The only thin consolation, at least for Erich and Andreas, is that Walter was not involved.

The other bolt was a letter for Erich, who's already in trouble for missing his reemployment interview on Monday—it seems that receiving news of your mother's death on the very same day is not considered a sufficient excuse. This morning's official communication demanded his appearance at the local Wehrmacht induction center on Monday, December 5, a mere ten days from now. There was no explanation of what for. Is he actually being called up several months short of his eighteenth birthday? If so, that's terrible news for Walter, who will have only a desperate Verena and an ailing grandfather to look after him. Fewer than two weeks have passed since Erich's return boosted everyone's spirits—losing him again will send them through the floor.

I shall hate to leave them in such a state, but if I stayed, what could I do? Erich, Verena, and Andreas are brave, intelligent people and will do what can be done. All of Germany is at the mercy of these scum, and war is coming. Happy endings will be few, and most of them, I suspect, will be more attributable to love and courage than any survival skills that I possess.

✦ ✦ ✦

SATURDAY, NOVEMBER 26

This morning I set out for Essen and my final *treff*. On the journey there, I went through my fictional reasons for not doing all that I'd promised to do—the suspected informers, cautionary rumors, all the doubts raised that needed allaying—and wryly noted how good I was getting at lying to those whom I needed to trust.

Dieter raised an eyebrow when he saw me walking towards his table in the Stadtgarden café, but otherwise refrained from expressing surprise until I was seated beside him. "What has happened?" he asked, sounding as angry as anyone who didn't want to be noticed could.

I went through my litany of problems, ending on the happier note that all were now resolved. All but one. Moscow's embargo on Dariusz Müller.

"The group won't follow anyone else," I told Dieter.

He stared into the distance for several seconds, then went to buy us hot chocolates as he worked on his response. "The committee won't be happy" was the best he could manage on returning.

"The committee has made a mistake," I said, pushing my advantage and earning another raised eyebrow. "They don't know the people involved," I insisted. "That's why they send in people like me."

He sighed, and I waited for him to accept the inevitable. The chocolate was awful, tasting as bad as it had at the end of the last war. And this one hadn't yet started.

"You will have to defend this decision when you get back to Moscow," he said, after searching in vain for any alternative.

I told him I'd be happy to.

"So when?" he wanted to know.

"This coming week, and then I'll be on my way." I asked if the number to call was still the one I'd been given.

It wasn't. He recited the new one from memory and had me repeat it several times. He didn't say why it had changed.

"An arrest?" I asked.

"Yes," he said, in a tone that discouraged further questions.

Something else occurred to me. "If two of us turn up, will they take us both out?"

Dieter looked alarmed. "Who are you taking with you? Moscow doesn't want any Jewish refugees." It might have been a joke but probably wasn't.

"A twelve-year-old boy," I said.

He looked at me as if I were mad. "Out of the question."

I had thought it would be, but in the unlikely event that Andreas renewed his request that I take Walter out, at least I now knew where I stood. I nodded my acquiescence.

"And next month I shall expect to see someone else," Dieter said coldly. He gave me a place and time, and the identification procedure the new man should follow. "By then you will be in Moscow," he concluded, as if saying so made it more likely.

I said I was looking forward to that.

There was nothing more. He left first, and I sat watching the ducks upending themselves in the water for fifteen minutes before heading back to the station. There was a band playing on the forecourt, and as I joined the small crowd that had gathered to listen, the music segued from "O Tannenbaum" to the "Horst Wessel Song," like some ageless horror breaking the surface of a beautiful lake.

SUNDAY, NOVEMBER 27

My time here is almost over. Müller came to see me earlier this evening and told me I must leave within forty-eight hours.

When I saw him waiting in the hall below, I knew that

something was up, but what he told me here in this room was still a shock. It seems the Gestapo intend to arrest our whole group at Wednesday night's meeting.

"Someone has told them we're done with just talking," he explained.

"So it's not about Giesemann."

"Not directly. They haven't found a body, but they must have their suspicions."

"So why wait until Wednesday?" I asked. It seemed too good to be true.

A grim smile from Müller. "I've been told to swell the meeting as much as I can—to tell all the regulars to bring along anyone they think might want to join us. That's one reason. And I doubt they have enough men to make simultaneous arrests all across town. Better to get all their eggs in one basket."

Seventy-two hours, I thought.

"They wanted to know why I hadn't filled them in on our new plan of action," Müller observed.

"And what did you tell them?"

"That I was waiting until we decided on something concrete."

"So there must be another informer," I said, drawing the obvious conclusion.

"Yes."

"But you've no idea who it is?"

"No, but they wouldn't still be looking for Giesemann if it was one of the men who saw him off on Thursday. So those are the ones I'm warning. And I'm telling each man the same—that he shouldn't make a run for it until after work on Tuesday. Some need a couple of days to sort things out before they go—family stuff—and if anyone jumps the gun, and the Gestapo notice, they won't wait around for our meeting to make their arrests."

All of which made sense. "What about the others in the group?" I asked, already knowing the answer.

"They'll be arrested. But none of them have actually done anything, and if they've got any sense, they'll blame it all on those who've vanished. I know," he said, seeing my expression, "but I can't see any other way."

Neither could I, even knowing that not having "actually done anything" was unlikely to save Ottilie and the others. It hadn't saved Anna.

When Müller asked if I knew where I'd be going, I told him no, not yet. After we'd shaken hands and wished each other luck, I took him down to the door and watched as he cautiously stuck out his head, like a man half expecting an unpleasant surprise. But there was no one out there, and with one last look back, he disappeared down the street.

I stood in the hall, hearing the music on the common-room wireless, aware that my heart was beating faster than usual. Two more days in this house, assuming the Gestapo didn't change their minds. I doubted they would. Catching everyone in one fell swoop would reinforce their sense of who they were. People who pounced.

Two days to say my goodbyes. To Walter, to Jakob, to all of them. But how should I do it? I could hardly hold a farewell party.

I would tell Andreas, I decided, and maybe ask him to tell all the others once I was gone.

The light in the boys' room was still on, and I could hear them talking to each other. None was showing under Andreas's door, but why would it be? I rapped softly and heard him say to come in. "And turn on the light," he added, aware of how dark the room would be to anyone else.

I did so. "It's me, Josef," I said.

His head jerked up from the pillow. "Ach, is it time?"

"For what?"

"For you to leave. I heard that Müller came around to see you."

"Yes, he did. And yes, it is." I told him I'd be leaving on Tuesday evening but wouldn't be telling anyone else before I went. "I'm not the only one going," I added, "and we've agreed that the fewer people who know, the better. I'll say goodbye to Walter," I heard myself promise, "but only at the last minute."

The blind eyes bore into me. "Josef, a question," he said, after what seemed a long silence. "Are you leaving the country?"

"I hope so."

"Could you take the boys with you?"

I hadn't expected it, and I didn't know how to respond. A voice within said yes, but was it one I should listen to? Who was it talking for—them or me? "I don't know" was what I said. "Do they want to go?"

"I can ask them," Andreas said. "Look, Josef, the doctor says I don't have much time—a few months if I'm lucky, maybe just weeks if I'm not. Verena has her hands full looking after Marco, and the army's coming for Erich. Walter won't have anyone."

"I'm sorry," I said. For the doctor's prognosis, for the whole damn mess.

He answered the former. "Oh, I've been on this earth long enough. But I'd like to know they're safe before I go. If I ask them and they both say yes, will you consider it?"

I said that I would. And that if I could think of a safe way to do it—

"Then I'll ask them tomorrow."

Back upstairs, I checked the street for any suspicious activity and allowed myself to consider the possibility. Had I been half expecting such a request when I asked Dieter about taking someone else out? His answer had been vehement enough, and I'd mentioned only one companion. But if that way out was closed, it was probably for the best—putting myself in the comrades' clutches was one thing, entangling Walter and Erich quite another.

We would have to get out on our own, which would be more difficult but not impossible. I work at one of the Reichsbahn's largest yards, from which freight trains leave in all directions, all around the clock. Getting onto one will not be a problem, and if I choose wisely, we should be close to a border long before a winter dawn. But there the problems will start. If I were on my own, I would find a hotel in a small town nearby and look for someone to help me across—there are always men smuggling something. But I have false papers that will probably stand inspection. Erich and Walter do not, and once the hunt for me and the other group members is underway, guests in hotels near the border will all be double-checked.

I don't rate our chances of getting away much better than fifty-fifty, but are Erich's and Walter's prospects any better here?

Should I decide, or should I let them?

MONDAY, NOVEMBER 28

Today's shift at work seemed longer than usual, and each time my eyes or my ears registered movement outside I could feel my heart speeding up. I didn't think it likely that any of the other five would put the rest of us at risk by leaving early, but you never know what fear will do, and by the end of the shift, I was more than pleased to be on my way home.

After supper, as I'd promised, I went to see Andreas and found both his grandsons waiting there with him. I still hadn't made up my mind whether or not to take them with me, but the difficulties I foresaw in getting all of us over the border were inclining me to "not" until Erich's surprise announcement.

"I can get us across the border" was the first thing he said once I'd closed the door. "I spent six months working on the stretch near our camp," he went on, "and I know the way into Belgium. If we can get to Hellenthal, we'll have less than fifty kilometers to walk, and we can do that in one night."

I looked at Walter, whose face seemed animated for the first time in days. "Please" was all he said.

It was clear they were both keen to go.

"Are you certain you can find the way?" I asked Erich. "At night?"

He said he was. After all those nights with the Dudes tracking groups of Hitler Youth, he knew how to find his way around in the dark. "And there must be a train from the yard that can get us close," he said, as if that were the only real question.

There was. The night freight to Aachen always carried a few cars for Hellenthal, mostly supplies for the camp and border defenses. It left at 1 A.M. and was scheduled to arrive in Aachen at four-fifteen. I had no idea where it dropped off the cars for Hellenthal or whether they arrived before dawn, but it wouldn't be hard to get us aboard. And in truth, if I was to take them with me, I had no better plan.

Saying I knew of such a train had Walter and Andreas almost jumping for joy, but Erich remained all business. "There's one thing more," he said. "Verena and Marco have to come too."

My first thought was "crazy," my second "unwise."

"What difference will another two make," Erich was saying, "either in a car or walking in the dark?"

And I had to admit he was probably right about that. "You know what will happen if we're caught?" I asked.

"Yes," he said simply. "Verena and I will end up in camps and Walter in an orphanage. And Marco . . . I dread to think. But we want to risk it. All of us do."

"What about Andreas?" I asked.

"Oh, I won't be coming," the old man said with a mischievous smile. "No, seriously, don't worry about me. I'll be fine."

He had it all worked out. East Prussia would be "excellent practice" for death, and no, he wouldn't have any problem getting there. A blind old man abandoned by two ungrateful grandsons? The neighbors would bend over backward to take care of him, and his friend the block warden would put him on a train and make sure that Sofie was waiting at the other end.

I was getting used to the idea. Five people under a tarp were as hard—or as easy—to find as three. I looked from one face to another and knew I couldn't say no.

"All right," I said, and finally won a smile from Erich.

"When do we go?" he asked.

"Tomorrow night," I told them. "Just small bags you can carry over your shoulders—you're out for a hike, not going into exile. And don't do anything different during the day. Erich, you go to see your boss at the depot and eat humble pie. Walter, you go to school and look miserable."

Erich had already talked to Verena, so all I had to do was say yes, repeat my rules about luggage, and tell her to keep Marco in for the day. She nodded and gave me a kiss on the cheek, but the look in her eyes was that of a woman who's either been sentenced to life or death and has no way of knowing which.

TUESDAY, NOVEMBER 29

The sun will soon be rising on my last day in Hamm, and before I go down to breakfast, I must put this journal back in its hiding place for the very last time. It's not something I want to be caught with.

This morning at work I shall find the chance to give

Müller the number I won't be using, along with a warning that he may find Moscow's welcome less effusive than the one he deserves. I shall also post the letter I've written to Jakob, in which I tell him what a pleasure he's been to know.

A last piece of Nazi news before I go: our government has forbidden Jews from keeping carrier pigeons. One wonders what message they fear might be sent.

Afterwards by Walter Gersdorff

THE CHAIN OF EVENTS THAT brought Josef's diary into my possession was one of those that make people wonder whether some things are simply fated.

Because of its importance as a railway hub, Hamm was heavily bombed in the war, and the fact that our house survived was something of a miracle. And when it was finally demolished in 1987 to make room for new apartments, how fortunate it was that someone should not only notice the plain-covered book in the wreckage but also take the time and trouble to hand it in at the local library. Where, in turn, the current librarian would pass it on to his friend and predecessor, an eighty-year-old named Willi Holstein who had lived and worked in the town throughout the Nazi era.

Holstein had reported on Hamm's denazification after the war, and he remembered hearing about the Gersdorff family—the arrest and death of the mother, the subsequent flight of the sons. Sensing that the diary was an important historical document, he thought about trying to get it published, but with his health already failing, he soon came to realize that the task was for someone else. And when he discovered that one of the Gersdorff sons was actually a historian, he decided to send the diary to him. Which is how I came, in July 1988, to open my mailbox in upstate New York and find a German-stamped parcel inside.

To say I was surprised would be the mother of understatements. To say I found reading the diary an emotional rollercoaster, much the same. It was, as Josef wrote in another context, like a journey in H. G. Wells's time machine—I was whisked back to witness my own growing up, in a time and place that had come to seem so distant but now felt far too real. I hadn't tried to forget that long-ago summer and fall, but I had succeeded in remembering it in ways that spared my heart. Coldly, dispassionately, as if it were a story that had happened to someone else.

FIRST, I MUST TAKE UP that story where Josef left off. More than half a century has passed since the night we said goodbye to Hamm, and when I try to remember it, I'm struck by how much I've forgotten. Some moments remain remarkably vivid, while hours at a time are only a blur.

I do remember the walk to the depot, the dark silent houses, the sound of our feet and our breathing. I was crying most of the way, having just said goodbye to my granddad and knowing how unlikely it was that I'd ever see him again. I remember squeezing through a hole in a wire fence and following Josef across the dimly lit yard to our chosen train. The car he chose was covered, and the coils of wire underneath the cover were large enough to leave human-sized spaces into which we could squeeze ourselves. The wire was for searchlights, Erich said, which somehow made the frontier seem nearer.

There was only a short wait before the train clanked into motion. Josef, who I now assume was accustomed to clandestine travel, was soon asleep, the occasional snore faintly audible over the noise of our passage. The rest of us just hugged ourselves and shivered as the train threaded its way across the Ruhr. Josef woke with a start when we rumbled across the Rhine, and I remember thinking that all we really knew about him was that he wasn't the man we had thought he was. That this made him seem almost glamorous didn't sit well with the resentment I felt about having been deceived.

He woke up again when the train was shunted around in a yard. After we heard our engine leave with most of the cars, we waited for what seemed an age for another to pick up those left behind. Another round of buffeting followed its arrival, and then we were off again, chugging down the branch line toward Hellenthal.

The sky was only just beginning to lighten when we arrived, the town and station still asleep. Fortune favored us where the setting was concerned—the yard backed onto woodland, and once the train was stationary, it took no more than a minute to get us all into the trees. Erich told us the road to his camp and the border continued on down the valley, and we should follow the edge of the wood until it was safe to rejoin the road outside the town.

He gave the impression of knowing where he was going, and I imagine everyone else was wishing and hoping that this was the case. The road was certainly where he had said it would be, and we walked along it for at least an hour as the sky grew steadily lighter and the birds in the forest found their voices. After one look up at the heavens, Josef led us off into the trees, where we soon found a dense enough copse to shelter us through the day.

I must have fallen asleep almost instantly, because the next thing I remember Erich was waking me up, and it was getting dark again. I don't think I've ever felt as cold as I did in those few moments, but a round of stamping, shaking, and hugging myself brought more relief than expected, and once we were back on the road I slowly began to warm up.

The sky above was clear, and for the first couple of hours, a sinking moon offered some light. This was generally welcome, but had the unfortunate effect of showing us one another's faces. The first thing I noticed was the fear in Verena's eyes, the second that Marco was worried for her. I don't know why, but I felt neither frightened nor especially anxious. Maybe it was Erich's confidence, maybe Josef's calm. Maybe I was still feeling numb from losing my mother.

There were no sudden shocks. The minutes and hours rolled by in a muted dream: the road winding on through the wooded hills, faintly trickling streams and rustling wild-life providing the meager soundtrack. Only once was this disturbed, when we heard the swelling growl of a motor up ahead and noticed the glow from its lights in the distant trees. We were all off the road before the headlights appeared, twin yellow orbs bouncing up and down as the lorry approached on the rutted track. The cab window on our side was open, and as it went by, a man took a drag on his cigarette, lighting his and his partner's faces. I can still see the two of them, fifty years later.

In the middle of the night, long after the moon had gone down, the road took a turn to the south. The camp was that way, Erich explained, about three kilometers further on. The lesser road in front of us, which looked like a recently bull-dozed path, would take us across the frontier.

On we went. I was exhausted by this time, and I could see that Marco and Verena were too. But no one complained or asked to stop—we knew the dawn wasn't far away. We'd seen no signs of habitation for several hours, and when, in the early morning twilight, we finally came across something man-made, it was a pair of concrete emplacements perched atop the flanks of the narrow valley we were following. There was no indication they were occupied—no lights, no sound, no warning rounds fired.

They had been built for the coming war, Erich told me later, not to stop people escaping the Reich. A visiting army major had explained that to him and his comrades while they were mixing cement for the one on the left.

We continued on down the path, which almost disappeared before growing back into a farm track. It was almost light when we crested a slope and saw houses ahead. Erich said they were Belgian, and Josef went forward alone to make sure. When he came back with thumbs upraised, Erich and I had tears in our eyes. Tears of relief, no doubt, but also, on my part at least, tears for our mother.

As far as I knew, we had no Belgian money, but Josef somehow persuaded the farmer to drive us in to the nearest town in his truck. Once we got there, Josef parked the four of us at a bus stop and went off on his own—something he would often do throughout our stay in Belgium. On this occasion I assume he was buying some local money with the emergency cache of gold coins he mentions in his diary.

At the time I was probably paying scant attention. This was my first foreign country, and I was entranced by how different everything was—the sound of the language (which Josef, it turned out, spoke fluently), the smells of the food, the look of the streets, with their strange architectural styles and surprising paucity of flags. A bus took us to another small town, which I now know was Verviers, and from there a one-carriage train took us into Liège. The journey took a couple hours, and with every mile that passed, Verena and Erich grew more relaxed, as if the fact of our escape was finally sinking in. We might not know where we were going, but we knew we weren't going back.

We arrived in Antwerp late that afternoon. I'm not sure how long we spent there—it felt like weeks, but was probably less than two. We stayed in two rooms in a small hotel near the docks, Josef and Erich in one room, Verena, Marco, and I in the other. The clientele were all workers, and they probably included a prostitute or two—at that age I wouldn't have noticed. I imagine that Josef thought the guaranteed privacy more than made up for the dirty sheets and cobwebs.

And of course he was hardly ever there. At the start of our stay, he told us he wouldn't be asking us where we wanted to go until he had some idea of what was actually possible, and that that was something he'd need several days to find out. So off he went each morning, returning briefly with food, but otherwise leaving us all to our own depleted devices. To top things off, we all had head colds, caught no doubt on our freight-train ride to freedom. We should have been feeling elated, but instead we felt anxious and miserable.

After three or four days of this, Josef relented and took us out for an after-dark walk. The nearby city center was full of beautiful buildings, the docks seemed to stretch for miles, and the sidewalks were packed with sailors of so many different skin colors that Marco and I had trouble not gawping.

Further days of seclusion followed, relieved somewhat by the pack of cards and German books Josef picked up in a pawnshop nearby. Our colds receded and the hours went by a little quicker, but I can still see the peeling walls and the imaginary countries I conjured up from the shapes of the stains on our ceiling. It must have been our seventh or eighth day in "captivity" when Josef finally said he had several possible destinations for us to consider.

We could take a train south into France or a ship bound for England or America. He advised against the former— France was too close to Germany and might end up occupied if the war he was expecting finally broke out. England would be safer, but he had no contacts there to help us. In America he did. He told us about this family in Pennsylvania whom he'd stayed with years before and who he was certain would find us a home. He admitted he hadn't heard from them "lately"—seven years, I later discovered—but said that the father and mother were only in their fifties and wouldn't have moved.

After all the Westerns I'd watched at the cinema, I was an easy sell, and I don't think Verena had ever considered anywhere else as a final destination. Erich's only objection was a fear that we wouldn't get in.

Josef assured him our arrival would not be noticed. And that once we got to Scranton, his friends would find a way to legalize our presence. They had, apparently, been helping immigrants like us for years.

It was at this point—somewhat belatedly, as now seems obvious—that I realized Josef wasn't coming with us. I asked him why not, feeling, I seem to remember, more surprised than upset.

He said he had things to do here, by which I assumed he meant Belgium, but in hindsight he probably meant Europe. When I asked him what things, he smiled and told me, "Better you don't know."

We left the hotel just after midnight—by this time being out in daylight would have felt like a novelty—and walked through the docks to a sailors' bar. It was closed, but hadn't been for long: the proprietor was still sweeping away the evening's debris, his wife rinsing out glasses. He nodded Josef toward a back room, where a sailor was waiting to collect us. He was Dutch and spoke a little German.

Josef hugged us each in turn and wished us luck. I felt sad to see him go, but, to be brutally honest, probably more from fear of how we'd survive without him than any sense of emotional loss. Perhaps I was suffering from a surfeit of the latter; more likely it never occurred to me that I might never see him again. I don't believe twelve-year-olds think that way.

We spent the next ten days in the hold of a freighter named the *Surabaya Queen*, sick as dogs for much of the time. Our sailor—a Communist, of course—brought us food and water each day and on one memorable evening took Erich, Marco, and me onto an open deck for a view of the ocean. The waves weren't as high as they felt in the hold, and the moon sliding in and out of the clouds was beautiful, but having no land in sight was scarier than I'd imagined. I took the opportunity to dispose of my Hitler Youth dagger—I don't know what had possessed me to bring it along in the first place, and Erich had pointed out the obvious, that should we run into the American authorities, they were unlikely to consider it a suitable import.

Being smuggled off the ship in New York was much like being smuggled on in Antwerp—done in the early hours of the morning with only our sailor for company. We were quickly passed on to another comrade, who looked like a Hollywood gangster but spoke better German than our previous guardian. He took us to the train station, bought our tickets, and gave us a handful of dollars for food. It was still growing light when we left the city, and try as I did to take a look back, a sight of the famous skyline escaped me.

That afternoon, we found ourselves outside the house in Scranton, each with a shoulder bag of belongings, all looking up at a door we didn't dare knock on, in case we should find that Josef's friends were gone. And then a woman came out—older than my mother, younger than my granddad, with a face that said, "Welcome, whoever you are."

She asked if we were lost.

Erich asked if she was Esther Brennan, and when she said yes, he passed her the letter Josef had given him.

She opened it, read it, and when she looked up, her face was smiling. "You'd better come in."

⊷ ⊷ ⊷

AFTER READING JOSEF'S JOURNAL FIFTY years later, I knew I had to go back to Germany. I had never before felt any desire to do so—I was and am an American, and though I sometimes indulge a nostalgic interest in how Schalke are faring in the Bundesliga, I'm far more invested in baseball and hockey scores. But the journal hadn't so much piqued my curiosity as sent it into overdrive, and when a publisher told me that readers would want to know what had happened to Josef's "cast of characters," I had the excuse I needed. My wife wasn't happy at the length of separation entailed, but commitments of her own prevented her from joining me, and in the late fall of 1988, I took a solitary flight to the land of my birth and childhood.

I won't go into the hows and wheres of my research; as this is not an academic tome, I intend to cut straight to the findings. My first port of call had to be Hamm, and I must admit to having been shocked. After fifty years the place was almost unrecognizable. I already knew our house was gone, but so were all the surroundings. The configuration of roads had changed, and I found it hard to overlay the new urban landscape of spaces and blocks with my memory of how things had been.

The railway depot was still in existence, but hugely shrunken in size. A couple of windowless concrete buildings sat inside acres of overgrown sidings; a line of rusting cars covered in graffiti that looked like a permanent fixture. My school was gone, a multicolored high-rise block soaring in its place. The library was still there, but the toy shop where I'd spent all my pocket money was now a Turkish takeout place. Like they say, you can never go back.

And so to the people. Most of those that Josef mentioned in his diary were older than thirty in 1938, so even a peaceful half century would have drastically thinned out their ranks. Germany, of course, had not been so lucky, and I wasn't expecting to find many survivors.

All of Josef's fellow lodgers died in the war. Gerritzen died at Stalingrad. Buchloh—whom I only vaguely remember—was "shot trying to escape" by a British unit in Normandy. Ruchay, whose job at the depot saved him from conscription, was killed when a bomb destroyed his lodging house in February 1943. Poetic justice, I couldn't help thinking—if he hadn't betrayed my mother, he might still have been living in our house, which never took a hit.

Jakob Barufka was one of the more than forty thousand civilians killed in the Hamburg firestorm a few months later. I couldn't find out whether he'd moved there or was visiting his family, all of whom died in the same attack. As Josef points out in the diary, Barufka was not the sort of man to inspire a twelve-year-old like I was at the time, but reading it fifty years later, I can see what a decent man he was.

Four of my teachers and my school principal are named in the diary, but Berndt Skoumal is the only one I remember well. He, Memering, Scheringer, and Bodenschatz were all killed in the war, Skoumal in North Africa, the others in Russia. Principal Huelse survived, taking charge of three more schools before he retired in 1965. He died in 1981.

The almost sympathetic Gestapo officer Kriminalsekretär Appel was one of fifteen Gestapo officers summarily executed by American soldiers during the Battle of the Ruhr Pocket in 1945. Kriminalinspektor Jagusch was sentenced to five years by a denazification court in 1946, and following his release in 1950, he lived on his wife's earnings as a kindergarten teacher. He died in 1968.

I have had considerably less success in tracing Josef's political contacts. And for an obvious reason: he used false names—and I think false descriptions—for all but one of them. I have been unable find out why he made an exception of Dariusz Müller and can only assume it was because he knew that Müller was already known to the Gestapo.

It's not a very satisfying answer, but it's the only one I have. Müller did escape that night and not only found his way to Moscow but also managed to persuade the Russians and his fellow German exiles that he was a man worth keeping. He returned to Germany with the victorious Red Army and for several years played a not insignificant role in the new East German regime. Perhaps his spirit proved too independent, or perhaps he simply backed the wrong horse, because he died in the purges that followed the workers' rising of 1953.

The other members of the "Working Group" all proved impossible to identify with any certainty, as did the men on Josef's Comintern list. I talked to several long-retired railwaymen, and some had suggestions that fitted those few facts I had, but I got no further than that. I have no idea what happened to them or whether they ever moved on to active resistance.

The pseudonyms Josef used for his Comintern contacts probably weren't the ones they used for themselves, let alone their real names. I haven't found a single reference to a Dieter, but I have found mention of a female Comintern agent known as EP whose age and physical appearance are compatible with Josef's Elise. If the two women were one and the same, then she was one of the German comrades Stalin sent back to Hitler as part of the Nazi-Soviet Pact. "EP" died in Ravensbrück in 1941.

That was also the year that my grandfather died, having long outlived Dr. Offner's expectations. We were able to exchange letters even after the war began because America had not yet entered it, and the last we received in Sofie's neat writing, a week or so after Pearl Harbor, was the one announcing his death. She and all the rest of her family were murdered by Red Army soldiers in late 1944.

And then there was my mother. I knew that knowing more about her death would serve no useful purpose, but as my wife tells everyone, "Walter can never let anything be." Perhaps on this occasion I was right, because at least my worst fears proved unfounded. My mother had been ill-treated, but that had been the norm, and according to the octogenarian witness I finally found, she had, like so many others in the same weakened state, been easy prey for pneumonia.

I visited the memorial center at Lichtenburg and stood in front of the plaque above the mass grave, watching her bustle around the house in Hamm, seeing her smile as she kissed me good night.

BUT WHAT OF US WHO escaped?

The four of us stayed in Scranton for almost a year, Erich and I with the Brennans, Verena and Marco lodging with friends of the Brennans who lived just down the street. During that time Bill Brennan moved heaven and earth to win us immigrant status as refugees from Nazi Germany, and his efforts eventually bore fruit. We were Americans at last!

Once they were legal, Verena and Marco moved to New York City. I didn't get the impression that Marco's background was as much of a handicap in Scranton as it had been at home, but I must have been wrong, because Verena decided that a cosmopolitan city would suit her son better. It proved a wise move. Verena had always been a hard worker, and they soon had somewhere to live on the outskirts of Harlem, where he finished school. Marco was called up in 1943 and ended up back in Europe, at least for a while. While he was away, Verena met and married a widower with two grown-up children, and as far as I know has never regretted it. I have met him on a couple of occasions and on both was struck by his basic decency and their mutual devotion. They're both in their eighties now, and in her last Christmas letter, she said they'd spent the previous fall campaigning for Dukakis.

Marco has had a more checkered time of it. Once back from Europe, he eschewed the opportunity offered by the GI Bill, and settled for a series of dead-end jobs that just about paid for the girls and fun his earlier life had denied him. Eventually tiring of this, he decided to look for his father in Africa and after saving and borrowing enough for his passage set sail a couple of weeks before the Korean War broke out. He found his father, Jean Diallo, who had greatly prospered in the last twenty-five years and was a leading light in the anti-colonial opposition. Jean had a wife and other grown-up children but was willing to take Marco in.

He's been living in Africa ever since, and though I sometimes get news from his mother, I've seen him only once in almost forty years, when he came to New York in 1975 as part of his country's UN delegation. He's currently a government minister and has just survived a corruption scandal. No one could deny that over the years Marco was dealt some truly terrible hands, but he has never been bitter or resentful and despite every sign to the contrary has always seemed to believe that things turn out for the best.

Erich, the teenage outlaw, turned into Erich the satisfied adult. He lived with the Brennans until he was called up and after surviving four years in the Pacific came home to marry their youngest daughter, Mary. The army had trained him as a mechanic, and like Marco he saw no attraction in further education. He got work in a local garage, and when the owner suddenly passed away, the Brennans helped him buy out the widow. He ran the business for more than thirty years and became a local institution. He and Mary have four children, all of them now in their forties and each with two of their own. When he's not playing granddad, Erich plays pool rather badly and takes people out for drives in one of his beautiful antique cars.

⚬ ⚬ ⚬

I AM TOLD BY MY wife that fifty years later I am still very much the boy in the diary, which should probably give me cause for concern but actually feels quite comforting.

By the time I was called up in late 1944, the war was almost over, and I never saw combat. Unlike Erich and Marco, I made the most of the GI Bill, studying history for several years before going on to teach it. I won't say I've loved every minute, but I can't imagine a more fulfilling career. Life should be like history, something you never get tired of, a never-ending opportunity to use two of God's greatest gifts, endeavor and curiosity.

I met Ellie in my last year as a student, and we married two years later. Three children followed, two sons named Richard and David, a daughter named Anna. All are very much still part of our lives. We have one grandchild and are expecting another.

Scranton is only a two-hour drive from our home in Cortland, so we visit Erich and his family quite often. I always enjoy seeing my brother, and I think he feels the same. The two of us are so unalike—in interests, opinions, the lives we lead—but there's something brothers share that's not subject to any of that.

The last family gathering was a few weeks ago, at Bill Brennan's funeral. Esther passed on almost ten years ago, and Bill had been ill for quite a while. I visited them often over the years and remain quite close to several of their children. In all my time in Scranton, in all the years since, I never heard anyone say a bad word about Bill or Esther; if ever other lives were worthy of emulation, then theirs surely were. And over the years, whenever I've thought of Josef, it was with heartfelt gratitude for sending us to them.

AND SO, FINALLY, WE COME to Josef, or whatever his real name was. Many readers of his diary—American readers particularly—will find it hard to forgive him for being a Communist, let alone a self-confessed terrorist and murderer. I am not here to condone what he did, but as any historian knows, context is everything. When the First World War destroyed one set of moral precepts for organizing our world, many saw the Communist ideals of the Russian Revolution as a natural successor, and by the time it had become clear that this new dream was also prone to corruption, the Nazis had seized power in Germany. People like Josef, who worked and fought for the Communist dream, then had to choose between nightmares—one they believed still showed flickers of hope, one they knew offered only darkness.

As the diary makes clear, working for the Comintern was not for the fainthearted. You lived with the threat of torture and death; you got used to comrades not coming back. But he was doing what he wanted to do, which was fight for what he hoped and believed would one day be a better world. And no matter how wrong he might have been to think that such a newborn world could have a Soviet midwife, I can't help but admire the intention and the effort.

I am of course biased. He is the reason I'm here in America and have led the life I have. But what was the price? He seemed relieved when we said our goodbyes in that bar's back room, something I then put down to his being finally free of his burdensome charges. After reading the diary, I wonder. We all assumed he was meeting the local comrades to arrange a passage somewhere, but now I suspect that he was also negotiating his own immediate future. His bosses had ordered him back to Moscow, and the comrades in Antwerp—then an important Comintern base—would probably have known as much. And after reading Josef's account of his last conversation with Dieter, I find it hard to believe that the Belgian comrades would have shipped the four of us off to America just because Josef asked them to.

Did he make a deal? Offer them something—perhaps himself—in exchange for our passage? Then again, why would they not just take him by force and put him on a Russian-bound freighter?

Either possibility assumes an Antwerp apparatus unanimously loyal to Moscow, which in 1938 was probably not the case. Josef had mentioned an old friend when we were planning our escape from Hamm, and perhaps he persuaded this dissident comrade to help us while intending all along to follow the apparat's orders.

My attempts to find out more have been largely unsuccessful. The *Surabaya Queen* was sunk on convoy duty in 1942, and I haven't been able to trace the sailor who looked after us. One thing that Erich remembered was thanking him for all his help, and the sailor wryly remarking that he'd been well paid. With Comintern money, I have to assume. Probably paid by Josef, rather than the local CP.

I doubt we'll ever know, though having said that, the continuing news on TV of a Soviet Union falling apart suggests that the relevant records may one day become available. Watching the coverage in light of reading his diary, I find it hard to believe that Josef would have thought his old inspiration worth saving.

I have found no further trace of him. I think he went back to Moscow, either as payment for our escape, or because, in spite of the growing disillusion so evident in the diary, the Comintern was still where he felt most at home. A bullet in the back of the head may have been waiting for him, but given the fact that the terror was past its zenith by then, it seems more likely that he ended up in some godforsaken corner of Stalin's gulag. He might have simply died there or been given a brief reprieve in one of those prisoner units that the Red Army used to clear mines or use up the enemy's ammunition.

If by some miracle he survived the war and Stalin's last few years, I think the man who wrote this diary would have found a way to leave the Soviet Union, if only to work for a socialist future in a more conducive setting. And he would, I think, have made his way to America, if only to see what the people he'd saved were making of that gift.

Cortland, NY
October 1989

Acknowledgments

My heartfelt thanks to Juliet Grames, Rachel Kowal and Katie Herman at Soho for making the book better than it was, to Charlie Viney for believing in the original idea, and to my wife and partner, Nancy, for being just that.